"Violent and twisted."

"Cinematic and visually sumptuous."

*Enter the mysterious world of **La Madonna Negra**.*

LA MADONNA NEGRA | VOLUME I

She never dreamed.

Until the nightmares started.

Forced to flee the scene and the only home she ever knew, Yael finds herself in the shadows of the Ybor slums. For years she hid the truth from those around her, wearing her smile like a mask as she spiraled into the abyss.

With her whole life behind her, she has no need for hopes and dreams. Alone and beyond broken, she chases her nightmares to avoid her grim reality. So when she finally sees the chance to join the living, she can't help but question if it really is the light at the end of the tunnel? After all, the last time she was this close to freedom, she lost herself.

Is redemption near? Will the terrifying curse that stole her innocence be lifted if she follows the light? Or will her double life catch up with her in the bitter end?

Find the FIRST book in the adventure series at your local retailer!

"Beautifully complex."

"Exhilarating, with unexpected twists."

*Enter the mysterious world of **La Madonna Negra**.*

LA MADONNA NEGRA | VOLUME II

Yael Phillips never dreamed

of becoming any man's hero.

Yet, for five long years, she dutifully followed the orders of her nightmarish premonitions to the letter. Hiding in the shadows wasn't exactly a life plan, but on-call killers didn't get to make plans. Or so she thought . . .

As if cleaning up the streets of Ybor City weren't enough, the summer of 2010 saw a world of darkness brought to light. Though vigilante regulations would require she toe the line, she had long since grown tired of leading her life in the night.

Faced with the reality of maintaining her secret identities and the once in a lifetime chance at an indescribable love, Yael can no longer sit and wait for instruction.

Is it too late to take back her life?

Will fate have other plans?

Find the SECOND book in the adventure series at your local retailer!

LA MADONNA NEGRA

VOLUME III

GRACE FIERY

This edition contains the complete and original text.
It is the third in the La Madonna Negra mystery series.

LA MADONNA NEGRA | VOLUME III

An FGP Book
All rights reserved.

Copyright © 2022 by Grace Fiery

Cover Art by Stephanie Luk Oprea

This is a work of fiction.
Names, characters, businesses, places, events and incidents are either the products of the author's imagination or used in a fictitious manner. Any resemblance to actual persons, living or dead, or actual events is purely coincidental.

For information address: Fierce Grace Publishing

ISBN: 978-1-956930-99-3

To Professor Peterson.
For teaching me about the
transformative powers of
vision and direction.

WELCOME BACK

AND BUCKLE UP!

PROLOGUE

YBOR CITY, FLORIDA | 2011

Frederico paced anxiously across the hardwood floor, the creak of the ancient house going unnoticed as his mind flooded with possibilities. The phone rang a third time. He knew she wasn't going to pick up.

"Finish your picture and then we'll go get McDonald's, alright?"

"Okie, pops!"

Frederico stared at Tres, seeing himself in the boy for the first time in six years. "What'd you call me?"

"Pops!" Tres piped up, his voice cracking. "Deon calls his dad pops, so I'm gonna call you pops, too!"

"Sounds good," Frederico muttered, flipping his phone shut when he heard the voicemail greeting. "Be right back."

Opening the front door and slipping outside, he shut it behind him and looked at the short man on his porch. Though he was sure Johhny had no idea he knew exactly who *he* was, Fred wasn't about to let the man leave without an explanation.

"I called her four times—no answer."

Johhny's eyes darted back and forth. Then, he turned to the car waiting in the street and shook his head. The back window rolled down, revealing the eyes and nose of a bald man Frederico could only assume was the mafia Don of Ybor City.

Johhny turned to face Frederico, taking a long, deep breath. His eyes were blinking away as if the short man's mind was processing an immense amount of data. When he cleared his throat and nodded in departure, Frederico grabbed his arm.

"Hold up!"

Johhny's eyes stayed fixed on the spot Fred held until he released him. "Yeah?"

Eyeing the man in the sedan warily, Frederico tried not to sound desperate when he asked, "Why did you come here?"

Johhny didn't answer, only stared at him.

"Come on!" Frederico whispered harshly. "I know who you are. You need to tell me where she is man!"

Studying him for a long moment, Johhny turned to the street once more. The hair on Frederico's body stood on end as he wondered if he had just made a grave mistake. Though he didn't know much about the mafia, he was certain the average Don didn't make house calls.

To his surprise, Johhny held up his own cell phone and gave it a little shake. If Frederico wasn't watching in fear, he might have missed the imperceptible nod of approval.

Johhny opened his phone and pressed a few buttons, then turned on the speaker. Frederico listened to an Italian man with a thick accent deliver a message that brought more chills to his spine.

"You stupid fucks still don't know what you're doing, huh? Little moolie works for the feds and nobody sees a thing? Lies of a liar! Samuele, you never deserve to be the Don. Tomorrow, I return to Sicily to have you removed. Permanente! Tonight? I clean your mess, but not for you! Per la mia famiglia."

Frederico listened to the message, leaning in as he tried to understand. The voice stopped, and the message ended with a spat of disgust. It was then that he knew.

"Vitto?"

A small gasp escaped Johhny as he took a step back. "How did you—"

"She moved, man!" Frederico shouted, his voice wavering. "She moved out months ago, I don't know where? Somewhere in South Tampa! Did you check there?"

Johhny shook his head. "Didn't realize . . . "

Frederico buried his face in his hands, trying to remember the name of the street Yael had mentioned back in August. It was something she found . . . funny? Ironic? He couldn't quite recall. When he kicked his cousin out last summer, his primary focus had been keeping his son Tres safe from Vitto—the mafia cleaner who had been hot on Yael's tail all year.

They hadn't talked much since, but after five years of living together, Frederico hadn't expected their relationship to fall apart so quickly. While he was completely enthralled with daddy duties, Yael was wrapped up in a love all her own with her fed boyfriend Joe. For years, Fred and Yael knew everything about each other. But here in the eleventh-hour, he had no answers.

What did I do?

"I made her leave," Frederico cried, unable to catch his breath. "I made her leave when she saw the threat and now he got her!"

"We don't know that," Johhny retorted softly. "He left this message a couple hours ago, there's still a chance we can find her in time."

"In time for what?"

Johhny shrugged. "Your cousin is the best I've ever seen. She can handle Vitto, no problem."

Frederico forced the breath from his lungs and inhaled again, doing his best to trust Johhny's calm confidence. Yael was terrified of Vitto, and with good reason. The man disappeared people and cleaned up crime scenes before disappearing himself. He was a professional hitman—Yael was not. She might have come across as a killer to these men, but he knew better. She was soft and more vulnerable to the darkness of this world than she understood, naive as she could be.

Fred had only learned about her vigilante activities last summer, catching her red-handed after he discovered her secret lair in their shared attic. When Vitto became a threat, it set off a chain of events that had led Yael and Frederico on a crusade to fight the new wave of trafficking a few blocks away at the Port of Tampa. But what had they really accomplished?

After Fred's arrest a few months ago, their smalltime investigation had all but ended. He had been lying to himself this whole time, believing he and his cousin could one day make a difference in their city. Now she was probably dead. He bit his trembling lip and sighed.

"What do we do?"

Johnny glanced over his shoulder and then cocked his head. "Any chance you are 'the feds'?"

Frederico's face said it all, but for good measure he replied, "Fuck no!"

Nodding at him and sliding his phone into his jacket pocket, Johnny pulled out his cigarette case and lighter from the other pocket. Lighting it as he stared at the porch ceiling, he returned to his thoughtful processing and took a long drag.

"Way I see it, you're safe for now. If she's been gone for a while and you aren't 'the feds', you probably ain't on Vitto's radar. I'm gonna get a tap on her phone—"

"I can do that myself," Frederico snapped. "And I'm not worried about me!"

Johnny gave him a look. "Not to pry, but did I or did I not hear a tiny human on the other side of that door."

Fred paled. "Fuck."

"Get a hotel," Johhny said quietly. "Tap the phone and watch her credit cards. I'm gonna figure out who the fuck Vitto was talking about. You sure you don't know anything about that?"

"No," Frederico lied, wondering if he could find Joe's contact info before anyone else did.

Maybe I should call the FBI? Fred mused, his stomach sinking. He'd have to find some way to warn Joe the mafia might be looking for him.

"I'll let you know if I find her. You do the same?"

Frederico nodded, though he knew he would do no such thing.

CHAPTER ONE

TAMPA, FLORIDA

Yael stared blankly at the phone screen, her eyes still refusing to cooperate as she attempted to read the latest message from Frederico. The ride across town should have taken less than thirty minutes, but her tears of anguish would not wait. Having only been an hour since she left him there in the mud, it was likely Joe's body was still warm . . .

Throwing her phone onto the passenger seat as she wiped away fresh tears, she made the turn into the Tampa Executive Airport lot and searched for the long-term parking spaces. Pulling in to a spot next to the large hangar, she put the car in park for the eighth time since she left home and broke down in wretched sobs.

Vitto had finally done it. After almost a year of this stupid, bloody game, he had finally gotten what he was after. All this time, Yael thought he wanted her life. Tonight, Vitto had taken her very soul. No matter how many bullets she put through his skull, it could not take back the one's Vitto left in Joe. It could not give Yael back the only joy she ever knew. She would never be the same.

Searching the glove compartment for a spare napkin, Yael blew her nose and wiped her face, grimacing when she saw the brown and black smudges of her makeup. She almost never cried and rarely ever wore makeup, but of course she had tonight.

Angrily flipping open the visor, she swore when she saw her puffy eyes and bright red nose smeared with mascara. Rubbing vigorously, she did what she could to wash away all signs of her dinner with Joe. His blood was—figuratively—on her hands; she didn't need it showing on her face, too.

Just as she was about to close the visor, she saw it. The look in her eyes.

Numb.

Cold.

"Dead," she whispered, unfeeling.

But that was a lie. She was not dead inside, though she wished it were otherwise. Tonight had broken her, and yet, it had also shown her just how alive she truly was.

Alive and . . . alone.

Forever.

The buzz from her phone on the seat beside her gave her a start. Picking it up and squeezing the new tears from her eyes, she read the instructions through blurred lenses.

"Time to go," she moaned dejectedly, sniffling and dabbing the crushed napkins in her hand at her nose.

She knew she should at least try to clean herself up, but what was the use?

Her phone rang again. Frederico was calling for the fourth time.

Maybe I should just go home?

Home? she heard herself scoff. *What home?*

Yes, only hours ago she had intended to return home, to Fred's, but that was before she'd killed the man she loved. That was before she lost her soul.

Yael knew the truth. She had no one. Nothing. And nowhere else to go.

Reaching for her go-bag in the backseat, she checked for any miscellaneous items she might have left in the car. Her rifle would have to stay in the trunk, but she decided to bring her small roll of knives just in case.

Yael walked to the passenger door and sat inside long enough to flip the trunk lock mechanism inside the glove box and lock that too. She clicked the fob twice for good measure, then started toward the opening in the fence next to the massive building. A plane was landing as she approached, and she wondered if it was her ride out of town. Seconds later, she had her answer.

The plane she was told to board was the Bombardier Global 5000 sitting to her left on the tarmac. The tiny Cessna she'd seen arriving was a third of the size of the behemoth ahead. If she didn't know any better, she would think the man had diverted a commercial flight just for her!

A woman in a stewardess uniform came into view, waving to Yael from the doorway of the plane. Shaking off her stupefaction, she continued hurriedly across the tarmac and up the steps.

"Ms. Peachy, I presume?" the stewardess asked cheerily. Taking Yael's bag in both hands, she waved her on hurriedly and continued, "Come, come! Master Olivier is so excited to have you with us. We'll take off in a few minutes, and then I can show you around the cabin."

When she sank into the plush carpet, she found herself rooted to the spot staring at her feet. The squish reminded her of the muddy, blood-soaked ground under Joe's lifeless body. Choking back a sob, she lifted her head slowly and met the woman's wide eyes.

"Oh!" Yael gasped, wondering if she'd already made a mistake.

"Come now," the woman said, patting her gently. "Why don't we get you set up in back?"

Allowing the woman to lead her into the belly of the plane, she followed her through a slender wood-laden walkway into an open space. The three sections of the plane were more obvious from the back after walking through. The first section nearest the cockpit held a kitchenette and storage cabinets made from the same shiny, stained wood lining the entire cabin. It opened up to reveal two seating areas in the center section: one standard seating area with cup holders built into the walls of the plane, and a second dining area complete with table and credenza. It was here in the rear section of the plane that Yael was most surprised to find a fully made bed ready for sleeping.

"The loo is just through there, as is the storage for the bags, but I can leave this with you for now. I need to finish the flight preparation. I'm Marge if you need anything."

When Marge closed her in to the makeshift room, Yael was overwhelmed with gratitude. The woman was kind and an unexpected companion on this trip into the unknown. Doing her best not to give in to the urge to break down, she went into the bathroom and washed her face.

Five minutes later she returned to the room, an unsettling feeling flooding in when she saw the door was no longer closed. Olivier's voice in the near distance let her know he had boarded. Was this his bedroom? She hoped not and prayed Marge hadn't assumed she was here to entertain him in that way.

A tear slipped down her cheek as she realized she would never have sex again. Sure, she had spent almost twenty-three years as a virgin. It wasn't as if she needed it. But knowing that she would never feel secure loving anyone—for their safety—meant she would have only the last few months with Joe for her memories.

Hopefully I won't be around much longer.

No! Stop it!

Why?

She felt her legs give way and braced herself for the fall, the bed beneath her forgotten. Head in hands, she silently released the new wave of grief, the world around her fading into the background.

"Peach?" Olivier called for her, poking his head into the doorway. "We've been cleared for . . . oh, Peachy!"

Placing a hand on her shoulder, he tried to console her with a cluck of his tongue.

"Aww, come on, Peach. I know it's been hard, but there, there. We're together now."

Yael looked up at him, mouth agape.

"You look terrible, Peach."

She huffed.

He leaned toward her and drew her into his arms, surprising her with the show of strength. She had never been this close to him before, and his suits—tailored as they were—did little to expose the truth of his physique. Olivier's scent enveloped her and she recalled the first time they'd met. His swagger of wealth and power was ever-present, but tonight she sensed something new in him.

"Peachy," he murmured, leaning in to kiss her.

Yael's palm hit the crook of his nose as she mushed his face away from hers, the force knocking him into the chair behind.

"Damn it, Peach! You waited all this time and you're still on this?"

Yael stood and scooped up her bag. "I've obviously made a mistake."

"Now wait just a minute!"

"No! Fuck you, Olivier! I'm literally crying in your face, and you try to kiss me?"

Olivier smoothed his hair back, still looking affronted. "I understand your tears, dearest. You almost lost me—and I'm a real catch. I'd be crying, too."

Watching incredulously, Yael stared at him and wondered if he was serious.

He stood and placed one hand in his pocket, motioning casually with the other. "I turned around the moment you called. If you didn't want to join me, why reach out?"

Yael took a step toward him, incensed. "I am a murderer. I needed help fleeing the country."

"Murderer?" Olivier's eyes lit up. "What kind of murderer?"

Dropping her head to the side irritably, she shook it and asked, "Is everything a joke to you?"

"No!" he said seriously, placing his hand on his chest. "I believe you! Can't I be curious?"

"Curiosity killed the cat," she said smoothly.

Olivier smiled. "And satisfaction—"

"You know what! Just . . . shut up!"

Marge knocked on the wood and peered into the room. "Master, we've been cleared."

"Well, Peach?"

Yael looked at Marge and then back at Olivier. "Fine, what now?"

"Just buckle in anywhere," Marge said as she left.

Walking to the seat across from Olivier and dropping her bag beside it, she sat and buckled her seatbelt. Meeting his eyes and shooting daggers his way, she fumed at her predicament.

The plane taxied for a minute, then the engines roared. Seconds later, they were floating.

"That was fast," she said, lifting the window cover to confirm she was really in the air.

"Hmm?" Olivier asked, peeking out his own window. "Ah, yes. The Bombardier has one of the fastest takeoff speeds in the world in its class. Rolls Royce Pearl engines and all that . . . now, where were we?"

Yael crossed her arms. "You were assuring me of your willingness to cooperate, without strings."

"Strings?"

She rolled her eyes. "Olivier, I am not interested. I will never be interested. I need your help, and since I'm still here, I am guessing you are willing to aid and abet an international criminal."

"International, you say?"

Her brow shot up. Was he calling her bluff? She decided he wasn't and embellished further.

"Olivier, I'm a killer. It's what I do. What I've always done." She gave him a steely look and set her voice to the most menacing tone she could muster. "If you make me, I will kill you . . . just like I killed Stacey."

"Why would I go and do that?" he asked cheekily. "Oh, this is *exciting*! Are you wanted in Canada? Though we are headed to an island, perhaps you would just need a disguise . . . "

Yael stared at him. The man was calculating her next steps without question. What kind of man was he, the Brit?

A soft ding rang through the cabin. Olivier removed his seatbelt and stretched his hand to hers.

"Hungry?"

Yael carefully unbuckled the belt at her lap and took his hand, allowing him to help her from her seat. He released her and walked out of the room.

"What the hell?" she grumbled with a shrug.

Marge was up and about, setting up a small feast at the table. Most of the platters held beautifully prepared sushi rolls and exquisitely garnished sashimi, but two small charcuterie boards sat between an array of crackers and flatbreads. Yael followed Marge toward the galley and offered the woman a smile.

"Anything I can help with?"

Marge grinned. "Absolutely not, miss! You have a seat and enjoy yourself. I'll bring out some fresh cut fruit in just a minute."

Yael gave her a shrug and a smile and returned to the table, sliding in across from Olivier and taking the plate he handed her. Building out a meager fare as she considered the current state of her stomach, she slid open the window cover and stared out at the clouds.

"What did poor Stacey do to deserve her death?" he asked blithely as he mixed a pea of wasabi into a small bowl of soy sauce.

"She got in my way," Yael said ominously.

"Oh ho ho! Well then, here, here!"

She accepted the glass Marge handed her and lifted it with a tilt of her head. Taking a long sip of the sweet wine, she stared at it and made a face of pure delight.

"I think this might be the best wine I've ever had."

"Pity," Olivier said, his tone filled with amusement. "I hope you've come prepared to spend your money, Peachy. No use living like a pauper on the run—they might suspect it's you!"

Yael shook her head, her mouth tightening the smile to a smirk. "I'm sure you can help me coordinate things with Sampson."

"Righto!" Olivier exclaimed, popping a piece of sushi into his mouth and giving her a wry smile.

They ate in silence for a few minutes until Marge returned with the promised tray of fruit. Yael wondered how they could eat this much, but remembered that Marge and at least one pilot that she knew of would both need a meal at some point.

"How long until we land?"

"Eager to get started, are we?" Olivier checked his watch. "We'll arrive in just over seven hours, give or take. Checking in a bit late, but the drive to the resort is only about twenty minutes. I'll be busy with business, but that will give you some time to get your affairs in order, yes?"

Yael nodded, suspicious of his calm demeanor. "What do you get out of helping me?"

"I'd like to think we've become friends, you and I. And soon we will become the best of friends. We can plot new schemes and be thieves together all over Europe."

She rolled her eyes. "I am not a thief, you freak."

"Yes, I know. That's why I said new schemes. Do keep up, Peach."

Yael shook her head. Ever since her attorney Mr. Sampson introduced her by her real name—Philomena Piccirillo—Olivier had insisted on calling her Peach. Everyone always found a damned nickname for her.

"I have an important meeting on the Island, but once things die down we can have some fun. We can fly home and you can see the estate, then I have an engagement I simply cannot miss. You are always welcome to join me, Peach, but I understand if you prefer to *hunker down,* as it were."

She giggled at his use of the terminology, then nodded. Yael wasn't sure what she was going to do next, but all in due time. Her focus at the moment would be keeping Olivier at arm's length.

"So, what shall we do in the meantime?"

She shot him a scowl. "What do you usually do on your flights?"

Marge snickered as she came to pour them each a glass of water. Olivier looked at her from the corner of his eye, but otherwise ignored her.

"Mmm hmm," Yael groaned. Thinking of the two flatscreen TVs she saw in the front and rear quadrant, she asked, "How about an in-flight movie?"

"Marge stocks the entertainment area every flight." He stood and opened the credenza across from them. "A few books in here and some movies there. But you know what just occurred to me?"

"What?"

"Friendships can also have benefits."

"Let me off the plane, Olivier."

He chuckled and plucked out his choice. "A movie it is."

Yael stared at the cover and grimaced. "What kind of books are in there?"

Sitting with an absent-minded shrug, he placed the movie on the edge of the table and returned to his plate. Yael searched the small library and selected a book called *See Jane Run*.

Very appropriate, she thought with a hint of amusement.

"I'm gonna lay down," she said shaking the book in his direction. "I'll see you when we land."

Olivier tapped his chopsticks at her and winked at Marge, who had returned to pick up his selection and hand him a pair of headphones.

"There's another lavatory up front, miss. You can rest up and get changed if you need to, we'll make do."

Yael nodded. "Thank you, Marge."

Closing the door behind her and locking it soundly, she slumped against the door and felt a deep pang of sadness flood her system. For a moment, she had almost forgotten her sorrow.

I've got to keep moving.

Yes, stay busy.

Olivier seemed to stay busy. Maybe she could learn from him? Though she didn't believe for a second he really wanted to be friends, he still came across as harmless. Annoying—actually, *very* annoying—but harmless nonetheless. She could fend for herself against his advances, especially if there were others around. As incorrigible as he was, something about the Brit said he honored his duty to sensibility and decorum.

Climbing into the chair in the corner and angling herself to look out the window, she pressed the button to adjust her seat and melted into the soft leather. She reached down to pick up her bag, rifling through it until she found her phone.

Another missed call?

If Frederico was contacting her, that meant he was finally free. She didn't really need to talk to him to figure that out, right? And now that she was on the run, there was no use trying to work together on the trafficking case. Yael was done living her life for everyone else.

Besides, Fred shouldn't have been involved in any of that anyways. Now that he had Tres, it was time to be a *normal* father. Would he listen to reason? No, of course not. There was no way she could explain any of this to him. Until she had answers to the myriad of questions he would send her way, it was best she didn't speak at all.

Turning off her phone and sliding it into the pocket, she scanned the contents of her go-bag and pulled out her pistol. Removing the clip, then placing it and the gun into the large side pocket, she tossed the bag on the floor. If she ever packed another go-bag, she'd need to remember important things . . . like clothes.

Just like last time . . .

Yes, this was a lot like the night she left her father on the hardwood floor, clinging to his wife's lifeless body. That night, she'd packed a go-bag of sorts. Tonight, she'd grabbed a bag she was never supposed to need. That night, she had Fred. Tonight, she had Olivier. But unlike that night, she had no reason to trust her rescuer, no visions to keep her busy, and no worthy distraction from the pain. That night, she had found her freedom. Tonight, she had found . . .

Shaking the image of Joe's dreadlocks in the dirt from her mind, she tried to think of something positive. Yes, she would need new clothes for this new life of hers. More important, she would need a new identity. Who did she *want* to become this time around?

After she left home and moved in with Fred, she became his shadow. Then she became her own shadow, wandering the streets of

Ybor in the cover of darkness. Trying to live in the light had only made things worse, but maybe she could find a happy medium between pitch-black and gunmetal grey. It wasn't like she had much of a choice.

A twinkle out the window caught her eye. When she leaned forward to look at the stars, her reflection in the glass stopped her in her tracks.

She tried to smile, but it felt foreign. Would it ever seem right to feel joy again?

A chuckle from Olivier at the front of the plane gave her pause. He was working hard to be disarming and it seemed to be helping. As long as he behaved, his charm and spirit would no doubt be good for her.

Sitting back and clutching the book against her stomach, she imagined herself traveling the world with him. She had never been one to enjoy air travel—especially takeoff and landing—but in this jet she'd barely had time to notice the jarring sensation.

Maybe it'll be fun, she thought hopefully.

Opening the book to the first page, Yael began devouring a story about a woman who went to get groceries in springtime and forgot who she was.

CHAPTER TWO

PRINCE EDWARD ISLAND, CANADA

Yael awoke with a start, clutching her chest as the terror faded from her sight. She had been dreaming, and for the first time in her life the dreams were not related to her *work*.

After years of nightmarish scenes, one would think she was prepared for the awful visions of the night. But these seemed more like the fever dreams of Hollywood, with their *Alice in Wonderland* twists and turns that always led her back to him.

Dream Joe.

She shuddered.

Dream Joe was the name she gave the monster lurking in the corners of her mind, chasing her to and fro as she died a thousand deaths. Dream Joe was angry. Dream Joe was a ghost she was sure would haunt her for the rest of her days.

He flashed into her mind, his face contorted as he raged against her from the other side of his gun barrel. Yes, this was the most likely outcome for them. She, the serial killer, on the run, and he, the straight arrow, doing the one thing that came natural to him.

No! Joe loved me.

Joe didn't even know you.

Shaking her head tearfully, she drew the covers over her face and prepared herself for another day of wallowing. A knock at the door startled her.

"Open up, Peaches!"

Yael gasped at the intrusion, wondering if the staff had given Olivier a key to her room. The door didn't budge and wouldn't, locked from within as it were. She snuggled deeper into the lush comforter.

"Peach, I know you're in there!"

"Go away, Olivier!"

She giggled hysterically at her unexpected rhyme.

Oh, God. I need help!

She did indeed. And wasn't Olivier supposed to be providing that? Groaning, she rolled out of bed, wrapping the massive duvet around her frame.

"I'm sleeping," she shouted through the door.

After a moment's pause she heard, "No, you're not."

"What do you want? Are we leaving already?"

"Open the damned door!"

Yael lifted her chin and gave a little sniff. "I'm not decent. Come back tomorrow."

"Peach, I never thought you were."

She stared at the door, puzzled. "Were what?"

"Decent," he said mirthfully, laughing as he leered into the peep hole. "Now open up. Let's see you."

"I'm only in a robe, good sir," she lied, putting on her best British accent.

Olivier chuckled. "You truly are a peach. Now, open the door."

Yael pulled the comforter over her head and adjusted her grip on the fabric at her chest, then opened the door a few inches.

"What?" she barked.

Lifting his head and leaning forward in an attempt to look down into the opening at her chest, Olivier drew in his cheeks and gawped at her.

"Terrible robe," he murmured as he looked past her into the room. When she sucked her teeth at him, he met her eyes. "Why so puffy? Crying again, are we?"

She gave a sniffle and a blank stare.

He lowered his voice. "You know, I sent for you last night. Why did you decline?"

"I was busy."

"Busy?" he guffawed. "What business do you have here?"

Yael narrowed her eyes and pushed the door shut, but Olivier put up a hand to hold it steady.

"Alright, Peach. Friend to friend? You look absolutely wretched. Why don't you put on a nice short skirt and meet me in the lobby?"

She rolled her eyes and opened the door. "Did I leave my magic suitcase on your plane?"

"You haven't been shopping yet? Bloody hell, what have you been doing all week?"

"It's been like, two days!" she corrected. "Not even. And how am I supposed to go shopping without money and a car?"

"Why didn't you say something when I called for you, darling?" He stepped into the room and walked over to the phone to dial out. "Hello, Jacques? Is Susan available? Wonderful, my companion needs her measurements taken, and then we'll need something suitable from the boutique. Very good then. Bye-bye."

He turned to Yael after hanging up the receiver, a smug look on his face.

"I could have done that," she said irritably.

"And yet, you didn't." He sighed. "If we're going to have to deal with this every time we do a job, I don't think we can be partners."

"What the hell are you talking about?"

Olivier slid his hands in his pockets as he strolled around the room. "If you wanted to be taken on a shopping spree, you only had to ask."

"I did—"

"And," he interrupted loudly, "if you wanted to handle things yourself, you should have done so by now. We don't have time to waste, you see."

She exhaled sharply and stared at the ceiling.

"Susan is the resort seamstress. She will be up momentarily to get you fitted. Let her know your preferred styles. Susan will send word to a few shops around town and we'll make a day of it tomorrow."

"What about my money?" she complained. "I need access to an untraceable account, no? And I don't want to be indebted to you, so don't even offer."

Olivier opened his wallet and slid out a card. "Take this. Come on, Peach! Be reasonable. This is my emergency AMEX—I rarely use it. You'll charge everything to this card and then have Mr. Sampson facilitate a monthly payment from one of your accounts. Do you find my solution acceptable?"

Yael studied him for a beat, trying to find issue with it. She couldn't, so she nodded and took the card. The man was a pompous windbag in almost every way, but he obviously knew a lot more about having money than she did. And she hadn't thought about Joe once since he arrived.

"We'll have dinner tonight so we can plan our day. I thought you might like to pretend to be tourists?" He smiled. "When Susan arrives, let her know you need something for tonight and the morning outing."

"Okay," she said softly, following him to the door.

"Oh, and Peach?"

"Yeah?"

He leaned against the door frame and cocked his head. "This is the only time I'm going to say this: you are incredibly rich. It's time to start acting like it. No more ghastly barmaid costumes, if you please."

CHAPTER THREE

Yael felt like a British royal on holiday.

It wasn't the white couture mini-dress with its puffy sleeves, pearl embellishments, and accessories to match. It wasn't the hair style, a half-up half-down coiffure where every single long, glorious curl had been placed *just so*. And it wasn't the dewy, feminine makeup that left her virtually unrecognizable. Though she was a vision of loveliness, a walking example of the perfection money could buy, it was what she felt *inside* that mattered most.

Yael was absolutely and unequivocally *free*. Free of all burdens, free to be whomever she wanted to be, free to do anything she wanted to do.

It dawned on her that this was her first real vacation as an adult. Moreover, it was the first vacation she'd taken since her mother died. When she traveled with her parents in her youth, she would often be forced to dress, speak, and behave in certain ways.

Her father believed children were to be seen and not heard, and he was extreme in both rights. Stefano wanted silence—unless of course he needed Yael to put on a show. Then she had to be vivacious enough to prove she was his daughter. She often felt like a little doll, waiting in quiet perfection until he came and pulled her string.

After he remarried, his new trophy wife was all he required. Yael was often left at home when they took a lavish tropical vacation or attended a fancy soiree. Stefano would only bring his child along if it could gain him political favor. On the rare occasion he needed Yael to be present at an event her stepmother, Lilith, would whisk her off to the mall for a new dress and a blowout.

The last two days of her life were so different, even with Olivier as company. With no one to pretend for, she could finally enjoy being fun, flirty, and feminine. How she wished Joe was still alive to see it.

She sniffed.

Ah ah ah, none of that.

Yesterday after their shopping spree, Olivier had taken her around Prince Edward Island. They lunched at the Blue Mussel Cafe before a private tour of the quaint, historic home that inspired the book *Anne of Green Gables*. Then they saw a handful of the sixty-three lighthouses on the Island during their luxurious boat tour. The former provided a tearful moment for Yael, wherein she remembered watching a rendition of the play sitting on her mother's lap. She and Olivier ended the day eating some of the famous Charlottetown ice cream she couldn't stop hearing about; she was looking forward to trying another scoop before they left for Great Britain.

Today, Olivier had proven himself to be a good friend after all. She'd been waiting for signs of his usual creepiness since they landed, but it never came. The biggest surprise she found was in the level of comfort they shared, especially during long silent moments. Now as they headed to dinner, she found herself enjoying the company on her first holiday.

Yael heard her phone buzz for the tenth time today. She jumped and opened her new clutch to check it.

"It's at the hotel, Peach," Olivier said in droll voice, staring out the window at the rolling hills. "Look at that, another star."

They'd both been fascinated by the presence of a single large, decorative star on almost every house on the Island. She looked past him, her curiosity piqued by the seeming show of solidarity between the locals.

Canada was known in American popular culture for its niceness, but she never expected to experience it for herself. And nice didn't come close to describing the warm welcome they received everywhere they went.

Joe waved to her from across the street as they drove by.

What the fuck?

Not again, she groaned.

It's fine! This is probably normal.

She sat back and smoothed her skirt. She *hoped* it was normal, if that was the right word. Her mind seemed to be slipping away. It started with the dreams . . . then the imaginary buzzing of her phone . . . should she really call seeing his ghost *normal*?

Yes, it had to be. Mourning the lost love of your life was no easy feat. Aside from a deep sense of sadness and the occasional wave of depression, she was otherwise okay. Thanks to Olivier, she was starting to have hope that it would be possible to heal.

Rays of sunlight suddenly appeared from behind a big, fluffy cloud. Yael caught sight of her reflection and stifled the small gasp that nearly escaped her. The woman before her was stunning, but her eyes?

Dead.

Enough! she scolded. *You look amazing.*

Breathing deeply and swallowing the lump in her throat, she leaned into the seat back and closed her eyes. Though wasn't as lucky yesterday, she had made it through today without bursting into tears. This morning she'd realized she was likely PMS-ing, so she was determined to get through this time without an outburst or regression.

By the time they made it back to the resort, Yael had calmed her nerves and pushed Joe from her mind. After four days of feeling guilty for doing so, she was smart enough to see the benefits of a clear headspace. She thanked their driver and tipped him, beyond grateful for the cash Mr. Sampson had transferred to her, then walked alongside Olivier to the resort bar.

As per usual, all eyes were on them as they made their way to the only open stools. Olivier had casually explained that people believed them to be a handsome couple. He wasn't wrong.

Olivier was an Earl and the sole heir to one of the richest families on the planet. Though he was the last in his line, he expressed a deep devotion to the continuation of this legacy. Yael had become a lot more understanding where his brazen attempts at courting her were concerned. The man needed to start a family soon to give him the chance to raise and bear his own heirs. She hoped he found someone who actually loved him, though he claimed not to care either way.

Yael followed the feeling she was being watched and made eye contact with a beautiful blonde across the bar. The woman gave her a curious look when Yael smiled, then returned to her drink.

"I think you've got an admirer," she said softly.

Olivier popped an olive into his mouth. "Indeed."

"You think *she* thinks we're a couple?"

"Even better," he said wryly.

Yael didn't catch his meaning. "Why?"

Gazing at her lips and pushing her hair over her shoulder, he leaned in. "That woman is a jaguar."

Giggling softly, she asked, "Don't you mean a cougar?"

"Whatever. Women like her look at women like you and assume you'll be a dead fish."

"Gross," she countered.

"Not the smell, Peach," he chuckled. "A pillow princess? A starfish? Oh, bugger. Older women like her tend to tell themselves that all the young beauties of the world are sexually selfish. If she thinks you and I are together, she will convince herself that one night with her is all I need to see the light. Who am I to tell her otherwise?"

Yael let out an unladylike snort. "You're a cad."

"Excellent use of the word!" he commended. "A few months across the pond and you'll be a full-fledged Brit."

"We'll see. I'm going to get some rest." Yael shot the woman another glance as she downed a chilled double of Grand Marnier. "Ugh. First I need to get these clothes organized so I can pick the right luggage. And housekeeping hasn't been in since we got here."

She stood and placed her hand on his shoulder. "Now, I'm going to make it look like I'm asking you to come to bed. You're going to smile and pat me on the arm—I said the arm—yes, good. She's watching."

Olivier leaned in for a kiss.

"I will slap you."

Grinning, he leaned in and stole a kiss on her cheek. "What wife would leave her husband without a kiss?"

She glared at the woman over his shoulder and narrowed her eyes. "Blondie is going to know I've spotted her. When I leave, check for me at the door and then give her the look. She needs to think I've expressly warned you off."

"You are such a naughty girl," he purred through his smile. "Of course, I didn't need any assistance, but now—"

"Now," Yael said softly as she straightened his collar, "the jaguar is all revved up for you."

Grabbing her purse and shooting the woman a pointed look in parting, she turned to saunter out of the restaurant. To her surprise, Olivier pulled her back.

"You've proven to be a far more respectable woman than I initially believed. Tell me, have you been playing hard to get this whole time? Is this a test?"

Yael tilted her head in question. "Uh . . . no?"

"Oh, thank God," Olivier blurt out, obviously relieved. "I mean really, Peach. Anytime, anyplace. But that one looks promising."

Catching a glimpse of the smug look on the woman's face, she couldn't help but agree. "Have fun, Olivier."

Twisting her hips and walking on the balls of her feet ever so slowly as she left the bar, she stopped in the doorway and turned to face the blonde one last time. The woman didn't try to hide it; she was downright giddy. Putting on a pout, Yael shook her head in feigned disgust.

When she stepped out of view, she burst into laughter. "Absolutely ridiculous."

She hoped the seamstress was still on call, or she'd be cutting herself out of this dress tonight. Zippers were a real bitch. You'd think for all the money she'd paid for her new wardrobe, someone would have thought of that part.

CHAPTER FOUR

Olivier pushed in Yael's chair. "Madame Peach."

"Thank you, good sir," she replied demurely.

"*Claddagh* is my favorite place across the Island by far. On my first visit two years ago, they were kind enough to take my late reservation and save me a couple seats at the bar. A table opened up, but I was so impressed with my service here that I declined. The Oysters Rockefeller are to die for and you'll have to try the escargot."

Yael turned around in her chair. "Where is everyone?"

A broad smile spread across his face. "I love this restaurant. I couldn't possibly share it with anyone else."

She shook her head. "You're outrageous."

"I'm supporting my favorite establishment. Ah, yes. Hello, dear," he said in greeting as the bartender approached with a bottle of wine. "I presume we are right on schedule?"

"Yes, Lord Hulley. Robin will be right out with your starters."

"Very good, then. Nice to see you." Olivier turned to Yael and grinned. "She's a lesbian. Flirty little thing, but I learned the hard way."

"Why are you telling me that?" Yael whispered harshly.

Olivier lifted his palms, an affect of innocence on his face. "I thought maybe you might have good reason to deny me. What if you were only after my cousin's money? Millions of dollars is worth the sacrifice of taking a little—"

Yael kicked him, hard.

"I concede. You are far too masculine, so I'm not wrong to wonder. But there is no way God would make a woman like you for another woman. Not possible."

She took a long sip of her wine. "I'm going to hurt you, Olivier."

He smirked. "I doubt that, Peachy. You're far too magnanimous."

When she raised her hand to flick him, he growled and snapped his teeth. Her playful giggles floated around him, soothing his ire. There was something about the woman, damned if he could ignore it any longer.

The blonde had been a real tiger in the bedroom, totally willing to trash her cottage rental in the heat of her passion. Lamentably, all he could think about was Yael. He thought he had her that first night on the tarmac, thought he'd finally won her over. He could forgive her lifestyle and her prudent frugality. But if she made him wait much longer . . .

"Marry me, Peach."

She made a face. "We were having such a good time."

"Ha! That was a test," he said sharply. "I have to be sure this isn't some elaborate ruse to entrap me, you see."

Yael placed her glass on the bar and stared at him, completely devoid of expression. "You've been pursuing me since the moment we met."

"Exactly," he retorted with a point of his finger.

Her mouth dropped open. Then, she burst out laughing. "Ridiculous, really!"

Olivier sighed and finished his glass. He loved her sense of humor, but at times hated that she found him so amusing. As the present 15th Earl of Ravenscar and future Duke of Yorkshire, he was quite a serious man. The last in a long line of serious men, in fact.

He had to remember that she was American. She couldn't possibly understand—yet. Once they arrived in London, she would learn very quickly how important and respected he was as a nobleman. Once they arrived at his estate in Ravenscar, she would be unable to resist his power. For now, he would have to show her more than his charms.

"Tell me about Stacey," he said, keeping his tone nonchalant.

Yael sighed. "I'm good."

"I'll bet you are," he muttered. Clearing his throat, he tried again. "Tell me your secrets, dear friend. I'd like to know more, especially since I'm the one aiding in your escape."

"Now that I have my accounts in order, I can buy my own jet."

He looked at her and laughed. "Woman, I've just made a downpayment on my upgraded Bombardier. It isn't even in production yet."

She shook her head. "You might need a tiny apartment on wheels, but I don't."

"My tiny apartment can get us from London to Miami without refueling. Let's see your imaginary aeroplane do that."

Robin delivered their kale Caesar salads and escargot, giving them each a small appetizer plate and fresh cutlery. She offered Olivier a small bow then turned to leave. Stopping in her tracks, she examined Yael's attire, and upon meeting her eyes, instantly bowed her head. Backing away comically, she stumbled into the kitchen.

"She's new, that one," Olivier explained. "But she wasn't wrong. You look stunning tonight, dear friend. Dazzling."

Yael bowed her head and took a bite of salad. She moaned in surprise and picked up a small bacon lardon, studying the short strip of cross-cut bacon. Then, she carefully loaded a lardon, a large crumb of garlic, a small piece of clothbound cheddar and a leaf of kale covered in caper dressing onto her fork and took a bite.

"Exquisite."

Olivier knew she would assume he was referring to the food. Truth be told, he was finding that his barmaid was a full-fledged lady. Her awareness of etiquette went beyond courtesy and common sense. She had been *trained* to dine. The way she sat in public aligned perfectly with her new wardrobe. If he had never met her, he'd think her one of the gentry at the very least.

Glamorous as ever, she wore a long black dress that hugged its way up her curves and opened to a deep V at her chest. He wondered how she managed to keep such fullness in the confines of the halter top. And her waist to hip ratio was activating some primal awareness in him that she was ripe for the picking, ready for childbearing.

It was odd the woman was claiming to be deadly. He hadn't attempted to contact Stacey since their last trip together, but when he called her this week her number was disconnected. Could it be that Yael actually had taken her out?

"Why won't you just tell me?"

Yael frowned. "Tell you what?"

"About Stacey. Tell me something . . . anything!"

"Why do you want to know so bad?" she asked. "Seems to me you might be trying to pull a fast one."

"A fast one?" he scoffed. "Preposterous. I knew the woman, for God's sake. Don't I deserve a little closure?"

"She wasn't your wife, dude. She was your dead cousin's lover!" Yael shook her head in disgust. "I don't owe you a damn thing."

Olivier sighed. "I thought we were better than this."

"Sir, I have a very strong self-preservation gene. I would hate to see you lose your life over pussy."

"So vulgar!"

She rolled her eyes. "You're asking me how I murdered someone over dinner and I'm vulgar?"

"If you would just tell me—"

"Fine. You win. I killed her because she was trying to get to my money." She punched him in the arm. "By the way, thanks a lot, asshole! She told me *you* told her all about it."

"Killing for money?" he asked quietly, taking a bite of escargot. "Interesting."

"I can kill you for free, if that will make you feel better."

He looked affronted. "Oh ho ho! Really? Thank you so much."

She laughed. "Can it. I don't know why you insist on pushing my buttons."

Olivier almost griped about her insistence on doing the same to him, but it was no use. Yael—or Santamaria Philomena Piccirillo as he knew her on paper—was nothing like he expected her to be. Still, one thing he had right about her was this terrible sense of modesty. She was painfully humble, despite her air of confidence.

He believed her now, for he would go to just about any lengths to protect his future. Though he certainly could not see his young Peach killing Stacey in a fit of rage, he would not put it past her to defend what was rightfully hers.

"Stacey's life was nothing to be mourned," he assured her, hoping that wasn't the reason for her tears. "And if you can find a way to prove she was harassing you, perhaps you won't need to live like a hermit."

Yael's face paled in the dim amber light of the Edison bulbs above them. "I can't believe you would say that. You didn't even know her."

"Oh, I knew her well. Women like Stacey are a dime a dozen for men like myself. You know, I suspected she was a high priced call girl all along. If that type of woman was after *your* money, you did the right thing."

Olivier understood now. She was in mourning, though not entirely for Stacey. He suspected she was mourning her old life as a barmaid.

And I'm ridiculous?

"Let's go somewhere you want to go. Anywhere in the world . . . er, anywhere warm. Unlike you, I have no need for a new winter wardrobe. I've got time to spare and you need to relax."

Eyes glazing over as she reflected thoughtfully on his question, Yael stared off in the distance. "I'd love to go back to Sicily. I haven't been since I was young." She shook her head. "You know, um, on second thought, I should try something new."

Olivier rested his cheek on his fist and watched with fascination as her mind worked to find their next location. He hoped she would pick something exotic. Some place packed with scantily clad ladies on sunny beaches.

"Cuba!" she said, slapping her hand on the bar. "I can't believe I didn't say it sooner. Can you get me in?"

Olivier lit up, genuinely pleased by her request. "This is just perfect! I have an important meeting in the Caribbean in a few weeks. What a splendid arrangement. Couldn't have planned it better myself."

"Where we will stay?"

"Leave it to me, Peach," he replied with a wave of his hand.

Taking his Blackberry from his pocket, he sent a text to his flight crew. Then he emailed an acquaintance in Cienfuegos, Cuba letting him know to expect their arrival.

"And done." He put his phone away and picked up his glass. "We leave the second of June after my morning meeting. Looks like you've got more shopping to do."

CHAPTER FIVE

Olivier slid out of his chair and stretched forward toward the center of the cabin, his hands scraping against the Bombardier's low ceiling. Yael peered over the top of her book and gazed at him expectantly. Paying her no mind, he yawned and headed to the lavatory.

Based on the times given, she estimated they were halfway to Cuba. Leaving Prince Edward Island was bittersweet; she would cherish the memory of her first true taste of freedom for the rest of her life. But she was excited. Her mother was half Cuban and had always promised to take her when the government lifted the embargo. Luckily, Olivier's pilot had connections at most airports; she had no need for a passport and the custom's officers were quickly paid off.

Olivier's schedule kept him busy up until their departure that morning. When they boarded, he apologized in advance for his lack of focus. Working diligently with only one bathroom break, he was attempting to cross as many t's and dot as many i's as he could before their trip started.

She was surprised by his quiet concentration, this being the first time Yael had seen him in action. His job—whatever it was—appeared to require his undivided attention. Olivier didn't seem like the type of man to care about anything, yet it was obvious to her now that he took his business seriously.

Both the table and credenza in the center of the plane were covered in thick stacks of paper. And the tabbies! So many little sticky tabs! She couldn't even begin to understand what he was working on, and she didn't want to try. If this was the life of the super rich, she might give it up in the end.

Today, Yael found his silence bordering on bizarre. Olivier's attention was almost always solely on her and she couldn't stand it most of the time. She was sure she didn't want it, but this new tranquility would take some getting used to.

Olivier clapped his hands together. "Come, Peach. Time for lunch."

Finally! she thought.

"And don't worry, that's one project down and only one to go. I'll have time to finish up tomorrow morning. Then you'll have me all to yourself."

"Oh, joy," she said drily.

"Denial doesn't look good on you, madame," he sneered as he began organizing his many stacks of paper. "I'm not blind, you know."

She let out a snort.

"Looking sad and forlorn out at the great sky," he continued mockingly. "And not once did you offer to help. That must of have been hard."

Yael bit her tongue, knowing he was pushing her buttons—his favorite pastime. Some days he treated her like a delicate flower; on others she was a lowly, piteous poor person; and on others still, she was simply a woman in need of a man to care for. She had a feeling he was projecting, doing all he could to distance her from the killer he now saw her as in his mind.

Go right ahead, she thought with a smirk. Keeping him at arm's length would be easier if he underestimated her, as most did.

As soon as he finished packing up his makeshift office, Marge swooped in to sanitize the table. Yael liked the woman and appreciated her attention to detail. While she couldn't imagine having the gall to hire a full staff, she wondered if she might need an assistant one day. If she did, they'd have big shoes to fill. Marge operated on love and loyalty, and it showed.

"Miss Peachy, would you like a salad?" Marge asked with a smile. "I found some lovely greens fresh at an old farm just yesterday."

"If it's not too much trouble—"

"Nonsense!" Marge assured her, turning on her heel toward the galley. "Allow me to set the table, and then I'll bring it right out."

Yael grinned. "Thank you, Margie."

Marge looked over her shoulder, her open-mouthed smile displaying a mixture of shock and pleasure. "That's a good girl!"

Giggling to herself, Yael stood and crossed the jet to put away her book. It had been years since she had time to read for pleasure; she'd forgotten how much she enjoyed doing so. Though everything was falling apart for the main character, the story was finally coming together. She felt oddly connected to Jane, the protagonist who had forgotten herself. Yael was fairly certain things were about to take a dark turn, but she was also starting to see the light through the cracks in the story. Each time Jane had a new breakthrough, Yael felt her own reality was becoming clearer as well.

She had to admit that Olivier had a fascinating life full of adventure, a life lived in a world she hadn't known existed until now. Her father, Stefano, was wealthy, but he had shared very little of that lifestyle with Yael before she ran away from home at seventeen. Years of etiquette training aside, this was her first chance to behave like she came from money.

What good did living the old way do her? What had putting her life on the line for others really done, other than ruin her own? Nothing! Nothing at all. And so, with each passing day, Yael felt more comfortable with her new plan: doing nothing at all. For five years, she'd done the work; now she intended on reaping the benefits. The world could save itself.

"Marge, I've made *my* selection," Olivier whined playfully. "If you could be so kind."

Marge cackled as she took the DVD from him. "*Marmaduke*? Really?"

"I mean, we have it here . . . "

Yael giggled from the doorway. "I'm not watching *Marmaduke*!"

Olivier grabbed her hand and yanked her down beside him. "You will, and you'll like it."

"Play nice," Marge warned as she went to put on the movie.

"Yeah, play nice," Olivier said with a poke to Yael's side.

"Hey!" she replied in stride, slapping his hand away.

When he suddenly stopped and crossed his hands upon the table like a model student, Yael turned to find Marge staring at them sternly with hands on hips. The woman could only hold her composure for a few seconds before she burst into a fit of closed-mouth giggles.

Covering her eyes in pretend shame, Yael turned to Olivier and mouthed, *I will kill you.*

Olivier was laughing in an instant, clutching his chest as tears sprang into his eyes. "For God's sake, Marge, play the movie!"

A few minutes later they were all watching *Marmaduke*, with Marge sitting in a chair by the mounted television and Yael and Olivier munching away at their delicious cold fare. In addition to the promised salad made of leafy greens and tiny chunks of chopped veggies, there were two small fruit salads, a tray of Canadian cheeses and snacks, and two sushi rolls for Olivier.

Yael was stuffed by the time she finished her salad, even after Olivier picked at it without her permission. (She'd tried stabbing him with the fork, but he simply said *"En garde!"* and flicked her fork out of her hand with his.) As the credits began to roll, she grabbed a bowl of fruit salad and bit into the world's most perfect grape.

"Why is this so good?" she asked no one in particular, popping another into her mouth. "I don't understand."

"Oh, Prince Edward Island has got wonderful grapes," Marge piped up as she cleared the table. "Melons, peaches, plums, and pears . . . we always stop in at the local farms when we visit. Good potatoes, too!"

"Marge loves a good potato," Olivier nodded.

Yael shook her head and laughed. "You are so weird, dude."

"Hey, *dude*," he replied coolly, "What do you wanna watch next, *homeboy*?"

"I hate you."

Olivier ignored her, instead giving her a shove. She made a face in vexation, but pushed herself out of her seat and knelt before the credenza. Marge had updated the movie selection since her first trip. There were a couple of action movies—*Red* and *Salt*—but she wasn't in the mood for murder today. The full *Harry Potter* series— sans the latest and final movie, which didn't hit theaters until next month—was tempting, but she didn't feel like seeing *magical* murder either. Her last two choices were between a comedy and a movie she wasn't quite sure about, so she opted for the comedy in the end.

"Let's watch this one."

Olivier took the case from her. "*Date Night*? Are you trying to tell me something, Peach?"

She narrowed her eyes.

"This would be our . . . third?" He looked up and tapped his chin, then pointed at her. "Yes, our third date. That's the one where you put out."

Yael might have punched him, or at the very least slapped him one, but the way he said the last two words was so silly all she could do was shake her head. The man was incorrigible, but she loved how he could so quickly disarm her with his charm. He could almost make her forget . . .

She froze and swallowed the lump in her throat, casting her eyes upon her bare feet. Why was she pretending everything was fine? How could she be so happy—it hadn't even been a month!

"I changed my mind," she whispered solemnly. "I'd like to watch this instead."

"*The Book of Eli?*" Olivier asked in confusion, turning the case over to read the back. "Ruined landscape . . . humanity's redemption . . . yada, yada . . . oh, listen to this! '*Though Eli prefers peace, he will risk death to protect his precious cargo, for he must fulfill his destiny to help restore mankind.*' Really, Peach? This is the one?"

"Mmm hmm," she replied absently, her mind squarely on Joe. "I can read my book if you want to watch something else."

He handed Marge the movie and leaned against the chair. "What's happened to you?"

"Hmm?"

Placing his hands on Yael's shoulders, he leaned down to look her in the eye. "Earth to Peach? Where have you gone?"

Shrinking away from him, she turned to wipe the teardrop from her cheek only to lock eyes with Marge. Swallowing the sob rising from her belly, she blinked away the tears and forced a flat smile to her face.

"I need to use the restroom," she muttered, slipping past Olivier and shutting the door behind her. She didn't make it to the bathroom, though. Instead, she slumped into the closest chair and sank into the abyss.

Who am I fooling? she wondered. *I couldn't even make it a week . .*
.

She had done her very best to keep her mourning to the early evening, pushing through each day and promising herself she could collapse into depression later. *Just a few hours more*, she often told herself. And it worked, for the most part.

The times that it didn't, she was lucky enough to be on her own. Two days ago she'd broken down on top of a lighthouse; the woman who consoled her thought she was overwhelmed by the view. It had been beautiful, but it wasn't the majesty and splendor of the sea she was so emotional over.

It was Joe.

He was *there*. Well, of course he wasn't. But still, she saw him standing there plain as day—dapper as ever—looking out over the water alongside her. He was so close she could almost touch him. Sadly, when she tried, he disappeared.

The guilt she felt for laughing and enjoying herself today was nothing compared to the guilt she felt when she saw him then. He was in her dreams every single night, and those dreams often turned to nightmares. He was haunting her days, showing up in the strangest places at the worst times. He had been the love of her life, but all she wanted now was to be left alone.

How dare she? How dare she ask for peace from the ghost of the man she loved and lost? How dare she try to escape him? She owed him everything. She always would.

"Peaches?"

Yael hurriedly wiped her face and turned the chair away from the door.

"Can I come in?"

"*Occupado*," she sniffed.

Olivier walked into the small enclosure and shut the door silently behind him. "Woman, you will tell me what's wrong?"

She sniffed again.

He sat in the chair opposite her and clasped his hands together behind his head. "Something I said?"

She shrugged.

"I didn't think so. I'm far too charming for all this."

Yael wouldn't look at him. She didn't want him here, but did she really have a choice? Not only were they fifty-thousand feet in the air, but they were on *his* jet.

Just a few more hours to Cuba, she offered. *Then you can cry in peace.*

She cleared her throat. "I'm on my period."

"Ah," Olivier said knowingly. He sat forward and nodded. "Feeling guilty about denying me, are we?"

He pat her on the leg and stood, ignoring the daggers she shot at him. Walking to the door, he opened it and poked his head out.

"Marge, we've got a *code red* here."

Yael looked at him in alarm. Would he eject her from the plane?

Marge's voice rang out from the front of the cabin. "Ah, *having the painters in*? Not to worry!"

"What the hell?" she grumbled in confusion. "What's going on?"

Olivier shrugged and held the door open. "Movie's on. And it looks like ol' Marge has found another bottle of your favorite wine."

Yael sniffed and stood, drawing herself up to her full height as she moved to pass him.

But Olivier gripped her firmly and held her in place. "What aren't you telling me, woman?"

She stared into his eyes, discomfited by his closeness. "You have something in your teeth."

Squinting at her as he pursed his lips together, he shook his head. "You'll have to tell me eventually, you know."

Yael looked down at his hand until he released her, then leaned in close to whisper, "The less you know, the less likely you'll be implicated."

Lifting her foot and stomping on his pinky toe with her heel, she joined Marge in front of the TV and focused on her breathing.

CHAPTER SIX

CIENFUEGOS, CUBA

A gust of wind whirled around her, briefly lifting Yael's hair off her shoulder. The driver had offered her a scarf to wear for the ride into town, but she declined. Closing her eyes, she inhaled deeply and took in the sounds of the city.

They'd arrived at Jaime González Airport a little over an hour ago. Olivier explained it was only a fifteen-minute drive to a hotel along the coast of Bahia de Cienfuegos, a large bay situated on the south side of the island. She wished it were a bit farther—wanting to soak in as much as she could—but she was tired after a long day of traveling.

Yael's first surprise had been the presence of all kinds of well-maintained classic cars. Many of the cheap taxis were cars she would kill to drive, especially those in tip top shape. The shiny red and white Ford-O-Matic convertible they rode in was almost in mint condition—except for the newer Russian diesel engine. And the cars weren't the only things to shock her on the road. She was fairly certain she saw a cow in the distance when they left the airport and they'd even passed a couple of carts pulled by horses. On some roads, people were standing in the middle of the street having a leisurely chat. Modern cars zipped by at over one hundred kilometers per hour, while her current ride hadn't topped fifty.

Cienfuegos felt ancient *and* new, raw *and* refined. The duality was strange, and she couldn't wait to explore more in the light of day. Still, the cool breeze and the setting sun were a warm enough welcome. The bright reds and oranges were fading into the golden light, and the sky above her was becoming a rich palette of varying blues. She hoped they reached the hotel before the beautiful painting disappeared from the horizon completely.

"We're close," Olivier said as he leaned toward her. Keeping his tone low, he whispered, "We'll have to be on our best behavior this trip."

"When am I not?" she scoffed.

"No murders, no stomping of the feet," he continued, tapping each finger on his hand as he listed them off. "Definitely no mouthing off, and absolutely no pouting."

Yael looked up at the huge, teal mansion to her right. "I guess we won't be seeing much of each other."

He snorted. "In all seriousness, Mr. Alvarez is a family man. He is a champion for . . . good."

She watched him struggle to get the last word out and laughed. "What is your problem?"

Olivier shivered. "Good is so . . . boring, don't you think?"

Yael giggled.

"Mr. Alvarez is now retired and travels the world with his beautiful young mistress. His son manages the hotel—and the casino below— and his baby sister is the keeper of the house." He leaned in and whispered, "I'm trying to win a bid, so really butter them up. Love, kindness, respect—that's what I need from you this trip."

"I'll give it my best shot," she sighed.

"Thank God it's only for a week," he agreed. "Anything more than ten days and I'm *knackered*."

Yael was about to ask him to define yet another unfamiliar term when the car stopped. She gazed upon the splendid white and gold mansion before them and clapped her hands together. High above the tall stone steps, she could see the tower pinnacles covered by red tile roofs peeking through the thick palm trees.

"Breathtaking! It's like a fortress."

"If you like it here, you'll really love Europe. Cienfuegos is rather grandiose, they call it the Paris of Cuba," he explained. "You will find a lot of French influences, and not just in the architecture."

She nodded. Yael had a special place in her heart for fancy old things; she never understood why. Though she wasn't sure if she would enjoy any place outside of Sicily, she would have to give the rest of Europe a chance.

"Let's have a stroll while the driver collects our bags," he said, taking her hand and helping her from the car. "We should be able to watch the last few minutes of sunset from the boardwalk."

Taking her arm, he whisked her along. It was almost completely dark, but just ahead she saw clouds of amethyst dotting the deep violet pockets of clear sky. Standing together on the corner of the boardwalk, they took in the final moments of the rapidly setting sun.

"*Oye, lindo!*"

Yael and Olivier both followed the sound, finding the source waving to them from their car.

"Mama!"

Yael looked at Olivier quizzically. He took her arm and led her forward, waving enthusiastically at the older woman standing with hands on hips as she waited.

"*¿Qué es eso?* What are you doing?" she screamed. "We're waiting for you!"

"Yes, Mama!" Olivier shouted back. He tilted his head toward Yael in explanation. "Her first Cuban sunset."

The woman was four-eleven on a good day, but her strength was apparent when she yanked Olivier down to give him a tight hug and loud kiss on the cheek. Then, she tapped his face lovingly as she admired him.

"Too long," she said sweetly.

Yael pursed her lips, fighting off the urge to cry. Though tiny, the woman was overflowing with lovingkindness.

"Mama, this is my traveling companion—Peach, err—Yael. Yael, I am pleased to introduce Mary Jane Alvarez. She and her family run this incredible establishment."

Yael held out her hand and was surprised when Mary Jane took it and spun her around.

"Whoa," Yael said with a giggle, steadying herself. "*Gracias.*"

Clearly impressed, Mary Jane made a face and nodded at Olivier. "You knew better than to bring me another *gringa*, eh? This one, I like."

Olivier shook his head brusquely. "Oh, no no no, Mama. She and I? We are *not* together, not at all."

Yael watched as he stuck a finger under his nose and feigned disgust. Then, she and Mary Jane burst into laughter at the same time.

"*Dale, dale,*" Mary Jane said with a chuckle, ushering them up the steps. "The *canchanchara* is getting warm."

"Mary Jane is from Trinidad—Trinidad, Cuba that is—and she makes the best *canchanchara* in the country."

"The world," Mary Jane corrected.

"The world," Olivier agreed with a firm nod.

When they walked through the door, Yael accepted a small terracotta cup from the tray a staff member offered. The sweet rum drink was cold and refreshing, but as a bartender she knew it was a dangerous blend.

"Rum, lime juice . . . what else?" she asked as she squeezed the lime wedge garnish over the cup. "We need this at Margarita's."

Olivier shot her a glance. "I didn't know you still worked there."

Stunned, though only briefly, she blinked and realized he was right.

"You taste the honey," Mary Jane said matter-of-factly. "No chemicals here, so it's sweeter. I can show you."

Slack jawed, Olivier crossed his arms. "You never offered to show me!"

"You never ask me," Mary Jane shrugged, ignoring his outrage.

"She didn't," he whined.

Mary Jane shrugged again. "She is Cuban."

Olivier looked at Yael. "You are?"

She nodded, though her brows were raised in confusion. She wasn't quite sure how the woman knew that, but suddenly Yael felt right at home.

"Don't worry about it," Mary Jane said, patting his forearm. "There is plenty of Cachito in your room already ready. The boy will bring me more TuKola in the morning."

Clutching his chest dramatically, Olivier lifted his chin. "No TuKola?"

Mary Jane sucked her teeth at him. "At the bar."

"Mama? What are we doing here?"

Yael giggled. Olivier seemed to have a way about him, especially with older women. She suspected the women loved it, though they obviously knew not to take him seriously.

"Lord Hulley!"

"Ah! There you are," Olivier said with a grin. "Peach, this is Maximo Alvarez. Macho, meet the lovely Yael."

Yael bowed her head at the handsome middle aged man before her. He was awestruck, stopping in his tracks the moment he laid eyes on her.

"*Alabao*!"

She bit her lips to hide her smile.

"The saying goes: '*a man possesses beauty in his quality and a woman possesses quality in her beauty.*'" Maximo shook Olivier's hand and grinned. "Welcome back, *acere*. I hear you have come to play tourist?"

Olivier pulled him in for a quick bear hug. "Later, Macho. I've got work to do in the morning. For now . . . "

Maximo and Olivier walked toward the steps shoulder to shoulder, speaking in low tones. When Macho abruptly turned to look at Yael, she rolled her eyes. But he just laughed and slapped Olivier on the back. Together, the descended the steps and left her in the foyer.

Mary Jane barked a few orders to the men and women who had all gathered to see the new arrivals. Most of them scurried along, but two teenage boys launched toward her and fought over the luggage at her feet.

"Silvio!" Mary Jane snapped irritably, picking up Olivier's briefcase. "Take it. *Vamos*!"

Yael tried not to laugh at the look of disappointment on his face. When the other boy smugly picked up her bags, she covered her mouth in an unsuccessful attempt at stifling a loud snort. He blushed, then grinned and ran up the steps.

Mary Jane was studying Yael's face. "You tired, *nena*?"

When Yael nodded in confirmation, the small woman took her cup and placed it on a glass side table. Then, she beckoned her to follow.

"Let me show you the house," Mary Jane said softly. "Your room will be ready in a few minutes."

Yael stuck by her side, marveling at the gorgeous decor that felt straight out of a classic film she couldn't quite remember. Most everything was a deep burgundy or bright red, and each piece in the grand entryway was inlaid with gold. Ornate gold framed mirrors and paintings of all shapes and sizes adorned the wall as high as she could see. Red, white, and cream figurines and statues as tall as she was were strategically placed on side tables and displayed behind larger pieces of furniture. Yael was reminded of her childhood home, before her father remarried, and wondered if her mother had been inspired by this very room.

Mary Jane stopped at the edge of the archway leading out of the foyer and squared herself toward the front door. Pointing as she went, she tried to help Yael find her bearings.

"Those steps and those steps go up to the bedrooms and down to the basement. Your bedroom is on this side, so take the steps over there. The kitchen is on that side, so take those to the basement."

Yael made a mental note and nodded.

"*Dale.*"

Mary Jane walked deeper into the fortress and down a hallway, then turned to open a pair of French doors. Yael was blown away by the hidden tropical paradise within the large courtyard; packed full of flowering plants and fruit trees, she knew she would be spending much of her time here enjoying the breeze.

"Through those doors is the *cafetería*. You can see the pool tomorrow," Mary Jane told her. "*Dale.* To the kitchen."

They returned to the foyer and went down the steps opposite those Olivier and Maximo used to descend into the unknown. By the time they reached the last step, Yael could barely see a thing. When Mary Jane opened the door, Yael nearly fainted.

The scent of fresh Cuban bread and stewed meat instantly took her home. The air smelled just like *Mauricio Faedo's*, the only bakery in Tampa her mother would trust for authentic *pan Cubano*. She lifted her nose and tried to figure out what she wanted first, but it was no use. Whatever they were making, she needed it.

"Is the *cafetería* closed?"

Mary Jane smiled at her. "*Si, nena.* But the kitchen? Never."

Yael grinned, then gave the space the once-over. "Any *pan*?"

"There," Mary Jane replied, pointing at a large basket covered by a thick cloth. "Let me check the ovens."

Bouncing happily to the basket, Yael tore off a piece of Cuban bread the size of her arm and bit into it. She let out a moan of pure pleasure just as she locked eyes with her guide. Embarrassed, she tried to cover her overstuffed mouth with the rest of the bread in her hand, only to realize it made her look worse.

Mary Jane waggled her eyebrows and pointed into the oven. "Fresh," she teased.

Yael swallowed the bread in her mouth and said, "Thank you," before taking an even bigger bite.

Cackling loudly as she waved a hand at Yael, Mary Jane took a short loaf out of the oven and placed it on the counter. Yael watched as she opened a cabinet and picked out a bowl and plate.

"*¿Quieres algo de ropa vieja?*" she called back to Yael over her shoulder.

Lucky to have just swallowed, Yael gasped. "Yes! I mean . . . *Si! Si, por favor!*"

Ropa vieja—or old clothes—was her favorite Latin dish. The flank steak was slow cooked for hours until it could be easily shredded, and was paired with a sauce made of tomatoes, onions, bell peppers, and spices.

Her grandmother always made the dish when she and her mother would visit, but Yael didn't have it very often now that the two elders were long gone. In recent years, she would only eat it at an old cafe called *La Teresita*. In the rare case her grandmother didn't feel like cooking, the three of them would go sit at the stools in the *cafetería.* They always ate too much bread and drank too much *café con leche;* Yael missed them both dearly.

I wanna go home.

Maybe you already are?

Smiling at the feeling the strange thought gave her, she briefly wondered if she would ever see Tampa again. The door creaked behind her, providing the distraction she needed.

Yael turned and saw a woman standing just outside the door at the base of the steps. The light shined through the crack in the door, illuminating her lovely face in the darkness.

She's gorgeous! Yael thought, wondering why she didn't come into the kitchen. *Maybe she's shy?*

Yes, that made sense. Yael remembered those days herself, hiding behind closed doors until the coast was clear, doing all she could to remain unseen. The girl was probably a cook, unsure of who Yael was and what she might be doing in her kitchen. Walking to open the door and welcome her in, she was stunned when the woman disappeared before her eyes.

"Hey, don't go . . . "

She opened the door, but there was no one there. Lifting her head to look up the steps, she knew it wouldn't have been possible for the girl to run away *that fast*. And silently at that.

What the fuck?

Mary Jane rang a bell, causing Yael to jump. A large square of wood over the counter slid open, revealing a pass-through to what she had thought was a solid wall. A tall, thin woman appeared and smiled at Yael.

"Have Silvio take this to her room," Mary Jane ordered.

The woman took the tray and left without a word.

"This way," Mary Jane said to Yael, leaving the kitchen through a door on the other side of the room.

Yael stared at the open doorway behind her and peered up the steps. No one was there. She closed the door, shook off the eerie feeling, and crossed the kitchen to catch up with Mary Jane. They walked down a long hallway of closed doors until Yael heard the distant sound of rumba music.

A few feet ahead, a door swung open; a short man stepped into the hallway, turning back to the door to say something to someone inside. Mary Jane slowed her gait and Yael followed suit, watching the man curiously. Suddenly, a woman's hand grabbed his shirt and pulled him back in. He laughed and pushed her away, leaving her with a kiss on the neck and another on the cheek.

When he saw Mary Jane, it looked as if he were about to greet her. But when his eyes landed on Yael, his mouth dropped open.

Mary Jane tapped her foot and shook her head. He gave Yael the once over and sighed, as if longing for what might have been. Then, he raised a hand in surrender and walked in the other direction.

Yael's eyes darted back and forth as she questioned what she had seen. Mary Jane said nothing and continued on once the man was out of sight.

When they reached the far end of the hall, Yael noticed the steps that would lead her back to the front door to her left. She was starting to understand the layout of her home for the next week and a half. As far as she could tell, the fortress was just a big square building with an open courtyard in the center.

Though it was still muted, the music was getting louder. Mary Jane opened the last door in the hallway; sound flooded the corridor. They went inside and Yael knew exactly what she was seeing.

In many ways, the gigantic club reminded her of her underground bar in Ybor. The Lieu was much smaller, but she knew the telltale signs of debauchery all too well. Moreover, she knew what prostitution looked like.

"Mary Jane, is this a brothel?" she asked plainly.

"I knew the fool didn't tell you!"

She smiled. "I'm not offended, dear. Thanks for telling me."

Mary Jane turned to face her. "Here in Cuba, prostitution is a voluntary occupation. This is our casino. We are not a brothel, but *si*, this floor is for our girls. We keep them safe, we feed them, and we help them. And the men pay for it all."

Yael crossed her arms and checked the place out. "At my club, my girls do the same. We protect them and give them a place to do their business. In exchange, they drive ours."

Mary Jane was impressed. "So you understand. That is a good thing. I hoped we could be friends."

Tears welled up in Yael's eyes. She cleared her throat and smiled. "I think I am ready to see my room."

"Wait here," Mary Jane said.

Following her with her eyes, Yael saw Mary Jane approach Olivier and give him a whack on the behind. He gave her a saucy look as she seemingly ripped him a new one, pointing to Yael at the door and wagging her finger.

The women surrounding Olivier and Maximo all looked her way, many showing visible signs of jealousy as they sized her up. Yael gave them a finger wave and laughed to herself when two of them exhibited shock by her boldness. But then, Olivier made a joke and the entire group laughed hysterically. Mary Jane threw her hands up and returned to Yael.

"*Dale, mami.*"

Three flights of stairs and one long hallway later, Yael was handed a key and shown around her room. It was on the corner of the building directly above the spot where she stood to watch the sunset. Though the space was dimly lit, Yael could tell she would enjoy the gold and copper accents in more detail in the daylight. She wondered if her cousin Frederico could find a way to visit, because this couldn't be the only red room. Fred *loved* red.

Mary Jane pointed out the clawfoot tub and shower combo behind a floor to ceiling curtain of thick, plush velvet. Yael also had a fantastic view of the street and into the heart of Cienfuegos from one side of the room, and the Bay from the other. The full length windows had shutters on both sides of the glass to insulate the rooms from the Caribbean sun, and there was a balcony with seating on either corner. The building was not equipped with air conditioning, but the main spaces were cooled by portable units if the carefully designed breezeways didn't do the trick. She and Olivier had been provided with portable units, as all foreign guests were, which she was grateful for.

The food Mary Jane had sent up was waiting under a cloche. The blanket of the bread basket had a handy pocket for a warming device, so the loaf was the perfect temperature and softness for soaking up the juices of her black bean soup. A decanter of *canchanchara* was placed in a tub of ice, which Mary Jane told her not to consume. There were two large jugs of drinking water on a sofa table behind her, and she could request ice from bottled water anytime.

She didn't intend on finishing the entire decanter of *canchanchara*, but the loaf of bread kept calling her back for more, and the rum cocktail made it easy to wash down. Yael figured she was drunk when she confirmed with her olfactory memory that the *ropa vieja* tasted just like her grandmother's recipe. Then again, her grandmother was born in Cuba . . .

Yael was seriously tempted to move here and stay forever. Mary Jane was a wonderful mother figure, and—

"Hey!"

The girl vanished.

What the fuck!

Yael swore she saw her—clear as day—standing next to the tub. The beautiful girl from the stairwell was there in an instant and gone in a flash. And she was stark naked.

"Hello?"

She checked behind the curtain and opened both wardrobes, but no one else was in the room. She looked under the bed and opened the trunk, but she saw nothing. She opened the door to her room and checked the hallway. *Nada.*

First Joe, and now this?

She took a deep breath and exhaled sharply, recalling her decision to hang up her vigilante cape for good. If this was some sort of haunted mansion, that wasn't going to change just because Yael had arrived. The ghost girl would have to find another savior.

She could be one of the girls from the basement?

What if she needs your help?

"Not my circus . . ."

Yael poured herself a glass of water and went to sit on the balcony overlooking the Bay. The water beneath glittered along the coastline, with the shimmering light of homes, restaurants, and nightclubs twisting and curving as far as the eye could see. Straight ahead, it was as black as pitch.

In the past, before her double life fell to pieces, she and Joe would sit together on quiet nights like this and watch their own rolling bay of glistening diamonds. When the familiar sound of the water lapping at the boardwalk met her ears, a tear slid down her cheek.

It's time, she thought sadly.

His icy hand gripped her shoulder and rested there, a firm reminder that she had a duty to uphold. She'd learned the hard way that Joe's ghost would not be kept waiting.

CHAPTER SEVEN

Yael opened her eyes against the blinding light, only to instantly regret it. Bringing her fingers to rub the bridge of her nose, she closed her eyes to give them a chance to adjust. Her head was pounding and she felt swollen and puffy all over. Rubbing her eyes and trying them again, she sat up and blinked the blurred room into clarity. As much as she hated to admit it, she was hung over.

Some bartender, she thought irritably.

Oh, don't even start . . .

She made a face in response to the bickering voices in her head, wondering if they would ever shut up. The room was unbearably hot and inexplicably bright for what felt like the wee hours of the morning. The sounds outside her window caught her attention, and she finally understood why she was awake.

After she had consumed an entire decanter of *canchanchara*, she sat on the balcony and intermittently watched the water between bouts of silent, wracking sobs and fitful dosing until she could no longer hold her head up. By the time she made it into bed, she only had enough energy to slip off her silk robe and crawl under the covers. The balcony door was wide open and the portable A/C unit unplugged.

Hot, hung over, and depressed, Yael lay in her exhaustion for another several minutes until another issue reared its head.

"Aw, fuck!" she moaned.

Rolling out of bed and squeezing her thighs shut, she waddled toward the bath and climbed inside to rinse herself off. Luckily her cycle was almost over, so the mess she felt was only a personal problem. She would have hated to ruin a set of bed sheets the first night here.

The cool breeze of the previous evening had been replaced by a humidity she was familiar with, having been raised in Tampa. The few times she'd slept without air conditioning in her life were the few times she woke up just like this—dehydrated and overwhelmed by fatigue. The dangerous *canchanchara* had only made this morning worse, but she'd eaten enough bread to soak up the Bay outside her window. Hopefully she would feel better when the air kicked in.

Yael stepped onto the towel on the floor in front of the tub and decided to air dry, picking up her bathing towel only long enough to cover herself so she could close the balcony door. A blinding light flashed as she approached, showing a large boat in the harbor reflecting the rays of the rising sun directly into her room. She grumbled to herself, holding the towel over her bare breasts as she pulled the shutters closed and shut the door.

After she plugged in the A/C unit and turned it on, she stood naked before the vents like *The Vitruvian Man* until she began to feel cold. Remembering the dilemma that sent her to the shower, she opened her luggage and located her hygiene bag. With the room cool, but not cold, she opted to remain undressed for her morning nap.

As usual, she had a great deal of trouble sleeping during the night. And as usual, she found herself denying what she'd experienced. There was no Dream Joe, no ghost man coming to haunt her. There was certainly no ghost girl following her around the mansion. Yael knew she had to come to terms with the truth—if she didn't properly mourn Joe's death, she would never survive.

She sighed and searched for a towel rack. Finding one hidden on the wall behind the curtain, she walked into the bathroom area to put it away. A beautiful painting hung on the wall above, a plaque below engraved with a phrase in Spanish. Doing her best to ignore her father's voice in her head, she tried to listen for her mother instead. After she died, Yael's father did all he could to erase her Cuban side—including a restriction on speaking Spanish at home. Hearing it in her mother's voice always helped.

"*En vano se lava el cuerpo si no se lava el alma,*" she whispered slowly.

Clean your body, she thought quizzically. *Don't clean your . . . soul?*

No . . .

She studied it again, then frowned.

"One washes the body . . . in vain . . . if one does not wash the soul?" She threw her hands up and stared at the ceiling. "Fine! Okay? I get it!"

Stomping back to bed, she buried her face under a pillow and tried not to scream her head off.

"TELL ME THE TRUTH! Please? Tell me who you really are, Yael? Please, I'm begging you!"

"I-I can't. I'm sorry, I can't!"

"Jessum peace, woman! Why? Why, Yaya? How could you—"

Yael sat up in the bed and gasped for air, unable to breathe through the feelings of panic shaking her being.

In her youth, she didn't know what it meant to dream; as she grew older, she started to understand that people dreamt at night—even if she didn't. That worried her, for a time. When her vigilante visions began in high school, she had no idea they would one day lead her to kill. They worried her, for a long while.

She had learned a long time ago that her dreams deserved her full attention. Yael's dreams were inexplicably tied to the work she did as a vigilante and a hit woman for the mafia. After ignoring them for years and watching people get hurt, she understood she had no other choice.

But it was these sick, twisted scenarios and nightmarish images that concerned her the most. In the moments she found herself able to get some shut eye, she awakened in another world of terror and regret. It was absurd to deny the impact on her health; the circles under her eyes deepened with each passing week. What if she was cursed?

Oh great, cursed?

That is ridiculous!

She wanted to agree, but she knew the voices in her head weren't being logical. Whenever she was irritated or upset, they had a tendency to be contrary no matter what she was thinking. Maybe she wasn't being haunted. And maybe it was silly to think a curse was any different . . . but she *was* on the run. Without a direct order from who- or whatever sent her out to commit murder on the regular, she could neither confirm nor deny she was AWOL from her divine position.

Bullshit! she snapped. *Remember what happened last time you ignored your dreams . . .*

That was true. She had almost gone out of her mind. But it also proved her point. Yael wasn't dreaming her usual dreams—and she hadn't had a vision in weeks or longer. Rather, she was having what she thought might be *actual* nightmares. Like a normal person—well, sort of. If that was the case, there was not much she could do to fix it. Aside from never sleeping again, the usual tactic of playing out the dream in her reality was impossible.

Last night, she and Joe were dressed in old timey clothes and standing in what appeared to be a cabin or shack on a tall hill. He chased her and she chased him, each running to and fro as they dove deeper into madness. As was becoming the custom, Dream Joe's anger reared its ugly head and left her both terrorized and humiliated. Though she tried to give him what he wanted, she also told herself it would only serve to make things worse. No matter the setting or circumstance, Dream Yael was completely powerless to Dream Joe. Dream Joe hunted her each night, and she only pretended to be unwilling.

"Senorita?"

Yael froze. She looked about the room, but saw no one. The woman's voice sounded far away—dreamy. Was she going crazy after all? She swallowed, as an awful thought crept in.

Maybe I'm still sleeping?

The knock at the door made her jump, but she sighed in relief. If this had been a dream, it would have been the worst one yet. Though she was unaware of it while she slept, she knew the instant she was awake that none of it was real. She said a silent prayer of thanks, then jumped out of bed to put on her robe and answer the door. When her hand touched the knob, she stopped short.

There is no ghost girl, she told herself sharply.

How do you know? she asked nervously.

Just open the door!

She took a deep breath and swung the door open. Forgetting how heavy it was, she pulled a bit too hard and went flying to the side with it. When she caught her balance and met the eyes of a young woman, she questioned if she was awake after all.

Like her, the girl had long, thick, curly hair. Like her, the girl was well endowed and hippy. The girl wore little makeup, if any, and was modestly dressed in jean shorts and a white tee. If Yael didn't know any better, she'd say she was in the twilight zone.

The girl studied her curiously, her lip curled in amusement as she sized Yael up and down twice. When Yael tilted her head to the side, the girl copied her; amazed, she tilted it the opposite direction and watched as the girl did the same.

Fuck me, where the hell am I?

Yael tried to be reasonable, knowing she was visiting a locale where many of the people looked just like her. She lifted her hand to give the girl a finger wave, but when the girl imitated her again, she lost her nerve and dropped her hand. To her surprise, the girl's hand lifted and came straight toward her face.

"*Beso,*" the girl said, giving Yael's nose a boop. When Yael's mouth dropped open and her eyes tried to focus on the tip of her nose, the girl burst out laughing.

"I see *tía* María Juana wanted to play a joke on us both!"

Yael shook her head in confusion.

"I am Dulce," she continued. "Today my aunt told me I have a twin sister. She was not lying."

Smiling at the girl and nodding in agreement, Yael pulled her robe shut at her chest and caught her breath. Mary Jane was truly a character!

She looks a lot like you . . .

Yeah. A lot . . .

Dulce motioned toward the cart at her side. "Are you hungry? *Tía* said you would have an empty tray from dinner."

Yael knew she shouldn't be, but she was starving. She stepped into the doorway and peeked at a basket in the cart. "What's in there?"

The deep melodic sound of Dulce's laughter bounced off the stone walls of the hall. "And I thought she was exaggerating! Really, who else could eat two loaves of bread so early?"

Blushing, Yael bit her lip to hide the involuntary cringe. "I guess one loaf will do."

Dulce snorted and opened the lid of the basket. "Oh, I brought you one loaf . . . for later. It's under these, wrapped in brown paper for when you need a snack." She pointed at the two flat parcels of parchment paper and waggled her eyebrows. "The *tostadas* are for breakfast. Let me clear your table."

Stepping aside to allow her in, Yael watched Dulce whip the cart across the room toward the small dining table. Glancing about the room nervously, she hoped she hadn't left anything out of place.

"Since we are twins, I figured you would like the same things I like. *Tía* wanted to send you this big platter and I couldn't understand! *Pan, pan, pan*," she said with a giggle. "I told her, if you like *ropa vieja*, and you love *pan*, you must be a *Cubana*!"

Dulce shook the empty decanter of *canchancharra* and made a silly face at Yael. When she looked inside, as if searching for the last drop, Yael joined her in laughter.

"Cuban girl visiting Cuba for the first time doesn't need a fancy breakfast," Dulce said firmly. "You only need Cuban breakfast!"

Yael gasped. "*Cafe con leche*?"

When Dulce did a little jig and rhythmically moved her shoulders, Yael giggled and shimmied toward her from the door. Both of them continued dancing and giggling together as Dulce pulled the coffee pot from the bottom of the cart and poured her a cup. Yael ripped open the parchment paper and tore off a large piece of the loaf that had been pressed and buttered whole, then dipped it into the cup on the saucer Dulce handed her. She took a bite, stopping suddenly to savor the familiar flavors.

The rich saltiness of the bread and butter combined with the sweet yet bitter coffee brought tears to her eyes. *La Teresita* was a treasure; *The Columbia*, even more so. But neither of the Tampa restaurant staples had delivered like this. The little basement kitchen once again took her home, to her grandmother's table.

"You're making me jealous, *hermana*."

Opening her eyes in embarrassment—she'd forgotten she wasn't alone—Yael stared at the girl staring back at her. Not knowing what else to do, she offered her a bite of the *tostada*.

Hands squeezing her belly, Dulce closed her eyes and felt around for a beat. "No room," she said in disappointment.

Grinning and biting off another massive mouthful of the buttery bread, Yael wiped her tears on the sleeve of her robe and took a sip of the hot coffee.

Dulce finished cleaning the table and produced a small cooler from the bottom of the tray. "I thought you might need some ice," she said sweetly as she plucked a few chunks from inside and then poured Yael a tall glass of water. "Drink this before you have any more *canchanchara, chica*."

Yael snorted. "No more for me."

"Liar!"

They both chuckled. Dulce wheeled the cart toward the door and asked, "You need anything?"

Eyes watching the woman's plump derrière, Yael marveled at how similar they were in personality, demeanor, and even their figure. Dulce was definitely softer than Yael, which made sense; years of martial arts training had made Yael hard. But the softness did little to detract from her sensuality and was only enhanced by her stunning visage.

She really *looks a lot like you . . .*

Her eyes flared.

A lot like you!

An idea began to form in her mind, though she wasn't sure if it would work.

"*Hermana*," she said smoothly, "are you married? Or do you have a . . . a *novio*?"

Dulce whirled around, eyes narrowed and lips pursed. "Why do you ask?"

Wondering if they might be twins after all—or at the very least, related—Yael decided to be honest with her new friend. "The man I came with—"

"The *Lord*?" she asked, her eyes forming two flat slits. "What about him?"

"Can you keep a secret? Just between us?"

Dulce nodded and leaned against the door frame.

Yael cleared her throat. "My—my boyfriend just—"

A look of concern crossed Dulce's beautiful features.

"He died," Yael spat out bitterly, wiping the tears from her eyes. "But Olivier—Lord Olivier—doesn't need to know that. You understand."

Dulce started to nod, then stopped and shook her head.

"He wants me to have fun and be merry," Yael explained. "I can't do that right now—not most days. He's very fun, you know? And obviously he's rich, if that helps."

"Oh, I see," Dulce said smoothly. "You want me to keep him busy."

Yael swallowed, wondering if she'd offended the girl. She bit her lip. "Dulce, do you . . . uh . . . work, uh . . . "

Chuckling as she reached for the string of Yael's robe, she twirled it in her fingers absentmindedly. "No, no, chica. My uncle Macho would never allow me to, even if I tried. Not that I would," she clarified quickly when she met Yael's eyes. "My family owns this place, so the men know better."

"Oh, okay," Yael said with a nod. "I'm sorry, I didn't mean—"

"No, no! You misunderstand. I do not work downstairs, but I do come home for the summer. I'm a student in *La Yuma*—in Miami; well actually, I just graduated last month! Although I've never met this

Lord, I would not mind the company. You know what they say: jovial companions make this dull life tolerable."

Yael smiled. "He's definitely not dull."

"I've heard," Dulce retorted, a mischievous glint in her eye. "You know what? I believe it is time for lunch. Maybe I will find my uncle and his young *amigo* and join them?"

Dulce winked and turned to push the cart down the long corridor.

Staring after her, Yael called out, "Dulce?"

"Just between us," the girl replied knowingly as she strolled down the hall without looking back.

YAEL SAT on the balcony and watched the harbor, too full of bread and coffee to move out of the heat. She was dressed casually in her black V-neck and jeans, finding nothing more suitable in her luggage to wear for a day in. Perhaps in the next few days, she and Dulce could go shopping together. Either way, Olivier's obsession with anything and everything overpriced would no longer influence her habits.

Admittedly, she wasn't averse to all his ways and hoped to become more like him—though she'd never say it to his face. Even with his affairs and the structure he applied to their travels, Olivier was a fly by the seat of his pants kind of guy. Nothing seemed to bother him for more than a few minutes; when he was troubled he always recovered quickly and returned with a surprisingly solid solution or rebuttal. His commitment to himself was admirable and she was happy to take that note from the wealthy man's book.

Her first order of business was finding some sort of homeostasis where her mind was concerned; otherwise, she'd wouldn't be able to master the art of living carefree. Having decided to begin her mourning process today, she thought she should try clearing her head after breakfast.

The problem was, the daytime hours were usually her strongest hours of the day. Once she had eaten, showered, and gotten dressed, she was better able to keep her head above water. Not that she wanted to be depressed, but she needed to start healing and didn't know the first place to start.

A single knock on the door caught her attention, giving her the motivation she needed to arise from her seat. Crossing the room quickly, she opened it expecting to see Dulce.

"Peach," Olivier said blithely, studying his fingers with his usual nonchalance as he leaned against the wall in the hall. When he lifted his eyes and saw her outfit, he frowned. "Egads! What on earth are you wearing?"

She rolled her eyes and crossed her arms.

"Not speaking to me, are we?" He stood erect and straightened his blazer. "How was I supposed to know?"

Aggravated, Yael made a face. "What the fuck are you on about now?"

"Add a *bloody hell* to that and you're right on your way, dearie."

She exhaled loudly and moved to shut the door.

Olivier slapped his palm against the wood and stepped inside the room. "Look, I apologize. Prostitution is a voluntary occupation here, you see?"

Eyes darting left and right as she tried to recall where she'd heard that before, she finally understood what he was saying.

"Olivier, I couldn't care less that we're in a—" she shut the door behind her before finishing. "Well, a . . . a brothel, or whatever."

"Oh?"

She shrugged. "Have you ever considered that I just don't like you?"

Crossing the room to sit at the small dining table, he took a moment to reflect on her question. "No."

Chuckling and walking to close the balcony door, she joined him at the table with a long sigh. "To what do I owe the pleasure, sir?"

"There's a good girl," he said drily. "Now, why are you dressed like a peasant? Thinking of taking up residence?"

Yael frowned.

"In all seriousness," he continued, his tone low, "is there any chance you orchestrated this business with Dulce?"

Feigning innocence, Yael shook her head. "Who?"

"Come off it, Peach. How the hell did you manage that? You haven't even left your room."

"I'm sorry, sir. I don't have the foggiest idea—"

Olivier held his hand up. "She said *you said* that I was charming, dashing, rakishly handsome—"

"Then you must know it's a lie," Yael interrupted. "I'd never say such things."

"Exactly," he said, wagging a finger at her. "Which is why I know you've set this up. Are you trying to get rid of me, Peachy?"

"Yes," she said, staring longingly at the door.

He snorted. "Get changed, let's go for a drive."

"No," she said plainly, meeting his eyes with a blank stare. "I'm taking the day off."

"Day off?" he asked in exasperation. "You're quite literally on vacation. Unless . . . have you been committing murder without me?"

Yael rolled her eyes and groaned. "A day off from *you*!"

Olivier gasped and put a hand to his chest.

She sighed. He had been very helpful in distracting her in Canada, and she really needed it. But she knew it was time to get serious about healing, and Olivier was anything but.

"Listen to me, old chap," she said lightly. "I'm taking a day—no, fuck that, a week—for myself. I can find another place to stay if that is going to bother you. I just need some time to think and clear my head.

If you were traveling on someone else's coattail, you'd need the same. Right?"

Watching her curiously, he took a long, labored breath and exhaled. Then, he stood and stalked toward the door.

"Let's be reasonable," he said thoughtfully. "It's Friday afternoon. We're only here through next weekend. If I let you waste your entire pilgrimage trip, I'd be a terrible friend. You understand that, right?"

Yael, recognizing the tone as genuine, listened and considered his words. He wasn't wrong. She hadn't decided where she would go next —and they still needed time to discuss it—but she also hadn't made any plans to enjoy the present. She was in fucking Cuba, for goodness sakes!

Swallowing the lump in her throat, she asked, "What do you have in mind?"

His eyes darted between hers until she lowered her gaze. "You look terrible. Let's have a chinwag and we'll figure it all out."

She shook her head and wiped the tear from her cheek. "I need to be alone, Olivier."

"Are you *still* on your period?"

Yael's mouth dropped open. "Get out!"

"Why in the *bloody hell* do you need a week? What aren't you telling me, damn it?"

"Nothing!" she shouted back. Taking a breath, she tried a new tactic. "Have you never desired a moment to breathe? In all your life, you've never been through something you wanted to do alone?"

His gaze dropped to the floor, then returned to hers. "Alright, Peach. As long as you don't spend it cooped up in here, I'll give it to you. You've got three days."

"I said seven!"

He opened the door. "Four!"

"Seven!" she called after him, jumping out of her chair.

"Three?"

She sucked her teeth. "Fine. Six!"

"And six it is!" he yelled as he slammed the door behind him.

Laughing as she threw her hands up, she wondered if Dulce would find him at all tolerable. Olivier's manner of dry humor was so disarming she found it tough to stay angry with him.

Smoothing her hair back, she wondered what she would do for the next few days. If he and Dulce were busy together, she'd have to go shopping alone. She'd need new outfits if she wanted to be comfortable in the humidity and . . .

Joe's ghost stared at her from the balcony.

She did a double take but found the door closed and the balcony empty.

Shit! she cried, a disturbing chill prickling up her spine.

How foolish could she be? Had she forgotten today's dream? Or for that matter, any of the others? She was supposed to be mourning. Yael now understood that Joe wouldn't have it any other way.

CHAPTER EIGHT

The store clerk came around the counter and asked Yael what she was looking for. Or at least she thought that's what he said, given it was in Spanish. Taking a moment to think, she formulated her answer.

"*Para . . . la medicina,*" she said softly, wincing as she pointed to her forehead.

"Ah, *comprende,*" he replied, beckoning for her to follow him back to the register.

Yael stood at the counter and waited, surprised when the man pulled out a small box filled with odd looking prescription bottles.

"*Grande o pequeña?*" he asked.

She blinked.

"*Tu cabeza?*"

Is my head big or small? she wondered. *Oh!*

"*Grande.*"

He picked out two bottles and placed them on the counter then held up his hands. She looked at him and then the pills on the counter, trying to figure out what came next. When he stared at her expectantly, she picked up both bottles and studied the labels. One said *paracetamol* and the other was *ibuprofeno*. Opting for the more familiar of the two, she set the bottles down and pointed at the ibuprofen. He nodded, took out two pills, and gave them to her.

"*¿Necesitas agua?*"

She shook her head and waved her hand in thanks, then left the store. Though she ordinarily wouldn't accept random pharmaceuticals from someone, she was finding Cuba to be a culture she could trust. Still, four days of the dull ache in the center of her forehead was as good a reason as any.

Her week of mourning had been somewhat successful, but the first few days of crying led to this new pain in her head. She hadn't intended on spending the entire weekend in bed, but the parade of lovers on the boardwalk Friday evening worked to send her into a spiral. By Monday, she found her strength and ventured out for a stroll around downtown Cienfuegos. The palm trees, blue skies, and old brick buildings all reminded her of Ybor City back in Tampa; knowing she would never return, Yael found herself saying a tearful goodbye to her hometown from across the gulf. Tuesday and Wednesday had been spent recalibrating. Both mornings she started the day with a shopping trip, and in the evenings she reorganized her wardrobe and dresser drawers, respectively. Thursday morning came around quickly, and Olivier was there bright and early to let her know their plans.

Yael was feeling better and more ready to enjoy her last few days in Cuba—at least for her mother and family's sake. So many Cuban Americans missed out on the chance to come home, and she was here in the best position to have a good time! But when he told her they were going to live like locals with Dulce, she almost changed her tune. She wasn't sure how she would handle being their third wheel or if she could deal with watching a happy couple just yet.

She opened her bottle of water and took a swig, then swallowed one of the pills. She hoped it was enough—especially since she never took medications—and slipped the other pill into the button pocket of her shorts.

In spite of her worries, Olivier and Dulce had been surprisingly relaxed in her presence. She felt like she was reconnecting with old friends, not joining two lovers on an outing. The ride up the coast had been incredible, and Yael learned a lot about Cuba thanks to her unofficial twin.

One of the most surprising lessons was about *Playa Girón*, the bayside beach they'd come to for the festival. Fifty years ago, the CIA and the US military brought mercenaries to invade Cuba; using this same beach, they came in through the water and battled the Cuban people for three days. Though Yael had heard of the "Bay of Pigs" and vaguely remembered it being associated with JFK, she remembered little of the history or its significance. But here on the very land where the battle raged on, it was not lost. The alert and resourceful revolutionaries won, beating back the imperialists through sheer determination. She resonated with Dulce's pride, though she didn't really understand why.

You're Cuban.

And *you're American.*

Yael shook her head. Being mixed with so many cultures and ethnicities was far easier in America. The moment an American stepped foot outside of the country, however . . .

Joe walked up to her and stopped short only inches from her face.

Rooted in place, Yael took several spastic breaths and tried to regain some measure of calm. Last week, this would have ended her; today, she understood.

Joe's spirit would likely *never* leave her.

When the realization hit her a few days earlier, she felt terrible and very afraid. The idea of Joe's ghost following her around and tormenting her was scary, but what might that mean for him? Was *she* his unfinished business? If she was, he could kill her. She didn't mind. He deserved a good end, even if it had to be in the afterlife.

Deep in her love for him, she called to him and told him so, begging him to take her out and find his peace. And for the first night on her trip, he didn't come. She slept better, though she still had nightmares. She felt free, even though she knew they were bound. As the days passed, she was less frightened of his presence. He came closer and closer every day.

A little too close there, bub, she thought uncomfortably.

Joe stared her down until she met his eyes. A warm breeze encircled her, leaving her tempted to throw her arms around him. She didn't, instead choosing to close her eyes and pretend it was his breath on her skin.

When she opened her eyes, he was gone.

Good, she thought. *You did good that time.*

But she looked over her shoulder and saw he was standing on the corner, staring at her. *Waiting.* Turning away from the little town to face the beach, she located Dulce and Olivier playing fútbol on the sand with a few locals. They appeared to be having a great time, totally unaware of her sneaky departure. She looked back at Joe and found him another block away.

Just follow him.

Where? You have no idea where you are!

Yael walked toward the corner where he stood and took a look around, deciding that she wouldn't go far. If she stuck to the main drive, there would be plenty of witnesses. She took one look back and studied the street she was on, and then headed into town behind him.

Tailing a live person was one thing. Human beings had their limitations—mainly their fleshly bodies and inability to fly. Following Joe in this form was unnerving. One moment he was on a street corner, the next he was on a rooftop. And it was obvious he had no intentions of sticking to the main road.

Where are you, Joe? Show me what you want me to do.

Clearing the way for a couple of kids on bikes, she stood on another corner and waited. The buildings in the area were small, mostly one-story. She was able to see straight through to the end of the thoroughfare from the central street, meaning what she thought was a town couldn't be more than seven or eight blocks wide and maybe a few blocks long. Why would he lead her here and disappear? What was she supposed to see?

The sound of *reggaeton* music exploded into her mind, sending pain from her ears to the center of her forehead. Squeezing her eyes shut, she waited for the offending car to pass so she could think again. But when she opened her eyes, no one else seemed to notice.

Damn it, Joe! Where are you?

The music grew louder, forcing her to brace herself on the wall behind her. Suddenly, she was blinded by flickering lights. She could see people—were they dancing?

It's a vision! she tried to tell herself.

But it was no use. Her brain was fried and she was out of practice. A wave of nausea broke through, and she was forced to stand perfectly still or risk losing her stomach. Breath ragged, she gave up on the vision and focused on staying upright.

Joe, please! Why are you doing this?

No answer. But that was the norm; he only spoke to her in dreams.

Please, damn it! Please, Joe!

The music in her head stopped, though it continued to echo in the distant crevices of her mind. She craved the peace of silence, even if just for a moment, but the echo would not cease.

That's not an echo, you idiot!

She quickly turned toward the sound, a sharp pain slicing through her spine. The voice in her head was right. The music was real, and it was coming from somewhere close by.

The sun was low on the horizon. Would she have time to do whatever she was here to do before dark? And why did she have the sinking feeling she was about to be *working* on her vacation?

Yael looked at the sky in warning, reminding her unknown divine employer know she was retired. She had come to the beach to enjoy herself and would not be deviating from the plan for some random—

Blindness overwhelmed her for an instant only for her sight to return in the same second.

Yael sighed. *And there it is . . .*

Yes, she'd seen it—her next kill—clear and plain as day.

But when she took a step forward to follow her *calling*, her legs were like jelly and the vision was gone. She knew she needed to go, *now*! If someone was in trouble, there was no time to waste paralyzed by fear!

Yael launched forward as if she were knee deep in thick tar. Just as she was able to cross the road, the very naked ghost girl from the mansion appeared on the corner and stared her down.

CHAPTER NINE

Yael stood perfectly still, though every muscle in her body was clenched tight. The naked ghost woman stood unmoving on the street corner, her hair blowing eerily in the wind. There was no doubt she was the same girl from the night in the kitchen and Yael's bedroom.

Was she *what Joe wanted to show me?*

As much as Yael wanted to turn around and move on, she was sure that the girl was close by and in grave danger. Retired or not, could she really ignore what she was feeling? Someone's daughter, sister, or mother might not make it home tonight if she didn't do her job today. Whether she was back in Ybor City or here in Cuba, Yael could not escape the darkness.

"American girl?"

Yael turned to find a man had approached her and was standing inordinately close. He was shorter and likely a little older than she, and it was obvious from his glassy eyes and sideways lean that he was intoxicated. She looked toward the street corner, but neither ghost was anywhere to be found.

Exhaling in frustration, she scanned the street until her eyes met the man's again.

"Life is . . . short," he said, practicing his English. "But! Only one second . . . to smile."

When he touched both of his cheeks and gave her a beaming, toothy grin, she couldn't help but return it. Then, she stepped away from him and waved apologetically before hurrying across the street.

Come on, Joe. What the hell is going on here?

The street was mostly quiet. The restaurants and storefronts on the main road were designed for tourists, whereas this block seemed to cater to hungry locals and small businesses. There were a few places for fixing everything from shoes to appliances, as well as an auto repair shop at the far end. She passed a bar and a small bakery, then heard the *reggaeton* music again.

"Yael!"

She spun around and searched for the voice. If she didn't know any better, it was an echo of *Joe's* voice she'd heard *aloud*. Was that possible? No one around her seemed to notice, though a pale older woman did give her a strange look.

A glimmer of light flashed in her eyes to the left. A long, dark alley way was positioned between the two wide buildings on the other side of the street. She blinked and heard the sound of a loud crack.

Shit!

Picking up the pace as she crossed the road, she waited until the coast was clear before slipping into the alley. She had no weapon; she shot a glance to the sky and hoped she wasn't completely out of practice. The years of honing her body as a weapon met a somewhat abrupt end when the dojo burned down, and her rooftop workouts were nowhere near enough.

The beat of the *reggaeton* music she'd been searching for was close enough for her to hear the vibration on the tin roof above. She was in the right place, but where was she? Peering around the corner at the end of the alley, she saw the hidden courtyard before her and groaned. This alley led to an open area with multiple other alleyways shooting off in every direction. There were no less than four bars—one on every corner—and she was pretty sure the two closed doors were nightclubs waiting to open.

Follow the music.

That was a good plan. Each bar was playing a different type of music, but it was the one straight down the way that seemed to be playing what she was looking for. Yael hoped that her *knowing* would kick in soon, or at least that the vision would refresh in her mental computer. It was darker here than anywhere else in the little town, and she was a lone foreigner. She needed something—anything—to go on.

Voices behind her in the alley spurred her forward. She stepped onto a paver that had been laid to form a makeshift sidewalk along the front of the buildings and met at a central block in the middle of the courtyard. Following the sidewalk to the second bar, she listened to the music and hoped for a clue.

Wait! What was that?

Yael stopped. She *had* heard something . . . but what? A whimper? She scanned her surroundings and searched for a small child or animal. Nothing.

The sounds of the voices from the main alley sent her flying into the alley beside her. Standing between the two bars gave her time to think, but it sure didn't feel safe. She needed to make a move.

Another whimper came, followed by a low grunt. Yael gasped and turned around. Before her eyes had adjusted, the alley appeared to end in darkness. But she could see now that the building of the bar she was casing was short, leaving a space to walk in back. She followed the sound of another low cry, nerves on end.

Creeping silently toward the edge of the alleyway, she crouched low and poked her head around the corner. At first, she only saw movement she assumed to be caused by a breeze. But here in the back alley of a back alley, there was no wind.

The groan gave him away before she understood, but once she did, Yael blushed profusely. A couple was in the far corner mid coitus, which made *her* a peeping Tom! She pulled her head back in shame and stood, steadying herself on the wall as she breathed through her spiraling emotions.

"¡*No!*"

Yael jumped and looked back at the couple, confused by the flash of light she saw in the man's hand. When the woman made a choking sound, Yael finally knew what she was here to do.

"¡*Cállate, puta*!"

Searching the ground for anything she could pick up and hit him with, Yael settled for an empty bottle of rum. She leapt across the dirt and drew back the bottle.

The glowing eyes of the ghost girl looked into hers with shock, causing her to falter.

The man, suddenly aware of Yael's presence, turned her way just as she swung the bottle. Instead of breaking onto the back of his head, it hit him square in the face and shattered.

"Ahhh!" he screamed in agony, dropping what she now saw was a large switchblade to the ground. He touched his bloody nose and stared at his hands.

Yael dove for the blade and came up ready to fight, but he'd focused his attention on the woman he had been raping and was swinging his fists wildly. The woman tried to get away, but he had her cornered as he wailed on her, punching her over and over again.

In her fury, Yael saw red. Her vision returned, showing her what she had to do. After what she'd just witnessed, there was no hesitation.

Running forward at full speed, Yael clasped the man's knife in both hands. Raising it over her head, she stabbed him in the shoulder with all the force she could muster. Then, she pulled his head backward by his hair and shoved him forward by the hilt of the blade. Tripping him in front of the cement wall this way brought a resounding *crack* to the darkness before he slumped to the ground.

The girl grabbed Yael's arm and yanked her away, pulling her toward the entry of the alley. Together, they ran to the courtyard, stopping short of leaving the alley to catch their breath.

"Okay?" Yael asked.

To her surprise, the woman was *not* the ghost girl from the mansion. She was older than Yael, rather than the same age or younger as she had assumed the ghost girl was. And by the looks of her attire, she was a prostitute.

Straightening her skirt with trembling hands and wiping the tears from her eyes, the woman tried to compose herself. She wouldn't look at Yael directly for longer than a second.

When Yael saw her nervously straighten her skirt for the fourth time, she drew the woman into an embrace and held her as she broke down and sobbed. The strangest part of all? Yael felt as though she could *hear* the woman's tears.

Not the sound of her crying or the liquid dropping from lid to cheek. No, it was the sound of words—or better yet, a story—coming through with each passing moment. She knew . . . this woman was a lady of the night, had been since she was young. Her name was . . . Maritza. She'd always lived here in *Playa Giron,* and she preferred to bed the tourists over the locals. The man Yael had just murdered was one of the few regulars she kept, and not by choice. He would force her each time, then throw a few dollars her way in payment. He had raped her hundreds of times in the last decade, and sometimes he even brought his friends. He was cruel, but no one had ever cared. Not until tonight.

Yael's tears flowed as she listened, listened to the wretched sound of a story never told. The story of a woman . . . and a man . . . and a city—a tale as old as time. Hidden beneath the surface of many lives lay a comedy or a tragedy. A fairy tale or a grim reality. And this woman? Her story was not yet over, not just begun. This woman cried for her yesterdays, and she cried for today, but she cried for her tomorrows, too.

By the time Maritza calmed down, the sky was nearly black. Yael stared at the darkness above and hoped Olivier wouldn't leave without her. Releasing the woman and helping her fix her hair, Yael tilted her head and met her eyes.

"*Te amo tanto,*" Yael said softly. Taking her hands and giving them a squeeze, she whispered, "*Cuídate, hermana* Maritza."

Maritza gasped and jumped away, mouth agape. Staring at Yael and shaking her head, her chest heaved and her eyes filled with wonder.

Feeling only slightly uncomfortable, Yael gave her a half smile and stepped into the courtyard. A man was standing at the front of the door to her right, smoking a cigar outside the bar. He studied her curiously, eyes darting into the alley and then back at her. When Maritza came out of the alley behind her and walked his way, his expression changed to concern.

"Maritza?" he asked, approaching the shaken woman with his hand extended.

Yael followed her feet along the pavers and made her way toward the main alley. When she looked back, the man was staring at her with the same expression of shock that Maritza just had. He nodded at her and she nodded back. Then, she slipped into the alley and hoped she still had a ride home.

CHAPTER TEN

Olivier watched Yael settle in to the plush leather booth and take a sip of *canchanchara*. Ever ready, she had made sure to request a bottle of water with each new decanter today. She told him it was helping her maintain a nice buzz and decrease the likelihood of developing another hangover.

"*¿Quieres un poco de pan, hermosa?*" Dulce asked Yael as she slid out of the booth. "There should be fresh loaves by now!"

Olivier whacked her bottom and drew his fingers back quickly to avoid the swat of her hand. Ignoring him when she stepped out of reach, Dulce looked at Yael and waggled her eyebrows. Nodding and biting her lip, she shimmied away happily.

"*Y mas mantequilla!*" Yael shouted after her.

Dulce gave her a look that said 'no duh' before she disappeared around the casino bar.

They sat in the booth quietly, listening to the final song of the jazz band on stage. Once they wrapped up their set, the club of the mansion basement would turn over and welcome a younger crowd that was ready to dance. Most of the girls who lived in the rooms had been here for the earlier hours of the jazz show; they were all occupied now.

Once they showered and refreshed their rooms, they would join the locals for a night of dancing and more.

The music ended with a blasting crescendo, the trumpets blaring as the remaining patrons cheered and whistled. A thick silence quickly blanketed the club, then a record player scratched and the sound of samba drums joined the low hum of the small crowd.

"I saw you, you know."

Yael frowned. "Saw me what?"

"Where did you go, Peach?" Olivier pressed.

"When?"

He took a sip of brandy. "When you went off alone."

The look on her face said she'd just been splashed with cold water.

"Exactly," he said, taking another sip.

Yael opened her water bottle. "I don't know what you're talking about."

"I thought we were better than this," he whined.

"Why are you so nosy?" she snapped. "Can't you just enjoy your vacation?"

"I'm not on vacation," he whispered in reminder. "You're hiding things from your very best friend, and I am simply trying to help clear the air."

Yael choked on the water she was sipping. "We are not best—"

"As your one and only very best friend in the whole wide world, it is my duty to be sure *you* are enjoying *your* vacation."

She chuckled.

"If we are going to maintain our powerful, *life-giving* friendship, we will need to catch up. Kill anyone this week?"

Gasping as she frantically searched to see who might be nearby, Olivier decided she had just given herself away.

"I don't need to know about every gruesome murder," he explained. "Actually, I still want to know what happened to Stacey—

whenever you're ready of course. But you will have to tell me something, otherwise we might lose touch."

"You've lost touch," she grumbled, tossing back the last of her cocktail.

Olivier smiled. His little Peach was finally starting to loosen up.

"Tell me something," he said as he refilled her glass. "Why are you still blocking me out? It's absolutely baffling."

Yael eyed him over the rim of her glass, then took a sip. "I can't decide whether or not I trust you."

"Honesty," he said with a nod. "Refreshing."

"Even though we are definitely not friends, I guess you are starting to grow on me."

"Ah, like a new set of plugs."

She stared at him perplexed, then made a face. "B-What?"

"You were saying?"

Eyes darting back and forth, she found her train of thought and continued. "If I agree to tell you more—not yet, but soon—will you stop asking?"

"I will think about it," he replied. "But tell me, why not now?"

She shrugged. "I just need time. I have to deal with what brought me here, you know?"

Olivier saw Dulce bouncing over with a tray from the corner of his eye. "Alright, I agree. But, in the name of friendship, you and I will be spending the afternoon by the pool."

Yael's eyes were on the tray in Dulce's hand when she said, "Sure. Sounds good."

Smiling at his own brilliance, he stood to help Dulce with the tray and then went to find Mary Jane. He was going to need her help to pull this off. That and a bottle of rum.

CHAPTER ELEVEN

Yael was positive she was drunk. Though she couldn't quite understand how it happened, and so quickly at that, she felt slightly out of her wits. She liked to think that, aside from her rare moments of rage, she never lost control.

"What time is it?" she asked Olivier.

"Time for another drink," he replied smoothly, leaning over to snatch her glass before she could object. "Can I ask you something?"

"Do I have a choice?" she slurred in question.

Olivier handed her the cup and shook his head. "Are you really betrothed?"

She blinked a few times, her head wobbling as she tried to focus. "Betrothed? He's dead."

"So the day we met . . . that was a lie?"

Yael's brows furrowed in thought. "No. Well, kinda."

He stared at her.

"I didn't *lie* lie. It was a good word to explain my situation." She sat back in the lounge chair and closed her eyes. "Where is that bread? Sheesh."

"You've already had your bread. So, you were *kind of* betrothed? What does that mean in American English?"

Yael snorted and reached out her hand, aimlessly grasping at the air until her fingers could pick up the mango at the edge of the fruit platter beside her. She ate it and licked her fingers clean. Opening one eye and fighting to find her focus, she looked at him and shrugged.

"Means I had someone. Someone great," she cried.

"Oh, no! Peachy, look at that," he whispered, waiting for her to follow his finger with her eye. "That bird is trapped!"

"What bird?" she asked, searching for it until her eye rolled shut. Closing it tight, she relaxed into the chair and asked, "Where's that bread?"

"So you ran away . . . from love? Leave someone at the altar, did we?" Olivier poked her in the leg. "You aren't a murderer at all, are you? You're just a scaredy cat."

Yael slapped at his hand, though she ended up hitting herself. Opening her eyes to squint at him, she said, "I am not scared."

"And you're not a cat," he said in agreement.

She frowned and tried to figure out what he meant by that. Shrugging it off, she decided she might as well tell him the truth.

"I killed them. So I ran."

"I knew it!" he exclaimed proudly.

She sucked her teeth and rolled her eyes, her whole head following without warning. "You don't know anything, man. See, I didn't *kill* kill, but I might as well have."

Olivier sat back in his chair and sipped his fruity cocktail. "I killed someone once."

Yael leaned toward him, grabbing the arm of the chair when she felt herself falling forward. "How'd you do it?"

"Her name was Emma Kate, and I loved her. We rode horses all our lives, and one day she made me so angry that I sent her horse off into the woods. She jumped on my stallion to give chase, but he bucked her off as they made their way down the path. Died instantly."

Studying him with her good eye, Yael wondered why he would tell her such a story. Was it possible he was telling her the truth? He was deep in thought, paying her no mind as he reminisced.

"Emma Kate?"

He looked up at her and nodded solemnly.

"Did you ever have another love?"

"No," Olivier replied flatly. "Never wanted my temper to be someone's end."

Yael frowned. "Maybe you should try. Might make you less of a fucking creep."

"Real nice, Peach!" he scoffed, downing the rest of his drink. "Took me years to get over that one. You know what finally did it?"

"What?"

"My nursemaid gave me old knob a gobble—"

"Nursemaid?" Yael exclaimed loudly. "That's disgusting!"

"What! She was gagging for it, what was I supposed to do?" Olivier asked angrily. "It's not like she was a boiler. Plus, she had perfect, round jubblies and would do just about anything for my baby batt—"

"Stop!"

"But, Peach—"

"Nope!"

"I thought we were sharing," he whined.

"Ugh!" She shook her head. "You know you went British on me?"

He chuckled. "I *am* British . . . but, noted. I do stand by my point, though. You need a rebound."

"Right," she snorted. "Get over one by getting under another? Pfft. Whatever."

"I think, in your case, it might be the only solution. As your friend,

I'd be happy to oblige, but I know that would create some complications. Do you have any ideas of who you might want to do next?"

"No one is next, you weirdo!"

Olivier gasped, appalled by her statement. "What do you mean by that?"

"I'm done with all that, man." She closed her eyes. "I've got work to focus on."

"Look at me, woman."

Yael opened her eyes and tried to focus on his face. He seemed more serious than usual.

"Where will you go?"

"Huh?"

"Our trip is quickly coming to an end. I have to make arrangements for you. Will you stay here or return home? Have you decided yet?"

Shaking her head and biting her lip, she tried to reflect on what she really wanted next. Unfortunately, her mind was so clouded with drink and sleepiness that she couldn't think straight.

"I could also return on my way back to London in a couple of weeks." He paused. "Then again . . . you might need to come to Paradise after all."

"Paradise? This is paradise."

He grinned. "Thinking of staying? I can't blame you. A lot of American fugitives are said to have found asylum here."

Yael shifted uncomfortably in her seat. The word *fugitive* was a bit of a reach, right?

"In truth, this is a lovely place. But there is such a thing as Paradise, and I know because I've seen it with my own two eyes."

She gazed at him and wondered if he were being facetious. The punchline never came. Olivier was in his own world, a small smile planted on his face as he stared into the distance.

"What is this place?" she asked, unable to stop herself. "Or, where is it?"

"Hmm? Oh, right." He sat up and turned toward her. "Not far from here. And they have a lot more to offer, specializing in *fantasy* as it were."

"Fantasy, huh?"

Yael looked at the pool and imagined herself in a resort commercial. She saw herself walking naked on a private beach and then joining her masseuse in the cabana for a hot stone massage. Then she imagined a grotto hidden behind a waterfall; she could see herself there, dressed as a mermaid and sipping something out of a coconut. When she imagined herself flying through the air screaming '*weeeee*', she shook herself.

"I'm in!"

Olivier smiled. "Are you sure? I'll warn you, it can be very expensive."

"I'm drunk, I'm feeling reckless. I say it's time to put some of this damn money to good use."

"We leave tomorrow!"

She smacked her lips. "Where's that bread?"

"Peaches, you've had enough bread for today."

Yael couldn't remember having any bread. In fact, she hadn't eaten anything since this morning other than the fruit and vegetables from the tray beside her.

"Olivier," she groaned. "I don't feel so good. Can you find someone to help me to my room?"

He stood and took her hand, pulling her up slowly. "Let's go."

"Mmm mmm! Not *you*, Mr. Touchy-Touchy."

Olivier snorted. "Come on, woman. You're heavier than I thought you'd be."

Yael fell forward and went limp in his arms, then laughed when his legs briefly trembled beneath them.

"I will drop you into the pool," he warned tightly, pulling her forward toward the door.

She giggled and tossed her arm around his shoulder. It was a long clumsy walk down the hall, with Yael enjoying herself a little too much along the way. By the time they got to the slim, winding stairway in the corner of the mansion, Olivier was beginning to sweat. She looked up and sighed.

"Almost there, Peach"

They carefully climbed the steps with only a few words of complaint from his end, then traveled the short distance to her room and went inside. Olivier tried to take Yael to her bed, but she steered him toward the table instead.

"*You're never gonna get it,*" she sang as she opened the paper bag sitting in the middle. She pulled out a piece of bread and finished her song, using it as a microphone. "*Never gonna get—whoa whoa whoa wow!*"

Olivier stared at her as she took a bite and smiled in satisfaction.

"Did you bring me up here for that?"

She grinned and chewed louder. "You thought you were gonna get it, huh?"

He threw his hands up and made a face of innocence. "Of course not! Well . . . maybe a round of snogging. But I thought you were out of it. Completely off your trolley! Where's the fun in that?"

Yael swallowed enough of the bread in her mouth to let her get a word out. "Speak English, good man."

"I've no interest in a shag with Sleeping Beauty, alright? Rather find me a slag or a nice tart—*John Thomas* ain't too picky when he's randy if you know what I mean."

"Never would have guessed," she said as she took another bite. "Now, go get me a *tostada*."

CHAPTER TWELVE

Yael ran from one room to the next, searching for the phone. When the ringing first started, she thought she could ignore it. But it had driven her mad, and now she would stop at nothing to find it. She was sure it was Joe. It had to be. She hadn't seen him in—how long had it been? Not that it mattered. One moment away was a moment too long.

She ran into the next room, frustrated at how similar it was to the previous. And like the other room, she could swear there was someone here watching her. Should she check in the last place she expected, or the first? What would she do if it stopped ringing?

No, it wouldn't stop. She had to answer it or it would never stop. She ran into the next room and shuddered at the sight of blood dripping down the walls. She was running out of time. She had to find it. She had to answer the call.

She ran to the next room and came to a screeching halt. There was no floor! How could she answer the phone if she couldn't walk inside?

"Joe!" she cried, praying he would come to her rescue. "Joe, please? I'm scared!"

Tearing her eyes from the abyss below, she ran to the next room.

She had to find the phone. It wouldn't stop ringing until—

"Peach?"

Yael sat up in bed, gasping for breath. A knock at the door tore through her panic. She forced herself out of bed. Her body was sore and she was exhausted; it felt as if she'd been running all night.

"Yes?" she called through the door.

"Are you ready? We've got to load the car."

Shit!

Wait. Where are we going?

She looked over at her luggage and nearly cried, grateful to her drunken self for being so oddly prudent.

"I'll leave the bags outside. Give me a minute."

"Righto," Olivier replied.

YAEL WASN'T sure if she was hungover or still feeling the effects of the drinks from the night prior. In spite of herself, she'd ordered one last decanter of *canchanchara* and a small platter of food to help soak it up. The bad news was, the food hadn't done it's job; the good news, though, was that she didn't feel nauseous or otherwise ill.

Just a little off, she assured herself.

Yes, she was. As the bits and pieces of her day at the pool emerged, she began to wonder if Olivier had hoped to take advantage of her. Did she unexpectedly get too drunk too fast? Could he have been telling the truth? As far as she knew, her ex-fiancé preferred his women unconscious; maybe Olivier's proverbial apple had fallen further from the family tree than she'd originally believed.

Much of her behavior toward Olivier was based on their initial meeting and all the things that had happened to her leading up to it. She'd never thought to ask him what he really thought of his cousin. Yael always assumed Olivier was just as bad as Xavier, if not worse.

He might have thought I'd be a sloppy drunk?

That was true. Olivier could have been liquoring her up under the assumption that she couldn't hold her liquor. She tried to think about his behavior yesterday. Other than getting her plastered, he'd been a perfect gentleman.

Maybe even . . . a friend?

She gazed out the window. In spite of his constant attempts to sleep with her (and could his silly propositions really be called attempts?) she couldn't deny he was an excellent companion. If he said he would do it, he did. Though he was a businessman at heart, he was direct with her about his dealings—unscrupulous or otherwise—and forthcoming about his appointments. Not once had he left her hanging or put her in a bad spot.

Yael sighed. If Olivier hadn't been trying to get her drunk, there was only one other option, right?

He cares.

The man was simply trying to help and she refused to accept it. Though she lacked the usual family and friend groups, she did remember what it felt like to be supported.

Kinda looks a lot like this . . .

Geez, nice going!

She shrugged off her guilt and put her seat up, then left the back room of the plane to join Marge and Olivier.

"Fancy a *cuppa*?"

She found Marge peeking over the top of a magazine from her seat up front.

"No thank you, dearie," Yael replied faintly. Forcing a smile, she sat across from Olivier and slumped against the wall.

"Changed your mind?"

"Huh?"

Olivier put down his pen and removed his reading glasses. "Have you changed your mind?"

She cocked her head in question. "I don't think so?"

"Oh," he said softly, picking up his glasses again. "Well, if you do, let me know. I can send you back to Cuba when we land."

"No, no," she replied with a shake of her head. "Best way is forward."

"Indeed." He put on his glasses and turned a few pages before signing his name at the bottom. "Alright, that's a good stopping point. Marge, time for lunch."

Yael opened the window cover and stared out at the clouds. After about a minute, she found the light to be a bit too much for her present state. Closing it and massaging the bridge of her nose, she took a few deep breaths.

"Are you sure you're alright?"

Yael gave him a look of suspicion. "Why aren't you feeling this?"

He shrugged. "I'm British."

Rolling her eyes, she lifted her elbows off the stacks of paperwork he was clearing and sat back. "You have a world famous British hangover cure for me?"

"Actually, yes. But I doubt ol' Marge has what we'd need for a *fry up*."

"What's a fry up?"

Marge handed her a bottle of water. "Ah, got a little *pishy* last night, did we?"

Olivier nodded.

Pausing to explain, Marge continued. "A *fry up* is a traditional full English breakfast. Everybody has their favorite, but usually it's made with sausages, bacon, eggs, tomatoes, mushrooms, baked beans, and toast. Me late husband preferred black pudding, though me mum always did chips instead."

Yael was horrified. "All that fried together? And you say American food is bad!"

Olivier snorted. Marge gave him a light slap on the shoulder.

"No, not together," Marge chuckled. "It's like a personal platter. But everything is fried—great for a morning after getting *sloshed to the gills*."

Marge finished her statement with a cross of her eyes, then headed to the galley to prepare lunch. Olivier put away his briefcase and stretched, then slid back into the seat to await the meal. Today's fare was lighter than usual, including a tray of tropical fruit, two long, flat Cuban sandwiches cut into triangles, a small bowl of lentil soup, and some assorted balls of fried, stuffed dough. When they finished their meals, Marge brought out a container of Cuban pastries for dessert.

Given they were in such proximity, the flight to Paradise had been much shorter than the others. To Yael, it felt like forever. The action movie Olivier chose had sounded unappealing, so she took the time to finally finish the book she'd been reading since last month. For some odd reason, she'd expected a happy ending. Though she did receive a sense of closure surrounding the mystery behind the plot, she was left with an uneasy feeling she couldn't shake.

Not long after she returned the book to its shelf, they were cleared to land. Olivier explained that the island they were landing on was an old plantation the owners converted to an executive airport. They would take a car to a ferry, then another car to the resort. She made a trip to the lavatory just in case.

Studying her pained expression in the mirror as she washed her hands, she gave in and acknowledged the chip on her shoulder. Yael had been working all day to tamp down the lingering feelings of guilt surrounding the ghost girl from the mansion. Though she had been exhilarated by the experience of saving Maritza, she'd made no further attempts to investigate the gorgeous glowing specter. A part of her wondered if the girl was a figment of her imagination, a distraction from her focus on healing her heart. But another part of her knew she wasn't the type to create imaginary friends. There was a good chance she'd left the girl to die somewhere on the island.

The beautiful ghost reminded Yael of the trafficking victims she'd freed from a sex dungeon last year. Their captors, Lorenzo Rizzolli and his sleezy girlfriend, had two naked underage girls bound and gagged in a BDSM trailer one county over when Yael found them. What if the ghost girl was actually back in Tampa, her life ticking away as she waited for Yael to return in the nick of time?

This isn't my job anymore!

Why are you acting like you have a choice?

Yael frowned. She'd been ignoring the question for weeks, but there was no use anymore. Five years ago, Ybor City had become a cesspool of debauchery, drugs, and violence. Understanding there were more variables at play than her nighttime vigilantism, she still wondered if the darkness had returned since she'd been gone. How many innocent lives had been lost in the last few weeks?

"Not my circus," she muttered to herself defensively, fixing her hair in the mirror. "I'm on vacation."

She no longer had time or energy to devote to life saving. She would never again set her sights on some high cause for the greater good. The last time she tried to play hero, she'd found herself on the radar of a madman. That man had ruined her life—and ended Joe's! Besides, she didn't want Fred on high alert, always looking over his shoulder to keep her nephew, Tres, safe. She had no interest in working for anyone anymore and had no reason to tie herself down to a specific location. In truth, she would probably always feel this guilt, but she would no longer give into it. She was finally free, no matter what anyone else had to say.

Chin up, she closed the lavatory door and shoved the thoughts from her mind. Olivier was sitting in the back cabin, already buckled in and prepared to land. He was looking out the window, his excitement apparent.

"I see someone is ready and raring to go," she said through her smile. She sat in the chair across from him and swiveled to open her window. "Wow! Is that it?"

Yael wasn't sure why, but she'd been picturing a tiny lone island with a single palm tree in the center. The rocky cliff below her was all she was able to see from this side of the plane, and it was big enough to hold a massive square building on its own.

"Is that the resort?"

Olivier shook his head. "No, and most of the buildings are hidden by the trees so you probably won't be able to see much. Each time I fly over, I try to look for a path or something that would lead there. Not possible."

"Why don't you just go there yourself?"

He shook his head with a sigh of longing. "Members only."

Yael stared at the square until it was out of sight. She had a fair number of questions about their next stop, but for now she only needed the answer to one.

"How is it that you've invited me if you aren't a member?"

Olivier grinned. "You have a certain amount of money."

She grinned back. "Yes, a certain amount."

"At any rate, if the rumors are true, I'll be a member by the time we leave." He beamed. "Been a dream of mine for almost a decade. My father was offered a seat, but he died before he could accept. I was this close to a legacy spot, though I do say earning it myself is a real honor."

Yael nodded. She could understand that. One of the reasons she never touched her money was because she hadn't earned it; she'd stolen it. Well . . . that wasn't exactly true, was it? Technically, her stepmother was the thief. And Xavier was a criminal; was taking money from a dead man really stealing? Either way, she knew the feeling and was surprised to find Olivier shared the same sentiment.

"On that note," he mused, "I might be a little busy this trip. Do you think you can manage?"

She shrugged. "I've gotten good at island hopping. Piece of cake."

They started their descent. Yael closed her eyes and braced for impact, still finding takeoff and landing to be her least favorite part of flying. When they touched down, she dug her knuckles out of the leather and exhaled.

"That bad?" Olivier asked in concern.

"Nah," she lied.

He reclined his seat and rested his eyes. Opening one, he eyeballed her and explained. "Small airport. I tried to get here before the crowd, but even in the slower seasons it can take a while."

Yael closed her eyes. She was anxious to get moving, to have new sights and sounds to distract her from her thoughts. All day, the only other thing she could think of was her dream from the night before. Though she knew it was just a trippy, looping scene, she could still feel the desperation. She had to check her phone.

Pick it up and turn it on.

It's not even two feet away.

You'll feel better. Just do it!

Yael reached down to grab her go-bag. The phone was still in the pocket, though she wasn't sure it would have a charge. She held the power button and crossed her mental fingers, then exhaled when it turned on.

"That won't work once we're off the plane," Olivier said softly, eyes still closed. "They block the signal at the resort."

"Thanks," she whispered in reply. She licked her lips and stared at the screen.

At first, there was nothing out of the ordinary. She tapped the menu button and wondered what she was supposed to be doing. But when the vibrations began and did not stop, she jumped and flipped it shut.

"Someone's popular."

"Hush," she said, her mind blanking on how to silence the phone.

She opened it again and watched as notifications for text messages and voicemails popped up, each new vibration interrupted by the next incoming download before it could finish. Frederico had called and left her messages, confirming he was still out of jail. Yael hoped his case had been dismissed, but felt sick when she considered the thought of checking in. When Johhny's name flashed across the screen, she held the power button and turned the phone off.

Tossing it haphazardly into her bag, she leaned into the seat and squeezed her eyes shut. She would have to check in with Fred when her rebound getaway was over. Hopefully by then, she'd be able to explain what happened with her, as well as the demises of Joe and Vitto, without bursting into tears. If she didn't, she was sure he would enter an anxious frenzy and demand she return home at once.

"I'm dreaming of seven buxom blondes. How about you?"

Yael didn't move, needing time to process his statement before she could answer his question. She sat up.

"What?"

He turned to face her with a stretch and a yawn. "I might have to try something new this time, but I want to hear yours first."

Mystified, she made a face. "What the hell are you talking about?"

"Fine," he snapped petulantly. "I'll keep it to myself."

Yael rolled her eyes.

"Come children!"

Olivier leapt from his chair and flew out the door. Yael burst out laughing and stood to join him. Plucking up her go-bag and tossing it over her shoulder, she stepped into the main cabin and met the golden eyes of a handsome man with long, blonde-tipped dreadlocks.

CHAPTER THIRTEEN

PARADISE, THE CARIBBEAN ISLANDS

Yael rolled over in bed and smiled. She couldn't remember the last time she slept so well. Her suite was beautiful, somehow immaculate in appearance while having a lived in feel. She imagined that she was somewhere foreign—well, somewhere else—in the heart of a city, miles above the ground in a penthouse suite. Everything about the trip so far had given her a sense of power and resilience, a feeling that she would one day take over the world.

The handsome dreadlock man tripped over his own feet several times on the way to the ferry from the plane, causing Olivier to behave like a jealous lover. Then the men on the ferry seemed to take turns checking on them on the boat's viewing deck. As each one came up and down, they would scan the area and then stare at Yael. Once caught, they would ask the same question and scurry off.

It was no different when they arrived on Paradise Island. The men and women running the resort couldn't help but stare at her, which would have been unnerving if it weren't for the looks she was receiving from her fellow guests.

She thought it was her age, as there were only a few people under thirty dressed as well as she. Then she wondered if it were her gender, as most of the people wearing fine clothes and tailored suits were men of means. Of course, she had considered that it might be her race—or at least, the ambiguity her skin tone afforded her—that was drawing such attention. But in the end, Olivier told her plainly: it was her beauty, style, and grace that confounded them all.

He wasn't wrong. Aside from the myriad of gorgeous, perfectly tanned and toned women flitting about in similarly fashioned sheer dresses, Yael was likely the only guest who could fit in with both the guests *and* the staff. She was happy the resort was air conditioned, because she intended on wearing only couture to avoid any mix-ups. If anyone was foolish enough to ask her for a menu, she'd make them eat their words.

Yael wasn't sure what time it was, but what did it matter? Olivier would be in workshops all week rubbing noses with members and other potentials. She had nothing but time, and she was going to take advantage of her time in Paradise—starting with the Jacuzzi on her lanai.

She crawled to the edge of the California King bed and pulled the resort phone toward her. Checking the menu, she dialed out for the spa.

"Hi, uh . . . the bellhop told me I could call you for a special bath. I want to try the milk and honey one he mentioned."

"Mistress, they're waiting for you at your welcome appointment. However, I can have them set it up upon your return."

Yael bit her lip. "Welcome appointment? I'm sorry, I wasn't aware."

"It's no trouble, mistress," he said cheerily. "I'll let them know you're on the way."

"Thanks." She looked around the room and sighed. "I'm going to need, like, an hour or so. Do you think I should reschedule?"

He laughed. "No, mistress! I will let them know to await your arrival in the lobby in approximately one hour. Will you need any assistance?"

"Um, no. No, thank you."

"Very good, mistress. Take your time and enjoy your day."

"You too, mister."

He laughed and hung up.

Yael was not really a fan of the whole "mistress" thing, but the island had a culture all its own. If that was the polite way to address a guest, who was she to give them a hard time?

What is the culture?

This place is weird.

It was indeed. Everyone she had seen since the handsome dreadlock man walked onto the plane was a staff member. Brown-skinned men of different races and ethnicities worked the airport, the ferry, and the transportation to and from the resort. The female staff, hostesses, and waitresses had one thing in common: they were scantily clad and incredibly attractive. Unlike the men—who were mostly black and Latino—the women were white, black, Asian, and everything in between. The diversity led her to believe the island might be run by Americans or the government, but she didn't know if other countries across the globe had similar melting pots. With no photos or historical landmarks to hint at the origins of Paradise island, Yael could only guess.

Frustrated at the thought of her appointment, she rolled her eyes and climbed out of bed, reluctant to be leaving so soon. Olivier had been so excited yesterday evening that he disappeared only moments after they arrived at the resort. She didn't mind at all, but she wished he had given her a little more information about the rules of this exclusive club he was joining.

What if it's a timeshare?

Don't give in!

Groaning as she crossed the room to take a quick shower, she prayed she wasn't about to sit through an eight hour "meeting". She'd learned a lot about timeshares from her regulars at Margarita's and would not be sold. Whether or not she ever returned would depend on the bill she received when she left, but she had no interest whatsoever in permanent membership. If Olivier was desperate to be a part of it, she wanted nothing to do with it.

Forty-five minutes later, Yael strolled into the lobby wearing all white. She'd found the off-the-shoulder linen dress in a boutique across from the mansion in Cuba. Creamy lace the same color as the linen had been sown along the seams and used to create an elaborate bow at her chest. The linen formed an under-bodice that started at her breasts and went down to her feet, with a lace wrap overskirt tied tightly about her waist. The elegant coiffure of her side-swept hair had been a happy accident; adorning herself with pearls and gold seemed only natural.

A tall, slender man approached her and gave her a dazzling smile. "Mistress Peach, I presume?"

She eyed him warily, wondering why Olivier would provide him with *that* name.

"Forgive me, mistress," he said, bowing in apology. "Word of your beauty has traveled quickly amongst the ranks. I meant no disrespect."

Yael smiled. "Uh . . . it's okay? Is this my welcome meeting?"

He blushed and bowed his head lower as he extended his hand. "Right this way, mistress."

She saw a sign above the hallway they entered letting her know they were headed to the resort business center. Vaguely wondering if Olivier would be in attendance, she sauntered down the hall and steeled herself for a long wait.

He called to a man just inside the door. "Mr. Conley? Mistress Peach is ready for you."

"Excellent!"

He held the door for her with his eyes lowered, then closed it behind her. Yael saw Mr. Conley wave her over, so she crossed the long, empty room and stood before him at the table.

"Madame Peach, what a pleasure," he said kindly, standing to take her hand and kiss her knuckles. "A pleasure indeed!"

She blushed.

"Oh, have a seat! Please!"

Motioning to the chair next to him, he pulled it out and waited for her to come around. Pushing it under her as she sat, he returned to his seat and opened the file before him.

Not wanting to appear nosy or out of touch, Yael casually looked about the space and wondered when the presentation would begin. The room was only about twenty feet wide, but it was at least a hundred feet long. It didn't feel like much of a business center, having only the one table and no computers or printers. There were no TVs and no projectors installed, but she knew that could be easily rectified with an A/V cart.

You were *late.*

They probably made an exception and this was the only room left!

She groaned, feeling terrible to have kept the man waiting. There were several doors along the wall behind her, one or more of which might hold the business center equipment. Not only was she holding up the welcome wagon, but she was interrupting the other guests.

"Thank you for your patience, madame. This is truly the perfect time for your first visit—the perfect time of year. So much excitement going on! There was a mix-up with your details, but we're ready for you now. The only question I have at this time is: male, female, or both?"

Blinking, she processed a litany of questions in an effort to break through her newfound sense of confusion. She was ninety-nine percent sure he wasn't asking this about her, so the only thing she could think of was the spa.

"Female," she blurted out, knowing she had taken too long to answer.

"Very good, madame." Mr. Conley pressed a button on a small square device at the edge of the table and said, "Female."

He scribbled a note into his file and turned the page. "Do you have any ideas?"

She shook her head hesitantly, not following his meaning.

"Not a problem," he replied with a smile. "You can always let your companion know and they will coordinate with me."

Yael nodded, though she had doubts she would be seeing much of Olivier on this trip. She was hoping to start taking care of such things herself. She was about to tell him so, when the wall at the opposite end of the room disappeared.

Only, it hadn't disappeared; she could see the edge was on hinges. She looked to Mr. Conley, but he was flipping through the file making quick checks along a form she couldn't quite read. A woman walked through the door, then another, and another.

Swallowing nervously at the sight before her, Yael felt adrenaline flooding her system. Blinking at the bare breasts of the unending parade of women, she felt an ominous sense of doom creeping down her spine. Her eyes settled on her hands in her lap as she tried not to vomit.

"Turn."

She looked at Mr. Conley through her peripheral, unable to move anything other than her eyes.

"Turn."

She heard the sound of their movements as if she were standing in line with them.

"Turn."

Yael looked up and saw the women turn on their heels with military like precision. They all faced the wall across from her, their bare backs and bottoms on display.

"Turn."

She saw their faces and couldn't help but search the eyes of those who watched her, begging someone to explain, to tell her this was all a joke. But when her eyes landed on the ghost girl from Cuba, they locked on her and did not stray.

What the fuck? Is she . . . glowing? How?

The line of women was perfectly straight, with each one touching shoulders or bumping elbows with the women beside her. The ghost girl stood between two women, shining brightly and staring deep into Yael's soul.

She's not real!

She's standing right there!

Yael glanced at Mr. Conley, who was watching her with rapt attention. She involuntarily turned back to the ghost girl, wondering what she was supposed to say.

"You may go," Mr. Conley said, his voice curt.

She looked at him again, terrified of what he would say of her inability to choose.

He leaned toward her and whispered, "Excellent choice. You've done well, madame."

Blinking in question, she saw the ghost girl had taken a step forward. The rest of the women returned through the wall, and the door closed once again.

"Edelira," Mr. Conley chirped, "sweet girl, take your companion to room seven."

The girl smiled at him and then bowed her head in Yael's direction. She crossed the room, seeming to float along as she made her way to Yael. Taking her hand, the girl lifted her from her seat and pulled her toward a door behind them.

Yael's legs felt like jelly, but she found her strength. She knew it was crazy, but right now she didn't have time for denial. The ghost girl was warm, solid . . . alive! Touching her hand!

Why the fuck is she glowing?

This is a dream!

This is not a fucking dream!

When they entered the room, the girl let her hand go and grabbed a thin, lace robe from a hook behind the door. She slipped into it and then stood by, as if waiting for instruction.

Yael looked around the room. There was a sofa next to a small bar on one side and a desk with chairs on the other. Yael sat at the desk, hoping to put some distance between the ghost and herself to give her space to think. The girl didn't move a muscle until Yael glanced her way.

"My name is Edelira," she said sensually. "You can call me Edel, or you can call me Lira."

Yael swallowed nervously.

"Or you can call me anything you want," the girl tried again, her throaty laughter filling the small room.

Covering her face with her hands, Yael tried to pretend the girl wasn't there. She didn't understand any of this, and Edelira's presence was not helping in the least.

"Would you mind if I joined you?"

Yael jumped. The girl had come to stand at the corner of the desk, but Yael hadn't heard a thing.

Calm down.

Nodding, Yael made sure to point at the chair across from her. She didn't want the girl getting any ideas.

"Thank you, mistress."

Groaning inwardly, Yael massaged the bridge of her nose. "Miss, please."

"Yes, mistress?"

"That," Yael said sharply, pointing at her. "Don't call me that, please."

Edelira lowered her head. "Yes, m-uh, yes."

Yael sat back and stared at the ceiling, wondering if there was anyone up there listening.

I could really use some help here, she thought wildly.

Edelira shifted in her seat, drawing Yael's eye. "You are . . . very tense. Can I help you?"

Blushing profusely, Yael shook her head.

The girl gave her a small smile, studying her intently. "Are you an angel? Or a bride?"

Yael blinked.

"I have never seen someone so beautiful," Edelira whispered. "Only my mother. Truth be told, you are far fairer than she."

Frowning, Yael marveled at Edelira's careful inflection of every word. Even with her deep, rich accent and raspy voice, she spoke like a noblewoman. Yael felt uneasy.

This is bad. This is a bad, bad place.

"I can see you are overwhelmed, *querida*."

Meeting the girl's eyes, she searched them and found her to be genuine. Yael nodded slowly.

"I can help."

Yael took a deep breath and exhaled until her lungs were empty. "I don't know what to do."

"I have wonderful news for you," Edelira said with a moan. "You don't have to do anything."

Though confused by her delivery, Yael felt instant relief. Now she could think! She dropped her head in her hands and calculated how much time she would have to find and murder Olivier before she commandeered a plane and escaped this hell.

A soft hand wrapped itself about her ankle and snaked its way up her calf. Yael froze, but she found her nerve when another hand pushed her dress up and over her knees. She peeked through her fingers, hoping she would find the girl in her seat. Of course, she was out of sight.

Leaning back slowly, Yael looked under the desk and found Edelira there just as she planted a soft, wet kiss on her inner thigh. When the girl moved higher and lapped at the same spot with the flat of her tongue, panic overcame fear.

Rolling the chair back, she brought her face down to the girl's level. Barely able to find her voice, she cleared her throat and whispered.

"Listen to me! I'm not . . . I'm not . . . Ugh! I am *not* supposed to be here. I'm not gay and please don't tell Mr. Conley because I definitely can't go through that again. Who were all those women? And why are you doing this? Actually, don't tell me!"

Edelira's expression changed with every word she spoke. Her mouth opened and shut twice, then stayed shut tight as Yael finished.

"Lower your voice!" Edelira snapped, her own voice a quiet whisper. "If what you say is true, they'll kill you!"

Eyes wide with fear, Yael wondered who they were and how long she had to get away from them.

"Come closer," Edelira said, crawling toward Yael and pulling the chair forward by its legs. "Is this a game? A part of your fantasy? They didn't tell me anything about you."

"I didn't know this was what 'fantasy' meant!" Yael choked out. "Who would ever think that way?"

Edelira shook her head. "Lower your voice! Look at me. I am serious. This is a frame room; you are being recorded. No! Don't move, and don't look. Keep your voice low or you will be taken!"

What did the girl mean by that? And why wouldn't Olivier warn her before bringing her here? Tears formed in Yael's eyes. Olivier had set her up! He knew she would never be okay with any of this, that she would be found out and . . . taken?

"Do not cry," Edelira whispered, wiping the tears from her cheeks. "There is only one way out of this room. I can promise you, your tears will mean nothing."

Yael stared at her, pondering the meaning. "How many men would I have to fight? I could probably take a few, but no more without a weapon."

Edelira paled. "*Querida*, you misunderstand. In this room, you seal your fate."

"And what about your fate? Am I supposed to save you?"

"Save me?"

Knowing she would sound crazy if she said anything more, Yael simply nodded.

"Are you serious?"

"I'm sorry," Yael said quickly. "If this is where you want to be, I apologize. But if you want to leave this place, tell me how we get out."

Mouth agape, Edelira stared at Yael in awestruck wonder.

"Edelira?"

Eyes darting back and forth, she appeared to be deep in thought.

"Edelira?" Yael whispered harshly. "What is it?"

Lips set firm, Edelira nodded. "Have you ever faked an orgasm?"

Cocking her head back and doing her best not to look for a camera, Yael shook her head. "Please, I can't do this."

"That's the way out. Stay exactly where you are, and make it real!"

Edelira pulled Yael's dress skirt over her head and angled her face just above her mound. Yael stared at the large lump between her thighs and watched as the girl simulated the erotic movements of cunnilingus. When she felt a hard flick on her inner thigh, she jumped.

"Oh!" She remembered her objective and recovered quickly. "Oh, wow!"

When Edelira massaged her inner thighs and moved to her quads, Yael's eyes widened. Did the girl think this was all a ploy after all? She was embarrassed to find herself enjoying the fake intimacy. Had it really been so long?

"Yes," she moaned, only half faking now.

The pressure release she was receiving from the massage was only sensual because of Edelira's proximity to her nether regions, but she was ashamed nonetheless. Yael could never use someone so mercilessly, yet here she was with no other choice.

"Oh my," she moaned louder, wondering why she felt the need. She reset her volume and tried again. "Yes, Lira!"

Though she was only shifting her position, when Edelira's thumb grazed across Yael's underwear, Yael jumped.

Now! she told herself.

"Oh, fuck!" she screamed, covering her eyes with her forearm and wiggling her hips side to side to avoid any further contact. "Yes, yes, yes!"

Tears streamed down her face as she wondered who might be watching. It didn't matter that it was all a show. It didn't matter that she was one step closer to freedom. The island was no paradise. Yael had been violated and there was no way around it.

Edelira pulled her head out from under the skirt, gasping when she met Yael's eyes. She pushed Yael's chair back and stood, opening her robe and wrapping herself around Yael's head.

"Let it out," Edelira purred from above her. "I will tell them it was your first time receiving pleasure. Tears like this are not uncommon from certain female visitors."

In that moment, Yael did not care that the young woman was naked and pressed up against her. Wrapping her arms around her bare torso and receiving her embrace, she wept.

CHAPTER FOURTEEN

Yael was still shaken when she walked out of the sterile corridor into the guest hallway. Edelira explained that the only way out of the meeting rooms was through the hidden hall, and that she wasn't doing it for her benefit or to give them privacy. Pressing the elevator button and crossing her arms over her thin robe, Edelira gave Yael a weak smile.

"Are you sure you've never been here before?"

Frowning, Yael shook her head. "Why?"

She leaned in to explain in a faint whisper. "First timers cannot access the second floor."

Yael's eyes flared. "What does this mean?"

Edelira brushed Yael's hair out of her face and shrugged, then stepped onto the elevator. When the door closed, she shook her head again.

Swallowing and focusing on her breathing, Yael stared at her feet and tried not to cry. After weeks of living it up in the clouds, she had returned to earth. Or maybe this was hell? It would have been one thing if she'd mistakenly entered the wrong room, but if a denial of . . .

service . . . was met with death, she had a feeling every room in the joint was used for—

"Which room?"

Yael followed Edelira down the hall and pulled her key from between her breasts. When she opened the door, she was shocked to see the girl run inside and look up at the ceiling. Closing the door behind her, she stood in the foyer and crossed her arms.

Edelira shook her head, a puzzled look on her face. "This room is not surveilled. This doesn't make sense."

"I thought the cameras where everywhere?"

"No, no. Only in certain places, and for exactly this reason." She picked up the phone and dialed out. "Brenna, it's Lira. Can you send for my clothes? Thank you."

Yael looked around the room and wondered if she was being tricked. She had no reason to trust the girl . . . and Edelira had no reason to believe her, either.

She was literally glowing!

Wait, why isn't she glowing anymore?

"How did you come to find this place?"

Yael blinked. "An associate of mine has business here this week. He invited me to come have a fantasy weekend. I thought I'd be playing dress up."

"Who is your associate?"

She sighed. "His name is Olivier . . . Lord Olivier something someth—"

"You're a guest of Lord Hulley, the British Earl?"

She nodded slowly.

"I bet I know what happened," Edelira exclaimed. "The woman he brought last time he was here . . . the coordinator must have thought *she* was returning. Once the first timer cabins are full, new requests are waitlisted. They aren't even offered access to the resort! The Lord must be paying handsomely for this suite. Although . . . you are very beautiful. Perhaps they were willing to make an exception once you arrived?"

Yael took a deep breath, unsure of what to say. Edelira was lost in thought, barely paying attention as she tried to unravel the mystery.

"Wait," Yael said thoughtfully. "Only first timer rooms are recorded?"

Edelira nodded. "Yes, the frame room and first timer cabins were designed to protect the resort and the club members. They are the only spaces with both visual and audio surveillance."

"You said there was a reason for it?"

"Yes," Edelira replied, her voice low. "The new system was installed about five years ago. Somehow, a man was able to track his daughter here. He got all the way to the frame room, then he tried to get the woman he chose to help him find his daughter. She assumed it was a test, so she told her coordinator. The man disappeared and his daughter was moved to another island. A month later, the frame room was equipped with sound."

"Why aren't all the guest rooms surveilled?"

"I think the logic was, with the cost of private travel and the resort fees, a person with intentions against what is expected will reveal themselves sooner than later. The fantasy rooms are also watched, but in a different way."

Yael shuddered at the thought of fantasy rooms, imaging the Rizzoli sex dungeon she'd burned to the ground. "What do you mean different? How?"

Edelira looked at the floor. "Heat. There is no audio, but the walls have a thermal camera installed."

"Why? What's the point of that?"

Shifting uncomfortably, Edelira cleared her throat. "Long time guests and members are afforded many freedoms, including the right to enjoy their fantasy without fear of judgement or questions of their character. Most guests are looking to release their inhibitions, to receive pleasures that they would otherwise miss out of from prudish partners. But sometimes . . . sometimes it goes too far.

"The problem was much worse before the system was put in place. Some guests would lie, telling their coordinators that their companions had not lived up to their fantasy requirements. This was a scary thing, because we had no proof. The consequences of such an accusation were dire for us as companions.

"The frame room surveillance system was the first step in protecting us. New guests could be ruled out based on their behaviors during the frame meeting. The thermal system was more helpful; human nature is revealed behind closed doors. Yes, the frame room is private enough, but still so close to the normalcy of the resort. The fantasy rooms are underground, soundproof, and made to evoke only the most carnal of instincts. Many companions have been saved from cruelty and death thanks to these systems."

Yael did her best to appear calm. She felt sick to her stomach. Listening to Edelira share the reality of her work was too much, too soon. What had she gotten herself into? What had Olivier done?

"You said there was a woman . . . the Lord brought her. Did you see her?"

Edelira nodded. "Mistress Stacey."

She felt like the wind had been knocked out of her. Stacey was *here*? Moreover, they had been expecting the woman instead of Yael. This room had been prepared for *Mistress Stacey*?

"Are you alright?"

Yael shook her head. "Just need to sit down, I think."

She stumbled toward the bed and collapsed, rolling onto her side as a wave of nausea hit. Her stomach was empty, thank goodness, but that wouldn't stop her from retching up bile. Taking a deep breath, she flipped onto her back and groaned.

The knock at the door startled her, but she could barely lift her head. Were they coming for her already? Had they discovered the truth about her intentions?

"I'll get it," Edelira whispered. "It's just my clothes."

Yael listened as she opened the door and cheerfully greeted someone outside.

Edelira laughed, then thanked them before returning. She got dressed in the middle of the suite then joined Yael on the bed.

"They said you ordered the milk and honey treatment? Good thing you chose me first."

"Why?" Yael wondered in horror.

"Uhh . . . you don't want to know. Trust me!"

Pushing herself onto her elbows, Yael gawped at Edelira. "Is there anything normal on this damned island?"

"Of course," Edelira said with a giggle. "Since you're going to be here for a while, you'll get to try all of it—the normal stuff. You can't exactly stay in your room."

"Why not?" Yael grumbled.

"We have minimum requirements for nonmembers who use the facility."

Yael sat up all the way and rubbed her eyes. "The Lord wants to be a member. What's the difference?"

"Members pay an annual fee and are required to attend meetings. Elite members also sponsor the younger girls until they are old enough to care for themselves."

Eyes narrowing, Yael took note of Edelira's verbiage. Sponsors, elite members, and surveillance for "protection"? She had to ask.

"How long have you been here, Edelira?"

"Since I was a child. Mama saved me and brought me here to live with Daddy."

Yael swallowed. "What did she save you from?"

"I don't remember much; it was so long ago." Edelira leaned back onto her hands and gazed up at the ceiling. "I was the youngest in my family. When my mother died, my father sent all the siblings to work, but no one could find any work for me. Travelers came and they offered him a chance to survive, so he sold me to a man to be his wife. I was so scared! But the morning came, and Mama told my father she could pay him much more and give me a better life."

"Oh," Yael said softly. "So you *do* want to be here?"

Edelira looked at her and shrugged. "I don't know. Where would I go?"

A small smile formed on Yael's face. "I guess you don't need my help?"

"No," Edelira said firmly. "But my sisters and brothers do."

Yael was confused. "Did she bring them here, too?"

Edelira chuckled. "Sorry, you misunderstand. The people here—the other companions—they are the only family I know. I am considered one of the most prized companions on the island. My life is incredibly rich and satisfying. But I will not pretend to be unaware, to ignore my privilege. If there is any chance you could help those who might need it, I will do whatever I can to help them be happy!"

Exhaling with a soft whistle, Yael nodded. She wished she could tell Edelira about her *calling*; after all, why would the ghost from her visions deny a chance at salvation? On the one hand, it was obvious this life was all she knew. How could she know better? On the other, there was a chance she really was happy here. It was her life—and her body—so who was Yael to interfere?

"Ugh," she groaned, lying back on the bed and staring at the mural on the ceiling above her. When she realized many of the figures were in various salacious positions, she clapped a hand to her forehead.

Edelira fell onto her side next to Yael and rested on her elbow. "I have to submit your fantasy to Mr. Conley by morning. We can use Mistress Stacey's plan as the foundation. And don't worry, I will downgrade it."

Yael turned her head and gave the girl a look.

She giggled. "I promise! It will all be very tame. There is a package available—though it is rarely ever used—designed specifically for female royals forced into marriage. Though the women prefer the company of other women, they maintain their marriages for the sake of propriety. They come here to be free and receive the pleasure they so deeply desire, without a potential scandal."

"That's what Stacey wanted?" Yael asked in confusion. She didn't know much about the woman, but given her obsession with Xavier, Yael would have been surprised to learn that Stacey was a lesbian. "She didn't stay with Olivier?"

Edelira shook her head. "The first time they came, yes. If I remember correctly, he changed his usual order at the last minute."

"What's his usual order?"

Closing her eyes, Edelira took a moment to think. "I believe it would be one of the standard packages. One man, multiple women with a similar look—I think he chose blondes. But when he arrived with Mistress Stacey, he changed the order to curly haired brunettes with brown skin. Come to think of it . . . "

Yael blushed.

"Oh," Edelira said, her eyes looking everywhere but Yael. "They came back for another visit soon after, but this time Mistress Stacey had her own fantasy to play out. I was almost called in for it, but my sponsor extended our relationship until the annual meeting."

"Should I even ask?"

Edelira tilted her head in question. "About what?"

"What was her fantasy?"

"Oh! It was quite strange. She wanted a combination package. In the daytime, she required an entourage of five women at all times. They were at her beck and call—I heard she treated them terribly. Each night, five men would break into her room and kidnap her; they took her to a fantasy room and brutalized her. Once they were finished, her entourage would go to her and pleasure her until she passed out. She did this every day for three days, until Lord Olivier cut his trip short and took her with him."

"Geez," Yael whispered.

Edelira nodded. "Our female guests don't come frequently, and some of them are worse than the men. I heard Mistress Stacey was worse than any royal, save a few particular nobles."

"She's dead now, if that helps."

Edelira froze. "Dead?"

Biting her lip, Yael looked up and avoided her eyes. Why did she tell the girl that?

"Good."

"Good?"

Edelira pursed her lips together. "I got lucky. My sisters did not."

Shit . . .

Yael didn't know what to say. In a way, she had Stacey to thank. If they hadn't mistaken her for the woman, Yael might have been caught by now! She was lucky to be in a room without surveillance, lucky she had chosen Edelira over some other girl who might not have been so discerning.

You call this luck? She sighed, swallowing the lump in her throat. *I want to go home. I wish I was on the couch . . . with Joe.*

She closed her eyes and cleared her throat. "You said the girls were disappointed when Olivier changed his order?"

"Mmm hmm. And that would indicate he is a very generous lover. There are not many like him, but when they do visit, the girls often fight to win their affections."

Yael tried connecting the dots. "But he's not a sponsor yet . . . because only members can be sponsors?"

"Yes, only *elite* members. My current sponsor was the newest elite upgrade. Well, I guess he's not my sponsor anymore . . . "

"What do you mean?"

Edelira let out a heavy sigh and threw herself onto her back. "My eighteenth birthday was last week. Daddy offered him an extension one more time since we've been together for so long, but he has put a downpayment on his new virgin. That's why I'm here with you now, you know? I have to have at least one client before I go in *the box* . . ."

Yael looked over at her, hearing the crack in her voice when she said her last words. What the hell was *the box*? She was afraid to ask.

"I just lost my virginity this year," Yael admitted quietly.

"Oh? My first time was a few years ago . . . "

Trying not to make a face, Yael bit her lips shut. "I don't understand."

Edelira sat up. "The children are kept as virgins for as long as possible. Our sponsors pay for our housing, food, clothing, and training. My first sponsor chose me the month after I arrived and maintained my place here until a few years ago.

"He was in love with his younger sister," she explained. "She died the year before he found me, so I was able to help him face his feelings and mourn his loss. All he asked was for me to try to force myself upon him, to beg him to take me. As the years progressed, I was taught to dominate him, to make him hurt for denying me the only thing I wanted. And then, when I was fourteen, he gave in . . . barely. I never saw him again.

"I was set to move to the adult cottages when I was purchased again by my second and last sponsor. He knew my first sponsor was a soft, timid man. I think that is why he saw me as a prize, even after my virginity was won. I enjoyed his company far more and preferred being a mistress over being a sister."

"So I'm your first . . . client?"

Edelira nodded and smiled. "And what an adventure this has been."

"You said before that something like this happened? Why did you trust me? It could have been a trap . . . or a test, right?"

"This is going to sound crazy," Edelira whispered. "But I feel like I know you from somewhere . . . "

Yael swallowed. She hated to say it, but she was definitely in the right place. "Now that you don't have a sponsor and you've had me as a client, what does that mean for you?"

Edelira brushed her hair behind her ears. "Daddy says I can keep my gifts and remain in the cottage as long as I keep my rating high. I'm a little nervous about that. I've had the highest consistent rating on the island since the ratings began."

"Then why are you nervous?"

"Sponsors *always* give five stars. Nonmember clients can be . . . picky. They say some people will give a low rating just to receive a comp—I think that's why the ratings exist. The other girls have good ratings but more experience, so if a client lies, their experience rating can help them avoid any trouble. I've only had two people on my account; if you were to give me a one-star rating, I might have to be reprimanded."

She tried not to let the spirit of depression wrap itself about her, but Yael would be lying if she said she was alright with any of this. Though she felt terrible for pushing the girl, she still hadn't received an explanation about the one thing Edelira seemed upset by.

"Edelira?" she croaked. "Why do you have to go to *the box*?"

The look in the girl's eyes said she'd gone too far.

"I'm sorry," Yael tossed out quickly. "You don't have to tell—"

"You should know," Edelira interrupted. "The annual meeting is next weekend. I don't think you will be leaving before then."

Yael sat up and leaned onto her hip, giving Edelira a smile of encouragement.

"*The box* is a secret chamber that only Daddy and the other members have access to, and only for one day a year. The annual meeting takes place after the sacred ceremony, which can also include the new member initiation if there are any."

"How many members are there?"

Edelira smiled. "Only ninety-nine, plus Daddy. Some years, there are no new spots . . . but this year there are *two*! That's why the resort is sold out already; for the next week or so, everyone you will see is vying for a seat. The rest of the members are already booked and will arrive closer to the event."

"And the main event is the annual meeting? That's what happens inside *the box* every year?"

"Mmm hmm," Edelira confirmed with a nod. "The induction ceremony is held in the conference room behind the companion quarters. After it's over, the members strip down and take their march to *the box*."

"You mean that square building? I saw it from the plane on my way in!"

"Really? I bet it was a sight to behold. That must be why Daddy has all air traffic halted during the march to and from *the box*. I always thought it was about the sound, but now that I think of it, the trees don't grow on the rocky areas of the island. I guess they don't want to be seen."

Yael was confused. "Is there a reason a hundred men strip down for an annual meeting? Is it some sort of primal thing, or do they just have trust issues?"

"Each year, members are required to confirm their continued allegiance to Daddy during the sacred ceremony. He's the Grand Master. The men must participate in an orgy before the women arrive, and new members are thoroughly initiated during the orgy. Besides that, I've heard it can get very messy in *the box*. Maybe they undress to save their suits."

After processing her words, Yael blanched. She decided to stop asking questions.

"Once the men take their positions, the women join them and report to their stations. There are five levels to *the box*. Level one is actually on the second floor—that's where I'm stationed this year. Sponsored girls who have lost their virginity and high value women take the second floor; they usually won't see very much action.

"I've heard a lot of the members enjoy watching as much as they enjoy participating, so the second floor balcony is a popular place to take a break. Level two is on the main floor. Level one and level two have holes in the walls, with seats and beds built in—that's what I mean by station. The lower levels are where things get a little confusing."

"How do you mean?"

Edelira shrugged. "The stories are similar, but some sound too crazy to be true. People tend to exaggerate, especially during the slower seasons when there isn't as much to do."

"Try me."

"Well, level three isn't so bad. It isn't until they hear they are stationed at level four that the women become afraid. Level three is down on the next landing; it houses the machine stations. The women are strapped in to all kinds of contraptions and put into various positions. It is on level four where the women who cannot endure are tossed down for the men who prefer more savage encounters."

"And the fifth level?"

"The fifth level is a mystery. It is the only level without assignments. Every year several companions end up on level five and disappear forever. Two years ago, one of my roommates was assigned to level four due to misbehavior. Her lover was also assigned to level four; not long after the meeting began, her lover was badly bruised and bloodied.

"The last man who had her picked her up and tossed her onto the floor in the center of level four. My roommate saw two men climb up from a trap door and throw her lover inside headfirst. Stuck in her position on level four, she watched the door to level five as the men continued to brutalize her, waiting for her lover to climb out. Later, another companion's body was thrown down; when the two men returned again to retrieve her, they were covered in blood. My roommate never saw her lover again."

CHAPTER FIFTEEN

Edelira handed Yael an oversized glass filled to the brim with a tropical frozen cocktail. She took it with both hands and pretended to drop it, laughing alongside her new friend when the icy substance spilled onto her chest.

"Cold, cold!" she rasped, using her finger to scoop it up and into her mouth. "Mmm!"

"I told you!" Edelira said playfully, picking up her own glass. "The best in the world."

"I'll have to get this recipe," Yael replied, taking a long sip from her bamboo straw. "I work at a bar called Margarita's. Maybe you could come visit me one day."

"You *work*?"

Yael burst out laughing. "Um, I guess you can say I'm on vacation."

"Wow. And at a bar of all places? I don't believe it."

"I'll make the drinks at the party tonight and you will." Yael winked. "My drinks put you in the *danger zone*!"

Edelira blinked. "I don't think I want to be in danger."

Giggling, Yael shook her head. She didn't want to make the girl feel bad for missing the reference, so she let it go.

Olivier had been MIA since their arrival. She was glad for it. Yael needed time to figure out how she could help the slaves on this island. Then, she had to decide how to handle the members. If Olivier was offered a membership, it could present an issue when it came time to make a break for it. But that would all depend on the plan, once she figured one out.

She and Edelira had developed a fast friendship over the last two days, spending every waking moment together flitting about the resort. Yael felt like she was in a tropical adaptation of *Vicky Cristina Barcelona*, a movie she and Frederico accidentally watched a few years ago when theater hopping. Though she didn't remember much (other than the awkwardness of watching sexy scenes next to her cousin) she did recall the sense of whimsy and wonder the film had provided. This moment was the closest thing she would ever have to the lives the two travelers had led.

After the initial shock and horror of her circumstances wore off, Yael was able to see the bigger picture. This was a matter of life and death—and not just the life of one. Edelira estimated there to be at least one hundred and fifty stations in the box alone. There were more female slaves here than male, but even a low estimate of two hundred lives put this task far outside Yael's comfort zone. She wanted to believe that a dream would come, but she understood she might have to settle for a vision on the fly instead.

Yesterday was their first day of acting out Yael's fantasy package. She found the massages and pampering to be enjoyable, and was surprised that Edelira's constant nakedness stopped bothering her after the second session. The girl was beautiful, incredibly talented, and the perfect companion for a spy. When they weren't being serviced by slaves or other skilled companions, Edelira would lean in close and whisper secrets in Yael's ear. Though it appeared they were sharing an intimate moment or a public display of affection, they were actually building a case and providing Yael with the resort blueprint.

The place was a maze by design, but that hadn't phased Yael. Years of following the *knowing* and piecing together the puzzles of her dreams had given her an excellent sense of spiritual direction. Each time Edelira showed her a new location, Yael would add the spot to her mental map.

Today, they sat on the rocks above the grotto. Though she couldn't visit the underground fantasy chambers, seeing the three levels from afar was exactly what she needed. It was the closest thing Yael would get to a bird's eye view of the resort, which was helping to solidify her nav system.

"Come," Edelira said as she took Yael's drink and helped her stand. "You need to take a shower and I need to pick your outfit."

EDELIRA MOVED AHEAD of Yael on the path, her usual sensual saunter replaced by a youthful hop as she leapt barefoot from stone to stone. They were on the way to her cottage on the beach, a luxury afforded to only the high value women on the island. She shared the house with three other companions who were in their twenties, and proudly told Yael that *she* had the master suite.

The clearing opened up to reveal soft, powdery white sand on a private beach that went on as far as the eye could see before curving out of sight. The path continued until they passed one, two, three large cottages before turning onto a darker stone path to the fourth house.

"Wow," Yael said, walking inside tentatively.

Though Edelira had gotten permission for the night's event, Yael felt like she was intruding. She had yet to meet the other girls and didn't know how they would feel about her ideas. What if they felt the same way as Edelira? What if this was *home* to them?

Edelira linked arms with Yael and marched her up the steps, opening her bedroom door with a flourish. "Isn't it amazing?"

Nodding as she took in the space, Yael had to admit the house was nothing like she'd expected. In a way, it reminded her of her suite on Prince Edward Island.

Yes, that's it. It's like a hotel.

She froze, scanning the room quickly. No photos. No personal effects. Sure, the cottage was beautiful, but who did it *really* belong to?

"I'm going to take a quick shower. Make yourself comfortable," Edelira called from the closet. "Oh . . . take that braid out of your hair so it can dry!"

Yael crossed the room and opened the curtains, then sat in the chair by the window to watch the waves. She went to work on her hair, then shook it out of its confines. Edelira was dead set on doing her hair and makeup, wanting her to have her first ever *girls' night*.

On paper, things were expected to get wild. Yael's coordinator was told that she had recently discovered a deep curiosity for women, but was afraid of her feelings. Unable to connect with women in real life, Yael had come to the island to immerse herself in the fantasy and explore it further. Edelira told her she would be billed for an orgy whether it happened or not. The docket was jam packed with clients seeking companions and Yael would be occupying some of the most beautiful women on the island tonight.

"Are you ready?"

Edelira, naked as always, was still dripping wet from the shower. Using her towel to dry her hair, she looked at Yael expectantly and tapped her foot.

"Bossy," Yael quipped, brows raised.

Edelira laughed and tossed the towel on the bed. "We still have to set up the bar! Come on, *vamanos*!"

Shaking her head and standing to stretch, Yael waited for Edelira to throw on a dress. The girl handed her a black box and then picked up a large zippered bag before ushering her downstairs.

Yael watched as Edelira moved about the living room, shifting furniture around to open things up. When she saw her pull a wooden rolling cart around from the dining area, Yael decided to check out the liquor stock so she could determine the night's cocktails. She had been expecting to find an array of rums, given their popularity in the Caribbean, but there were quite a number of familiar brands available. Only one ingredient was missing for a Long Island Iced Tea . . . she always had other options.

"Are you excited?"

Sighing, Yael made a face. "Not exactly."

"Why not?" Edelira tilted her head. "They're going to love you!"

Clearing her throat, she tried to make her point clear. "Have you changed your mind about leaving?"

Deflated, Edelira looked at the floor. "I get it. I do. But my life here has always been . . . charmed. If you can help make it even better, why would I leave?"

Doing her best not to frown, Yael shrugged. "You're right. It's your choice. I don't know why you're so sure they won't feel the same way."

"I knew it!"

Yael jumped and looked at the door, shocked by the sudden appearance of two beautiful women in the foyer.

"It's you!"

"Oh, she's gorgeous!"

Blushing, she allowed Edelira to steer her to the living room and into a chair. Within seconds, she was surrounded.

"Your hair!"

"I know! It's so soft."

Edelira shooed them away. "Stop it, go sit down."

The front door burst open and three more women entered. Yael met their eyes and tried to smile, but when the last girl gave her a look of suspicion, she lost her confidence.

"Come in, come in." Edelira grinned and closed the door, locking it soundly behind her. "Everyone, this is Yaya. Yaya, let me introduce you."

"This is Petra. And this is Athar." She walked to the couch and playfully pushed another girl down. "Here we have Ana Claudia, Lucia, and Aminata."

Yael nodded to each woman in greeting, painfully aware of the daggers Lucia shot her way. She swallowed nervously, her fingers fidgeting in her lap as their eyes bore down on her.

"Where are you from?"

She turned to face Ana Claudia, a girl who favored her in many ways. "Tampa . . . er, Florida. In the United States."

Lucia sucked her teeth. "American?"

"*Cállate*," Edelira snapped.

Ana Claudia stood and approached her, leaning in close to study her face. "No makeup?"

Yael leaned back slowly and shook her head.

"She's the *girl* everyone's been talking about," Petra said, clapping with excitement. "So many rumors!"

"What are they saying?" Yael asked, her anxiety growing rapidly with each passing second.

Edelira waved her off. "Who is doing her hair?"

"Oh, me!"

Yael smiled as Ana Claudia jumped and raised her hand. When no one objected, she took a step closer and dug her hands into the thick waves left by the braid.

"Pretty," she said, giving it a fluff.

Aminata stood and rung out her hands. "Let me help."

Her expression made Yael question Ana Claudia's abilities, but she didn't have a chance to think. Petra jumped up and snatched the makeup box from the table, clutching it close and giving the rest a look of warning.

"Where is the thread?" Athar asked, standing and stretching. "Look at those brows."

Yael looked up, then closed her eyes in embarrassment. She couldn't remember what her eyebrows looked like, but she hoped Athar knew what she was doing. A woman's eyebrows were sacred.

"She's perfect already," Edelira told Athar, running up the steps behind her. "Stay out of my room!"

Biting her lips to keep from smiling, Yael took a deep breath. She was feeling overwhelmed and needed to get ahold of herself. There was no room for error tonight.

Thirty minutes of fawning and fighting later, most of the girls were standing in front of Yael admiring their handiwork. Only Lucia was missing from the half-circle, opting to lean against the front door instead.

"I can't believe I'm about to say this, but," Ana Claudia looked around, "she's even more beautiful than before. Is that possible?"

"Obviously!" Petra exclaimed, leaning forward to add a dab of color in the center of Yael's lower lip. She rubbed her lips together and indicated that Yael should do the same.

Yael followed suit, then gave a pout. When Petra shook her head as if amazed, Yael blushed.

"Her hair is normally curly," Edelira bragged. "You should see it! It's absolutely glorious."

"I like what Aminata did at the end," Petra said, pointing at the feathered style in Yael's blowout. "She looks like a *star*."

When the other girls agreed and continued gushing, Yael finally broke. She wanted nothing more than to run, to be anywhere but here surrounded by people she didn't know. She couldn't explain it, could barely understand it, but these women were being far too . . . nice.

"Why is she crying?" Lucia snapped.

Edelira gasped. "Move, move! Go sit down. I told you, she's new to this."

"New to what?"

"Friendship?" Edelira said irritably. "And girl time. And damn it, Lu! What the hell is your problem?"

Yael tried to stop the tears from flowing. She tried to pretend she was alone, back home in her room. It didn't work. This was all too much.

She stood, then froze when she realized Lucia was blocking the door. Was that her plan all along? Was someone coming to take her away?

"How did you come here?"

Yael swallowed. "I flew."

Someone snorted behind her.

Lucia rolled her eyes. "Don't play stupid!"

"I was traveling with a man," Yael snapped back. "The way he described it, I thought it was just a fancy resort. A place for rich people to waste money—an escape. I had no idea this place was so . . . "

She took a breath, turning to face the girls behind her.

"I'm sorry," she whispered.

Petra took a step forward to pat her on the shoulder. She was staring at a spot on Yael's cheek; her hand came up slowly to dab at Yael's makeup. The room erupted with laughter.

"Vamos," Lucia said with a chuckle, her voice softening. "Let's start the show."

Yael looked at Edelira in question, shocked by the sudden shift in Lucia's attitude, but the girl just shrugged and gave her a brilliant smile.

THE GIRLS RETURNED a couple hours later after a trip to the grotto. Lucia's reference to "the show" had been apt; many of the resort guests had stopped to watch them sip cocktails under the waterfall. Companions and staff alike came from all over to see the most beautiful guest on the island. Yael pretended to be living the dream, but she watched it all from the corner of her eye.

They showered and changed, with Lucia surprising Yael when she offered her a dress to wear. Then, Yael made them all drinks and joined the group in the living room.

"Who's in?" Edelira asked once everyone was seated.

Lucia sucked her teeth. "I think the better question is . . . who's out?"

No one raised their hands.

Yael saw the look of desperation in their eyes and knew she had found her team.

"We're going to need more people," Lucia said firmly, her fist striking the table. "There isn't much time, but we have to recruit."

They all nodded in agreement.

"What package is she using?"

Edelira bit her lip, studying Lucia before answering. "Basically the same as Mistress Stacey, without male companions and a few other downgrades."

Eyes narrowing, Lucia took a deep breath and wiggled her jaw.

"That will work well. We can confuse the guards easily in the chamber."

Leaning toward Yael, Edelira whispered, "She was a part of Mistress Stacey's entourage."

"You aren't whispering, you fool."

Edelira sat up straight and stuck her nose in the air. "I wasn't trying."

Yael looked away from the group, hiding a small smile. Her young friend was quite the character, but this was no time for fun and games.

"I'm assuming security will be an issue?" Yael asked. "I haven't seen any guards—what type of weapons are we talking about?"

"It won't get that far," Lucia assured her. "There are always people left out of *the box*, so we can send a team to distract the guards."

"How?"

Lucia looked at Yael as if she were mad. "I'm sure the girls will think of something."

Aminata and Petra leaned together and made kissy faces, then Petra faked a moan.

Eyes flaring wide, Yael stared into her glass.

"You know," Lucia mused, "Security guards the blackmail files. Petra, can you gain access?"

"Without question."

Lucia looked at Yael. "You know about the temperature sensors?"

She nodded.

"The guards should be distracted enough that they don't notice the switch, but you'll still be in the chamber."

Yael swallowed nervously and shrugged. "Are you sure it will work?"

"The temperature sensors are mostly for making sure no one is dead. Security scans the chambers to make sure no one goes too far . . .

unless they paid for it." Lucia shook her head bitterly. "Lucky for you, this isn't the island for that."

Ana Claudia crossed herself. Frowning, Yael watched the expressions at the table darken.

What the fuck is that *supposed to mean?*

"Once the guards have been thoroughly sidetracked, someone will retrieve you and take you where you need to go."

Yael looked pointedly at Lucia. "Where can I access weapons?"

"It is illegal for any of us to have any such thing in our possession." She shrugged. "But we have our ways."

The ominous nature of her tone led Yael to believe her.

"Lira, what are you doing here? Really?" Petra asked quietly. "Why do *you* want to help? Don't you love it here?"

Edelira met the eyes of her fellow companions and shifted in her seat. "Maybe I'm a little nervous . . . "

"It's her first time in *the box*," Lucia interjected coldly, her eyes welling up with tears.

Yael studied her, watching as a single drop slid down her cheek. In that moment, Yael knew. Lucia was the roommate—the girl from the story—the one who lost her lover to the monsters on level five. She placed her hand on Lucia's and clasped it gently.

"Why are you willing to help me?" Yael asked, searching the eyes of each woman at the table.

At first, no one could answer.

"Faces of men we see, but not their hearts."

Yael stared at Lucia.

"I was one of the first slaves bred and born on this island. My mother? One of the first slaves brought to this retched place. She taught me about our home, about Dominica. This place is *not* my home. These men are not our family. They are our captors! Slavers!" Lucia looked around the table, her disgust evident. "I know I am one

147

of the few to believe that truth, but if there is a chance for freedom, for others to see the light . . . *that* is worth everything to me. Even my life."

Tears streamed down their faces as they all processed Lucia's words.

"How do you intend to kill a hundred men in one fell swoop?"

Yael blinked at Athar's question. The small girl had been silent most of the night.

"I think I know a way," Lucia whispered. "Mama always knew you would come. She just assumed you would be a slave."

"I once was," Yael admitted. "Until I found my freedom."

CHAPTER SIXTEEN

Olivier finished his drink and shook his cup in the bartender's direction. Spotting Yael in his periphery, he straightened his bow tie and cleared his throat.

"You rang?" she asked drily.

He turned toward her and feigned a look of shock. "Dear me, Peach. I didn't see you come in."

She sat down next to him and ordered a water.

"I came by your room for a *tittle-tattle*, but you were nowhere to be found."

"Sorry," she said, her eyes downcast. "This place is so busy. I didn't see you much this week. I really had no idea."

He shrugged. "You're alright, Peachy."

Yael cocked her head to examine his eyes. "Oh, you are *out of it*. It's barely three o'clock, where are you coming from dressed like that?"

Olivier's chin dropped to his chest as he confirmed he was wearing his tuxedo. He was regretting skipping brunch this morning, though he would have done it all over again. Being invited to rub noses with the elite members over a round of golf proved he was one step closer to becoming a member.

He flagged down a passing waitress to order a bite. "Do you have any bread?"

Yael snorted.

The waitress bit her lip thoughtfully, then jumped in excitement. "We have some fresh loaves being prepared for the mixer, but I'm sure I can snag one for you."

"Oh, I bet you can," Olivier replied saucily. He smacked her hard on the rump and gripped it firmly. "Run along, you little beauty."

The petite girl beamed with pride and adoration, then ran off.

"I wanted to update you," he said to Yael in a low voice. "We are still set to leave on Saturday, but it does seem there is a chance that this is my year. If I'm inducted, I'm required to stay another week."

"Okay," Yael replied quietly.

Olivier sat back. "What? No complaint? No witty rejoinder?"

"So, what have you been up to?"

He squinted his eyes in suspicion.

Yael looked at him expectantly, a small smile on her face.

"Well," he started tentatively, "I've been working the hell out of this resort, if that's what you mean. This morning I discovered that there are *two* open memberships, and one of them is for the elite club. I thought it was all conjecture, but it really *does* exist. Do you know what that means?"

She shook her head, an odd expression on her face.

"It means that my pool of competitors has been scaled down dramatically. Unless a current member decides to upgrade at the last minute, there are only a few other men on this island who can afford to be elites."

"Wow. That's huge."

Curious, Olivier thought as he sized her up. Yael wasn't herself today.

The waitress returned, running over to them with a white cloth cradled in her arms like a baby. "Mama Cita almost caught me," she explained as she put the parcel down onto the bar.

"Aren't you a brave one," Olivier told her, putting his hand in his pocket. He leaned toward the girl and held out his hand. "Give us a kiss."

The girl blushed and gave him a quick kiss on the cheek, then snatched the gold coin in his hand and ran away again.

"What about you, Peach?" he asked, tearing off a piece of the warm bread. "I'd like to hear it from the horse's mouth."

"Excuse me?"

He looked at her. "Come on, woman. Don't be silly. I know you're not a horse."

Yael shook her head. "I've been told there are rumors about me. Care to share?"

"Best one I've heard . . . I brought you here to seduce the Grand Master. As if I'd ever be willing to share."

"What's the worst one?"

Olivier sat back in his chair and tapped his fingertips together. "You came here to become the first female member."

Yael gave him a peculiar look. "I've seen a few women around this week. None of them are members?"

"No," he said with a grimace. "And believe me, Peach. If the stories are true, it wouldn't be a good idea for you . . . or any woman, for that matter."

"Oh," she said flatly. "So that's it? Nothing else you wanted to ask me?"

Olivier held a bit of bread in his fingers, pressing it into a round dough ball. "I was surprised to find you sharing the company of a number of . . . women? I thought we'd had this discussion."

"It's not what you think," she said quietly.

He tried to hold back his temper, her petulant attitude grating on his nerves. "You could explain! Why come to a place like this and spend time with a gaggle of beauties who have nothing to offer you?"

"You brought me here so I could explore my fantasies, right?" Yael stared into his eyes, her lips tightening as she took a long inhale. "Have you not considered that the companionship of good friends might be a fantasy for some of us?"

Thank God!

"Oh, Peach," Olivier murmured. "You're so complicated, it's simple."

She sighed. "Tonight we're going glamping on the beach."

"That's nice," Olivier replied, adjusting his crotch. "Skinny dipping and pillow fights, huh? Where's my invite?"

Shaking her head when he nudged her a few times with his elbow, Yael looked at the ceiling and smiled.

The woman was as stunning as ever. Effortless style and beauty perfectly accentuated by makeup she rarely wore, his Peach had taken his breath away this afternoon.

"I've got to get going," he said, brushing the crumbs from his fingers. "But I have a question."

Yael rested her chin in her palm and waited.

"Do you have any interest in philanthropy?"

She blinked. "Wh-where's this coming from?"

"If you were the founder of, I don't know let's say, *The Peach Foundation*, who would you serve?"

"Anybody who needs help."

Olivier shook his head in frustration. "No, no Peach. That isn't really how it works."

"Why not?"

He studied her for a moment. "Fair enough."

Standing and pushing in his chair, he took a step closer and gazed down at her. When she lifted her head to search his eyes, he couldn't stop himself. He leaned forward to kiss her.

"Oooh!" he coughed, wheezing as he cradled his balls.

"That's what you get!"

He turned to look at her and groaned in pain. "You punched me!"

Yael shrugged. "Reflexes."

"In me *dangly-bits*?" he asked, affronted. "You just punched a thousand kings!"

She tossed her head back and laughed out loud.

"Bitch!"

Yael gasped, but seconds later she was cracking up again. "Now we're even."

Olivier stood erect and shook the remaining discomfort from his leg. Straightening his jacket with a slight wince, he leaned toward her.

"I'll have my apology one day. If even one of our children has a wonky eye, I'm banishing you to France."

She made a face of exasperation and climbed out of her chair.

"Got to run, Peach."

"Can you stop calling me that?" she snapped. "I haven't gone by Piccirillo in years."

Olivier laughed and slapped her ass, gripping it and pulling her to him.

"I've always wanted to do this," he murmured, his free hand slipping to his groin to cover his member. "I call you Peach because you've got the greatest ass I've ever seen."

He squeezed it once more and then gave it a pat.

"Enjoy your evening, *Peach*."

CHAPTER SEVENTEEN

After a long day of spying and mapping the resort, Yael and Edelira came to rest on her lanai. She hadn't spent much time in her room, preferring the more peaceful energy the cottages afforded over the business of the resort.

With the annual meeting approaching on Saturday, the busiest weekend of the year was officially underway. The evening's masquerade party was open to all, but Yael had opted to use the time to her advantage. Lucia had invited the new recruits to Yael's room to pre-game, telling everyone who wanted to meet Yael to get ready well in advance. After she had a chance to connect with the ladies, they would head straight to the party.

Lucia, Petra, and Aminata arrived first, followed by Ana Claudia and Athar. The new recruits trickled in slowly, with the last stragglers joining them just before the clock struck eight.

"Yaya is here to help," Edelira told them. "She has proven herself to be a worthy leader. In just over a week, she has developed the workings of a plan that could give us all a new life. But without our help—our loyalty to what is right—the pieces will not come together and any plan we create will fail."

Lucia walked to the center of the room. "This woman has come to inspire us, to show us the way to freedom."

Whispers spread amongst the cabal.

A dark-skinned woman put up a hand, waving it at Lucia. "This is my home, Lu. The only one I've ever known. You are blessed to have your mother here, but what of the rest of us? Where will we go?"

"Edelira is here. She has chosen to stay and rebuild. Is that enough?"

The whispers grew louder, but Yael could hear many agreeing with that point. If the highest value companion on the island was willing to risk it all, so could they.

"How do we know we can trust her?"

The room erupted, with most of the women asking the same question. Yael focused on her breathing and scanned their faces, wondering if this had been the best idea after all.

A slim, pale girl stepped into the center of the circle. "If Lu trusts her, then so do I."

"Me too," another called from the opposite side of the room.

Petra stood and turned to address the women behind her in German. A few hands went up. She nodded at Lucia and sat down.

Lucia turned to Aminata and nodded her head. Aminata stood and said something in what sounded like French. Her speech was a little longer, but several more hands went up before she took her seat.

One by one, the girls stood and spoke in their home language. Athar asked in Arabic, Ana Claudia in Portuguese, and finally Lucia in Spanish. The room was silent. Only Edelira remained standing in the center.

"That's most of you," she said softly. "But we need you all. And then we need your friends and lovers to join the fight as well. You know the resources we have at our disposal, but you also know exactly what your life will look like if we do nothing. Whether you will leave and find a new home, or stay and build one here, I ask you: who will join our fight?"

"I will!"

"I will."

A round of acknowledgement lit up the room.

Edelira turned to Yael and gave her the floor.

Remaining seated, Yael said nothing at first. She went around the room and met the eyes of every woman, counting their numbers.

"Thirty-eight," she told them. "One hundred members?"

Edelira looked at her.

Sighing, Yael nodded. "Lira is right, you know. Thirty-eight people hungry for freedom is a wonderful starting point, but without the support of the rest of the companions and staff . . . "

"We can't risk a battle between companions," Lucia explained. "It is not our intention to lose, and we cannot turn on our brothers and sisters."

"What will *you* do?"

Yael stared at the woman addressing her, unsure of how to answer. Her plans had come to a halt and she was out of ideas. She decided the best thing to do was tell them the truth.

"When I came here, I had no idea what I was walking into. I wish I had a stronger plan by now." She took a deep breath to calm her nerves and continued. "If you think I don't take this seriously, it's only because you haven't considered my reality.

"You must understand this: I came here with a man who is desperate to be inside that room on Saturday. My only escape is on his plane. One mistake could cost me my life and my freedom, and there isn't anyone on the planet with the resources to find me and save me. We were all brought here having no idea what this place was. We're in it together now whether you see it that way or not, and it doesn't feel *right* to leave you here. I would rather die trying."

Some of the women were visibly shaken by her admission. A young girl she hadn't noticed came forward from her place by the door. She couldn't be more than thirteen.

"I believe you," the girl said, taking her hand.

Yael's eyes teared up at the sight of the bruise on her neck. She looked so familiar, almost like she'd met her somewhere before. Turning to face Lucia, she found the woman standing with her hands over her mouth, staring at the girl before her.

"Mama sent me to see if you were real," the girl whispered. "Lulu said you were the one. I think she's right."

Looking at Lucia again, she recognized the family resemblance. There was no doubt this child was her baby sister.

Wiping the tears from her own cheek, Yael swallowed and smiled at the girl. "Do you think your Mama might be able to help us?"

"Spread the word," the girl said loudly, with surprising authority. "The island has heard your battle cry. Mama Cita has spoken: I'm not going in no damn *box*! Paradise is ours."

As the room erupted in a victorious shout of tribal warfare, Yael proceeded to weep until she lost consciousness.

CHAPTER EIGHTEEN

Edelira splashed in the water, basking in the warmth of the summer sun. She had been feeling anxious for days, with all eyes on her as if she knew the answers. Unfortunately, she felt powerless, which was an unfamiliar feeling after years on top.

Leaving the water and jogging over to the blanket where Yael lay, she dropped to her knees and onto her stomach next to her. Yael had removed her top, resting her head on her forearms while she tanned her backside. She opened one eye and smiled at Edelira.

"What?"

Edelira blushed and looked toward the cottage. "Nothing, *querida*."

She wasn't sure how or when it had happened, but she was sure of what she felt. The question was, what did she intend on doing about it?

"Yaya?" Edelira called sweetly, rolling onto her side. She gazed into her eyes, hoping they expressed her passion. "Stay with me?"

Yael's face contorted in confusion. "Tonight?"

"Forever," she replied quickly, her voice cracking. "Stay here with me and be free!"

Mouth opening and closing, Yael didn't respond.

Edelira sighed and laid on her back with a huff. She knew she should have waited! Yael had so much on her mind and she'd only added another worry.

Was it really her fault? Edelira had only been in love once before, with her second sponsor. But he seemed different during their last few visits, preoccupied even. Whereas before, he would spend his entire stay wrapped in Edelira's embrace, he became cold and distant in the months leading up to her eighteenth birthday. Though he still had ownership of her until the annual meeting, he had dismissed her early and taken other, younger lovers as he awaited his first *official* virgin.

Yael was the only person she had ever known that made her feel safe, and not just when they were together. She understood that her sponsors would eventually move on; it was the way of Paradise. But Yael would never leave her . . . not if they were in love.

Hoping she hadn't ruined their last day together, Edelira tried a new approach.

"Where will you go?" she asked.

Yael faced her, a small smile breaking through her look of hesitation. "I think I have to go home."

"Isn't that where you were going all along?"

"No," Yael said, biting her lip. She sighed. "I ran away. Olivier and I were going to England."

"I know England!" Edelira chirped. "That's where my sponsors were from."

"Hmm." Yael swallowed. "Maybe you can go there one day."

Edelira looked up at the sky. "I'm afraid to fly."

"How would you know? Have you ever flown before?"

"When I was young," Edelira said, a smile crossing her face. "That's how I came here."

Yael nodded. "Is that why you don't want to leave? You know they have boats?"

Edelira chuckled. "I don't know, planes and boats sound pretty boring. I would rather be queen."

"Of what?"

"Paradise! Why would I want to see the world when everyone in the world dreams of seeing a place like this?"

"And who told you that?" Yael asked. "Sounds like something one would say to deter you from leaving."

Edelira thought about it, remembering the specific conversations clearly. Her last sponsor often spoke of his lavish trips when he brought her little trinkets. She would ask to join him, and though she wasn't entirely serious, his answer was always the same.

Why leave paradise?

She heard his words echo in her mind and shook off the growing sense of uncertainty within. "What is it like?"

"England? I've never been."

"No," Edelira said. "The world . . . out there."

Yael looked ahead, resting her chin on her crossed hands. "It's pretty cool. I never traveled much after childhood—except for this last month. This is the third island I've been on since I left home in May.

"In Canada, there is a place called Prince Edward Island. The people are so friendly and there was a lot of love in the little communities we visited. And Cuba? You've got to see it for yourself! It's kind of like this place, but with a lot more people and places, a lot more history. If you don't like planes, maybe you could take a cruise around the Caribbean?"

Edelira grinned. "I don't know, this Prince Edward sounds very handsome."

Laughing out loud, Yael buried her head in her hands.

"Perhaps I shall visit Nicaragua . . . " When Yael looked at her expectantly, Edelira elaborated. "I'm not one hundred percent sure, but I think that's where I come from. I was so young, but I remembered certain words and phrases from other girls. Maybe I'm wrong?"

"You should definitely go! Wouldn't it be amazing to find your hometown? Maybe you could meet a distant relative—or a handsome Nicaraguan prince?"

Edelira giggled when Yael waggled her eyebrows and shrugged her shoulders. Though she wasn't sure where the Prince of Nicaragua lived, she was positive she could marry him if she wanted to. But then she saw Yael's peaceful sigh and fell in love all over again. Everything the woman did was sensual, captivating; sometimes she couldn't bear the thought of losing her.

"Lira?"

She exhaled sharply. "Yes?"

"Tell me, what will you do here during your reign?"

Edelira shrugged. "Whatever I please."

"Queens have to lead, you know." Yael poked her finger into the blanket, leaving little dips in the sand beneath. "This place will need a leader if you all decide to stay."

"I *would* like to be more powerful."

"Let's try *empowerment* instead," Yael smiled. "It's always good to think about how you can help people, and also how you can empower them to help themselves. You have to believe in yourself first, though."

Edelira gazed up at the clouds. "I remember the first time I ever believed I could rule the world. Mama used to come visit me every year, and sometimes I would join her and Daddy for dinners with elite members. That was a time when they were still building the club— things weren't so organized back then.

"My mind goes to one dinner party in particular. In my excitement, I fell right to sleep. When the men left, Mama and Daddy had a terrible fight. I was so scared! I watched from behind a sofa, and to my surprise, it was *Mama* who had the upper hand. In the end, she scolded Daddy like a child, far worse than she'd ever treated me.

"After she berated him for what felt like an hour, she sent him away from his own suite! She caught me peeking and apologized for scaring me. Then she asked me to keep it to myself because it was very important for everyone to respect Daddy. I never spoke of it, but it is one of my oldest memories."

Yael bit her lip. "This might sound silly, but . . . your Mama and Lucia's Mama? Not the same person, right?"

"No, no. Lucia's Mama is Cita. She's the head chef here. I believe she got her nickname long before she was a mother. She was one of the originals."

"Mama Cita?"

"Mmm hmm."

When Yael reached up to her neck to tie her bikini top, Edelira helped tie the strap at her back.

Yael sat up and faced her. "This place has been around for longer than I thought. And if I understood correctly, it isn't the only island like this. Is there anything you can tell me? I think I'm meant to help the others." Wrapping her arms around her knees, she settled in to listen.

"I used to think I was Mama's favorite, but that was many years ago. When she first brought me here, I begged her not to leave. She promised to visit as long as I was a good girl and made Daddy proud. For many years she kept that promise—usually a couple months after the annual meeting. A few years ago, the visits stopped."

"What do you think happened to her?"

"Happened?" Edelira tilted her head. "Oh! She didn't stop coming to the island, she just stopped coming to see *me*. I wondered if it was because I knew too much. She always told me things and then said, '*I shouldn't have told you that!*'. I thought it was our game, the little secrets we shared, but maybe she couldn't help herself?

"I have such a vivid memory of the moment we met. I can see the auction block, the scary man, and then . . . Mama. We flew on a plane many times before we came here. Her life was so fabulous. And the men she took me to meet were so rich!

"Sometimes, when other companions get jealous, they remind me that I am just like them in the end. But it is hard for me to believe. I don't feel like them, and I don't think like them either. I was so young when Mama found me, I don't even remember what poverty looks like. Wealth and grandeur is all I have ever known. Who says I cannot be queen? And who can stop me?"

Yael bit her lips closed, a telltale sign she was trying to hold something back.

"What is it?" Edelira groaned.

Clearing her throat, Yael looked up at the sky. "You sound a little . . . haughty."

"Haughty? I am not!"

Yael bit her lips again, her laughter escaping through her nose.

"It's the training," Edelira admitted. "Both my sponsors required I receive a formal education. Many of the sponsors are split on whether or not their companion should be educated, but I've heard most that come from *old money* prefer it."

Yael sighed. "I know this is a long shot, but do you know where Mama is from? Or could you at least tell me what she looks like?"

"Of course," Edelira said proudly. "You know, most people don't even know Mama exists. The ones that do call her a ghost. Some companions use her to scare others or keep them in line. There's always a rumor that Mama is coming—or already here. But I know the truth; it was the same time every year and still is as far as I know."

"That's going to make it harder to find her. People who don't want to be found usually aren't."

Edelira frowned. She didn't want Yael to find Mama; she already felt bad enough about what she was doing to Daddy. More than anything, she didn't want Yael to get hurt.

"Why do *you* have to be the one to find her?"

Yael shrugged. "It's what I do."

Taken aback, Edelira asked, "I thought you made margaritas."

"That too," Yael said with a wink.

Edelira swooned.

Why was the woman so complicated? What kind of life did Yael lead and why was she so desperate to return to it? Beauties like themselves were supposed to be pampered and enjoyed. She would surely find herself in an early grave chasing danger as she did.

"You okay?"

Staring into Yael's eyes, Edelira found herself entranced. There was so much love there. How could she not feel it?

Help her feel it!

Edelira leaned forward and got onto all fours. Crawling to Yael, she looked her in the eyes and asked again. "Stay with me? Please?"

Moving closer, she tried to kiss Yael.

Turning her head, Yael began to cry.

Oh, no . . .

Edelira sat back on her heels and bit the inside of her lip. She watched as Yael wiped her cheeks and sniffled, her eyes on the sea before them.

"I love you like a sister, Lira. And I know that's not what you want to hear, but it gets worse." She looked at her and shook her head. "My heart will never heal."

"Oh."

"I have only loved two men in my life. Sometimes I think it was only lust for the first, but maybe that's only because of how deeply I loved the second. The first man broke me in inconceivable ways; he tortured me and called it intimacy. He would have loved this place. To put in context for you: The first man? He was Mistress Stacey's lover.

"The second man was perfect—and far too good for me. I never deserved him, but I held on because I was selfish. I wanted to have it all. And because of me, he's gone. Dead. I would give anything to be with him again for just one night. He haunts my dreams, my nightmares . . . he will never leave my side. I lost my soulmate. And for that reason, I could never love you if I tried."

Edelira's tears were for them both, though the last line ripped her heart in two.

"I know you believe this place is a paradise, but that is just a name Lira! The first man, the bad man? He pretended to be a good man the entire time I knew him. But he hurt people and killed people. He had no remorse. He was reckless. And in the end, he died a nobody.

"Mama might seem like a good person. I don't judge you for seeing her in the light you do. But this place is just like the first man. It pretends to be good, but it's bad right in front of you. If I gave you a rock and called it bread, would you eat it?"

"Of course not," Edelira snapped.

"You would if I convinced you that rocks were edible. You would if I told you it was normal to crack your teeth every time you ate. You would if everyone else was eating rocks, because that's how it works."

Edelira wiped her face. "Why are you saying these things?"

"Because I think you might have something called Stockholm syndrome. Or maybe something like it. Human beings can be programmed to think all kinds of ways. And sometimes, we can be programmed to see things backward. You were programmed your whole life.

"They told you it was okay to do things that weren't okay. They

166

told you this place was a safe haven, though you have never been truly safe. And it's not because you are bad or weak or anything like that. It's because you're a human being. Children need love. Adults need companionship. But this place has warped your understanding.

"Lira, you should *want* to leave this place even if you are afraid. Whether you do or don't, I know you will make a beautiful life for yourself. But it's important for you to understand that you should *want* your freedom, you should *want* to have the right to come and go as you please, and you should *want* the power to choose who you love and how. Do you understand what I'm saying to you?"

Edelira's chest heaved as she tried to hold back her emotion. "You think I'm a fool?"

"No!" Yael barked. "I think you, and hundreds of others like you, have made the best of a bad situation. I think you are incredible."

Blinking through her tears, Edelira sat up straighter. "It's not like I've never thought about it, you know. When I was young, I always expected Mama to return and take me away again. I thought I would have a chance to marry a rich man or a prince. But once I realized this was my home, I didn't mind the idea of being queen. My life has always been good."

"I think you mean that your life has been better than the other companions—or am I misunderstanding?"

Edelira thought long and hard. "I guess that is the right way to put it. Is it wrong for me to say that I don't hate the work I do here?"

"Well, let's think about it," Yael replied in a low voice. "You were blessed enough to be born beautiful. That helped you get sponsored, right? The thing is, you don't have a sponsor anymore. If I fail . . . you have to go to *the box*. Have you thought about what life would be like for you now that things are changing?"

Shaking her head as new tears sprang forth, Edelira began to bawl. "I try not to think about it!"

Yael scooted toward Edelira and rested her head on her shoulder. "I didn't mean to upset you. I just wanted to ask you to make me a promise."

Edelira sniffed and tried to steady her breathing. "What is it?"

Sitting up straight and looking her in the eye, Yael said, "Promise me that you will leave this island just once! Just a trip. It really is beautiful here, but I think it might be good for you to see a new location. There are a lot of islands nearby; you could make a day trip and take the girls. Promise me you'll at least think about it. Even if we fail."

Unable to stop her tears, Edelira shrugged and looked away.

"The first man, the one who hurt me? He drugged me and did things to me while I slept. But sometimes I think about what we did when I was *awake*. He had many fetishes, things I knew nothing about. He lied to me and told me it was all normal, and I believed him for *years*. He did all of it right under my nose and I worked alongside him almost every day. I'm sorry I hurt you, but I'll be damned if I ever let what happened to me happen to anyone else. Especially not someone as special as you."

Yael stood and grabbed Edelira's hands, pulling her to her feet. When they embraced, Edelira felt her sadness melt away. All that remained was an overwhelming sense of peace and understanding.

"If you ever decide to leave, you should come to Tampa and work with me. You know a lot, and it sounds like you were one of the few people who ever saw Mama aside from the club members. But I warn you, my life is dangerous. I take my work very seriously."

Edelira admired Yael's strength and intensity. As feminine and beautiful as she was, the warrior energy she exuded felt wholly masculine.

"If I come into power here, I will make sure we all remain free. I would even try to find a way to free all the other islanders."

Yael's eyes widened. "Where are they? Who are we missing?"

"Sadly, I cannot help you there. The only other island I am absolutely positive exists is the worst of the worst. There is a club of monsters—somewhere very cold—where the companions endure evils untold.

"Should any companion be exiled, they know what fate awaits them. And sadly, those who are scarred, injured, or maimed to the point of lacking usefulness, they are also sent away. This is why the companions here are so grateful for the thermal system in the fantasy chambers. They don't need that system there; the members pay to kill in peace."

"What is that island called?"

Edelira shuddered. "Kletka Isle."

CHAPTER NINETEEN

Yael sat unmoving, allowing the feeling to flow through her. After hours of nervousness, she'd fallen into a restless slumber on the lanai's plush chaise lounge. She wasn't sure what time it was—could only recognize that it was still daylight.

The dream was only a haze when she awakened, but in this moment she felt as though she could see and feel it all. The present and the future swirled before her mind's eye. It was as if she were simultaneously flying over top of the island and walking through the consciousness of every inhabitant.

At first, she felt the anticipation; the air was thick with it. So many hearts and minds were looking forward to an evening of excitement. She sensed the power, too, though there was some polarity in the energy she couldn't identify. But when she felt the vengeance . . .

A knock on the glass behind her brought her back to reality, the vision disappearing from her mind with a loud pop. She gasped and turned to see a man in the window gaping at her with wide eyes, his lips trembling in fear.

Yael watched him curiously, wondering why he was looking at her as if he'd seen a ghost. Why was he in her room?

"Yes?" she asked tentatively.

He shook his head and wiped his eyes, hitting his nose on the glass as he leaned forward.

Pushing herself up from the lanai, Yael eyed him warily. "Why have you come?"

Opening the door a couple of inches so only his lips fit through, he whispered, "I have come for your bags. I-I-I delivered the message. Lord Hulley is headed to the boat."

"What is your name?"

"Emmanuel."

She nodded. "You are very brave, Emmanuel. Everything is at the door. Thank you."

The man finally stopped shaking and took a breath. Bowing his head quickly, he closed the door and ran to collect the bags.

Yael exhaled all the breath from her lungs and inhaled until she felt a sharp pain in her chest. Olivier had been silent since their talk at the bar, only to deliver a message early that morning letting her know there was a fifty-fifty chance they would depart this evening.

True to Lira's intel, the no fly zone was announced for two separate, one-hour periods that evening. Resort guests had been clearing out as the weekend approached, but a mass exodus had occurred during the day. She was happy Olivier was a part of it. Now there would be no need for changes to the plan—if it could be called a plan at all. Besides that, he was her only way out alive.

She closed her eyes and tried to call the vision back, but all she could hear is her heartbeat thudding against her eardrums. When she did her work back in Ybor, she had relied on careful notes and divine plans she only had to act out, not think out. Here in Paradise, she had taken on the role of co-leader with a woman she had yet to meet.

Mama Cita, Lucia's mother, had an idea of how to take out the members, and Yael had to clear the fantasy chambers before she made her way to *the box*. If the vision did not return, Yael would have only Mama Cita and the islanders to rely upon. What if there were too many moving parts? What if winging it brought her life to an end? Or worse . . . what if she was taken?

No! That's not going to happen.

How do you know? This is nothing like the old jobs.

That was true. In Ybor, Yael usually took care of the bad guys one at a time. There were sometimes weeks or even a couple months between kills, but tonight she would have a lot more to deal with. On top of it all, it had been weeks since she worked out, months since she pushed her body to its limits. By the time she took Lucia's place in *the box*, she might be too tired to carry out Cita's part of the plan.

How am I supposed to do this without my gun?

Adrenaline!

She blinked. The voice in her head was surprisingly clear—shockingly helpful. And it was right. Once the adrenaline kicked in, she'd be fine.

You always are . . .

The voice was right again. In all her years saving lives, her life had never been in any real danger. She walked away from every fight without a scratch. Why would tonight be any different?

Yael walked into her room and met the overwhelming stench of cleaning solution. The lemon-pine scent had yet to clear away, so she left the lanai open as she went inside. After she had packed that morning, she and several staff members had sanitized her room from top to bottom. Edelira had warned her that failure was not an option because they had the resources to find her if Daddy survived. The island's technology was surprisingly advanced, and so they made sure to leave no traces of her DNA behind.

She felt a little off, waiting in the empty room like this. Needing to keep busy, Yael put on a pair of gloves the staff left so she could clear the room. It was the third time she'd had to follow the compulsion. She didn't feel at all like herself, and she didn't need to be wondering if she left the proverbial iron on the stove.

As planned, she was wearing one of Edelira's beach cover-ups and a pair of Aminata's shoes. After her shower, she had braided her hair and then wrapped it into a tight bun at the top of her head. She caught her reflection in the mirror and had a sinking feeling.

A knock at the door interrupted her morbid thoughts. She slid off the gloves and put one inside the other, then tucked the fingers until it turned into a tight little ball of latex.

Yael greeted Edelira with a kiss on the cheek and silently stepped into the hallway.

"Are you ready?"

Shrugging, Yael shook her head. "Ready or not . . . let's go."

YAEL RUBBED her fingers into Edelira's scalp as she moaned with pleasure. Moving her hair out her face, Yael brushed it back and caressed her soothingly. Every few minutes, she stopped to wipe the tears from her own eyes.

Water was all around them and the ceiling had a simulated sky that looked a lot like stars if you didn't stare directly at it. The six of them were all sitting or lying on the raised dais, supported by various steel arms wrapped in beige leather. Taking Yael's place as the object of affection in the fantasy chamber, Edelira was propped up in the center of the throne on a long, curving leather bench.

Yael sat directly behind her in the position designated for pleasuring the neck, face, ears, shoulder, and head. Ana Claudia laid on a bench beneath Edelira, where she was perfectly positioned to lap away at Edelira's asshole. Two girls Yael had not met were on two opposing benches that jutted out and away, giving them access to her clit and vulva. Athar moved about slowly, climbing all over to lick Edelira everywhere from her toes to her underarms.

Embarrassed by her own arousal, Yael cried in shame. Edelira had assured her that this particular group of women had often shared each other's beds over the years and enjoyed being lovers, but she still felt wrong to watch them. She knew security could be scrutinizing them, and understood there was no other way . . . but she hadn't expected to wonder, to ask herself why she hadn't simply taken the position rather than telling Edelira to replace her?

Yael felt sick. She was not interested in women, but she'd never felt guilty catching glimpses of lesbian porn on the TV at Fred's during parties. Her guilt was not in her arousal, but in her ability to become aroused at all. Joe would know of her betrayal—he was always with her. Even though she hadn't seen him since she left Cuba, she couldn't help but fear that he was simply biding his time. Once Edelira was saved, his ghost would surely return.

As her worry reached its peak, the cement door of the chamber opened along the far wall. Yael's heart stopped, then started and raced faster than before. Six more women entered and disrobed. Walking slowly and sensually toward the dais, they found open positions around Edelira's undulating body and went to work.

Edelira had told her that the dais was designed for one individual to receive pleasure by up to twenty people at once. She hadn't believed her, but there was no denying it now. Even with half that number present there were quite a few openings for more heads and tongues.

Yael took the hand of the woman who had come to replace her and climbed out of the cluster. She stood and walked toward the place where their clothes had been dropped, donning the sheer golden tulle dress closest to the door. The door opened again and a woman poked her head inside. Frowning, she came in and pushed Yael's dress off her shoulders. Turning it around about Yael's waist, she brought the thin gauzy material up and over her breasts and moved them into position.

Too nervous to feel violated, Yael let the woman put the dress to rights and focused on her breathing. Recalling the plan, she knew this meant the guards were no longer watching; if the plan had worked perfectly, they'd be passed out by now. She was counting on that if she was ever going to find Mama.

Biting her lip and glancing back at the mound of women behind her, she realized she and Edelira hadn't said goodbye. In a way, they had, but that was yesterday.

"Here," the woman whispered harshly. "Put this in."

Yael squinted her eyes in the dim light as she took the small item from her. It felt like squishy plastic until…

"Oh!"

Making a face of discomfort, Yael lowered herself into a squat. Sliding the tampon in with the help of the wetness between her thighs, she stood and shifted her hips around the stiffness. It wasn't her idea, but she had to give it to the girls. How else was she supposed to keep track of a microchip?

Stepping outside to join her, Yael asked, "Who's first?"

Following her down the dark cement hallway, Yael took deep breaths and tried to calm her nerves. She needed weapons. When did she find the weapons?

"This one first. Then we'll cut back."

Nodding, Yael stepped inside as the woman opened the door and hid behind it. When it closed, Yael stood in the corner of the room and took in the scene.

A tall redhead stood only a few feet away from her, screaming her head off about how worthless her slaves were. To Yael's surprise, several men were fucking other companions on the floor. The redhead was wearing red latex and had a black leather garter strapped about her waist and thighs. There was a man on his knees before her, presumably eating her out. Yael couldn't see his face. She noticed everyone else was wearing collars with leashes attached and had to assume the man before her was as well. Trying to focus on her *knowing*, she faltered. How was she supposed to kill this one again?

Looking at the wall beside her, Yael realized why they'd come here first. The room was designed like a medieval bedchamber, complete with a coat of arms and weapons on the wall. All she had to do was get to the sword before the woman saw her. Pressing herself against the wall, she crept toward the side table.

The redhead yanked the leash wrapped about her fist and shoved the man before her to the ground. "I'll do it myself! You're all halfwits!"

Yael made eye contact with him, remembering him from the pool. His eyes were filled with rage and loathing, and within seconds, so was Yael. She looked at the blade on the wall; it was probably sharp, but the tip was flat. Frowning, she stood on her toes and reached for the hilt.

The redhead crossed the room and grabbed the leash of a female companion, dragging her by her neck off of the man she was riding. Choking and scrambling to keep up, the girl fell to the ground and gasped for air as she pulled the collar away from her throat. The redhead released her and grabbed the man's leash instead.

"Do it right!"

The man lifted himself off the ground like a crab. The redhead straddled him and rode him hard. "Like this . . . yes! Keep those hips high. Be a fucking table!"

He groaned in pain from the exertion, his muscles trembling as she put all her weight onto him and ground her hips into his. When he saw Yael, he stopped moving and dipped his hips.

"What are you doing?" the redhead screamed shrilly, slapping his face with the knot at the end of his leash. She looked at the couple across from her and gasped. "Why have you stopped? How dare you defy—"

The man beneath her bucked hard, sending her flying onto the hard concrete floor. She screamed in frustration, stopping short when she met Yael's eyes.

"Who—"

Yael swung the sword over her head, her eyes on the concrete on the other side of the woman's shoulder. The blade cut through her jugular but stayed stuck in her neck as she gurgled in pain. Taking a step forward, Yael used the ground as leverage and pulled the hilt up with her.

She exhaled and scanned the room. The companions lay around her, panting with exhaustion. Looking into their eyes in thanks, she walked back to the door and pushed it open.

The woman on the other side exhaled in relief, peeked inside, and then ran into the room to the man still lying on the floor next to the redhead's body. Kneeling beside him and cradling his face, the woman whispered something in his ear and wiped the sweat from his brow. When she planted a kiss, he collapsed onto the ground in grief. She stood and looked at Yael.

"Is that all you need?"

Yael lifted the sword, noting it was heavier than any she'd ever trained with. She scanned the room and saw a few daggers on the wall. "I need a belt—that garter will do."

The woman rushed toward the redhead and unbuckled the leather straps, then spat in her face. Running to Yael with a quick glance back at the man, she handed it to her and returned to the door.

Putting the garter on over the sheer dress, she weaved the thigh straps along her waist and looped them together. Crossing the room quickly, Yael added three small, sheathed daggers and a broadsword to her belt. When she passed a spiked mace and flail, something in her said to pick them up as well. She had to clear the compound before she made it to *the box*, and she'd need weapons to pull that off. Hoping she wouldn't be too bogged down, she left the room and followed the woman down the hall the way they'd come.

When they reached the next door, Yael put down the heavy sword. Peeking inside, she saw what looked like a dungeon. Hay littered the ground and there was a distinct scent of stale urine and feces permeating the air. Her eyes adapted and she saw a small, fat man pounding away at a woman locked in stocks as she groaned in agony.

Stepping inside, Yael approached him silently on her toes. Swinging the mace a couple times to build momentum, she ignored the feeling of dampness against her soles. When she was only steps behind him, she gripped the handle with both hands.

"Hey."

"What the—"

The heavy spiked ball slammed into the side of his face, sending him flying.

The handle slipped from Yael's hands, but she didn't care to retrieve the weapon. Rushing to the stocks, she tried to find a way to open them and release the girl.

"Go!"

She froze. "Tell me how to open this!"

"Someone will come for me," the girl whispered harshly through her tears. "Just go!"

Yael looked at her and back toward the entry. Her guide was waving her over, urging her on. She let out a growl of frustration, then ran to the door and retrieved the flat topped sword.

"I will take you to the next room," the woman explained. "Then you'll need to go through another door. Athena will guide you to the next chamber on the other side."

"What is your name?" Yael asked.

"I am Cyrene."

"Thank you."

Cyrene shook her head. "They told me you were like this."

Opening the door before Yael could question her meaning, they both looked in and saw two pale, plump companions staring their way. As if they had been waiting, they leaped off the bed and tightened the straps holding down what Yael presumed was a man. She could only see a large belly poking up, and then his toes. Stepping into the room, she rested the flat tip of her sword on the ground and watched.

"What are you doing?" he asked nervously, his head lifting to reveal the blindfold covering his eyes.

The girls walked over to Yael and gave her a smile. She realized they were identical twins. Reaching for her waist, each girl slipped a dagger from its sheath and headed back toward the man. Climbing onto the bed, they began to stab him over and over as he screamed and screamed.

Yael stumbled backward and ran toward the door on the other side of the room. Pushing it and finding great relief when it opened, she stepped into the hall and waved back at Cyrene before following Athena.

An hour later, they were in a race against time. Nerves getting to her as her body began to ache, she jogged behind Athena and tried not to give in to what she was feeling. The sharp pain under her right shoulder blade was getting worse with every room. Not including the man the twins had taken care of and another who was beaten to death by an entire room of male companions, Yael had dealt with nine men and one woman. By her count, there was one more chamber to go. She had yet to encounter the brothers she'd been warned about, so she knew they were the last before she moved on to phase two.

When they reached the door, Athena hesitated as her eyes filled with tears. "You must be careful."

Now she tells me, Yael thought maniacally.

It was no time for jokes, but she needed something to break the tension. Her vision was still unclear, and she couldn't quite remember what would come next. If she didn't get a hold of herself, she was going to slip up.

"Open it," she whispered.

Athena quickly wiped the tears from her cheeks. Hands shaking, she pulled the door open and hid behind it. Yael put the heavy sword down, knowing she was too tired to wield it properly. The only remaining weapon was the broadsword in the hilt at her side. Poking her head in, she was surprised to find the other door was open across the way.

It was chaos.

She stepped inside, wondering if she was needed at all. The companions were wrestling with the two men within, with three male companions fighting one, and five female companions holding down the other. The brother on his feet was having little trouble with the men surrounding him. His quick movements and the smile on his face told Yael he was toying with them.

The brother on the floor yanked his arm free and slapped the companion sitting on his belly strangling him. She fell sideways, but the girl who had been holding that arm punched him in the throat.

"Agh!" he choked, still struggling beneath them.

Another companion stomped her heel into his crotch. When he screamed, she jumped into the air and landed feet first in his groin before falling sideways. He screamed and stopped struggling.

"Son of a bitch!"

The brother on his feet, having witnessed the move, shoved off the men he was fighting and ran to aid his brother. Yael pulled her sword from its sheath and ran to cut him off, screaming as she impaled his side and then jammed the hilt forward.

He fell to the ground in shock only feet from his brother, watching another companion climb on top of the younger man and squeeze his final breaths from his lungs. Both men died seconds apart.

The room was silent for a few breathless moments as they met each other's eyes. When Yael saw they were safe and dropped her head in relief, a male companion let out a whooping war cry. The others followed suit, kicking and spitting on the bodies of the fallen men as they rejoiced.

"Yaya!"

She turned to find two menacing guards watching her, hands resting on the weapons at their hips. Just as her heart fell out of her chest, Lucia's little sister stepped into the doorway wearing a matching sheer dress.

"Mama is ready!"

CHAPTER TWENTY

Yael gasped. "Mom?"

Mama Cita emerged from the shadowy hallway, a stern expression on her face. "I told them not to put you in that yet."

Shaking her head in confusion, Yael studied her features. The woman was not her mother, but damned if they weren't related!

"Don't worry," Mama Cita snapped. "I knew this would happen. Lu, bring me that dress!"

Lucia approached them and handed her mother another sheer outfit. Whistling softly toward the dark hallway, three women rushed over carrying bowls of water and cloths.

Standing perfectly still as she stared into Mama Cita's eyes, Yael allowed the women to strip her of the bloody dress. They set to work washing her body clean while Lucia fixed her hair.

"Listen to me and listen good," Mama Cita said hurriedly. "Every man must receive a glass, and if they look like they're going to drink it, you damn sure better stop them."

Nodding, Yael closed her eyes against the breeze cooling her bare skin.

"Step lightly. If you spill even a single drop, you're dead. You understand me girl?"

Biting her lip, she whispered, "I understand."

When the new dress was put in its proper place, Yael was handed a golden serving tray filled with ten small cognac glasses. Keeping it low and away from her face, she stared at Mama Cita curiously.

"You and the others will offer the drinks. If they don't take it, put one nearby. These fools won't risk upsetting Daddy. When it's time for the toast, they'll drink."

"Okay," Yael said softly.

"Look at me," Mama Cita said, grabbing Yael by her chin. "Not a drop."

Eyes wide with fear, Yael nodded.

Mama Cita clasped her cheek and smoothed back her hair. "You ain't tired. You've come too far now."

YAEL FOLLOWED the other companions down a long corridor, shaken to her core. Her mother was long gone, but Cita favored the woman so much that Yael still couldn't let it go.

She tried to hold the tray perfectly still as she trudged on. The round bases of the short stemmed glasses tinkled with every step, the sound echoing through the hallway like the early warnings of an earthquake.

Yael could see a male companion up ahead holding the door that would lead them to the path. The members had just left this hall, only a few minutes ahead up the path as they made their way into *the box* for the initiation.

A man's voice carried to her ears. She shuddered, knowing it was the infamous Daddy she was hearing. Each year, he gave a pep talk to the companions stationed inside.

They had little time to deliver the drinks and get out before he arrived at *the box*. Passing by the window, she looked inside and saw more than a hundred women dressed just like her, staring into the corner. She saw Lucia and several others she recognized from the recruiting meeting, but none of them looked her way. In fact, not a single person in the room moved their eyes from the man behind the door.

Yael stepped out of the hall onto the path, the pavers beneath scraping against her feet. Her arms were tired, but she didn't care. The night was almost over.

Just a little while longer . . .

Two minutes later, the trees overhead disappeared and the path opened up. When she stepped out of the tunnel, she gasped at the sight of the massive building.

From the sky, she had been unable to gauge the size of the place in relation to the cliff it sat upon and the sea beneath. As she approached, she was most surprised by its height. Towering over her, *the box* appeared to be taller than two stories high. Had Edelira misjudged the stories? What was Yael walking into?

Following the line into *the box* through dark metal doors at least fifteen feet tall, she did her best to maintain composure as she entered the warehouse-sized room filled with ninety-nine naked men.

"A gift from a member who hopes to be reconsidered," the lead companion decreed, bringing a round of smug looks and snickering amongst the members. "Grand Master will join you for a toast momentarily. Thank you for your patience."

Yael and the ten servers with her walked around the room, offering sensual smiles and wiggling suggestively as the men took their glasses. Some of the men watched her, not taking their eyes off her once she passed. She kept her focus on the ground, feeling her cheeks quaking beneath the forced grin. When she had only one glass left, she made her way toward the door as she searched for a man to serve. Moving past them as the whispers increased, she wondered if Mama Cita had prepared one too many. By the time she made it to the door, she was the only woman left.

Her nerves won out. The men looked hungry and she had no interest in satisfying their craving. Turning quickly to follow the companions back up the path, she stopped just short of spilling the drink on a man who had appeared in the doorway.

"What is this?" he asked, taking the glass from the tray.

Yael met his eyes and gasped, looking down. "I'm sorry!"

"Who are you?" He grasped her chin and studied her face. "You aren't one of mine."

Her stomach did a double flop. This was him? This handsome, unassuming man was Daddy? Yael tried to remember her vision, but her mind was blank.

"Are you . . . my Daddy?" she asked, biting her lip as she studied his face.

Taken aback, the man pressed his lips together.

"It was supposed to be a surprise," she said quietly. She tried to force herself to cry. It didn't work. "Master Olivier is going to be so upset!"

"Hulley sent you?" Daddy smiled. "Good man."

She smiled up at him, trying to appear hopeful. "You aren't upset with me?"

"Why would I be upset, kitten?"

Yael made a noise, the half-moan, half-squeal escaping her as she hugged the tray to her chest. "He sends his regards and asks that you all enjoy a toast and consider his elite membership next year. Until then, I will be here to convince you. I've only been training for a year, but I'm told I'm a fast learner."

She took a step forward, emboldened by the smoldering look in his eyes.

"Even Lira says I'm very good for a virgin. She was so excited for you." Biting her lip and looking him up and down, she smiled wistfully. "We have to finish preparing, Daddy. I hope I can make you proud."

Slipping by him, she tried to walk out the door.

He grabbed her arm roughly and pulled him to her. "Where are you going?"

Swallowing, Yael forced herself to smile. "I must find my sisters. We have a special ceremony for you, if you will allow us the honor."

"Come to me directly upon your return." Releasing her, he leaned down and murmured, "You and your sisters will join me on the roof to be deflowered before you meet the other members. Tonight will be the most magical night of your life."

Yael pushed herself further and lit up, running to him and throwing her arm around him. "Oh, thank you, Daddy! Thank you, thank you, thank you!"

Giving him a squeeze, she bowed three times and then ran out the door toward the path.

"Lord Hulley send his regards," he shouted jovially.

The room erupted in laughter.

She stopped when she reached the edge of the path and hid behind a tree. Two male companions pushed the doors shut, then waved to someone at the corner. A man emerged from behind a large boulder, signaling to someone out of sight. Yael saw the long object before she could see the men carrying it.

The beam that locked the door from the outside was dropped into place just as the faint sound of screams began from within. If the building really was sound proof, there was no doubt the men inside wished they were dead. The doors moved beneath the beam, but it mattered not. Daddy had designed *the box* to be impenetrable. Plus, Mama Cita's special concoction was created just for them, designed to provide an agonizing death. Whether it took hours or days, the men within had found their final resting place.

"Woo!"

Yael stood and watched as the men jumped in the air, running to hug each other as they cried out in victory.

The thunderous sound of a running herd met her ears. She turned to find the women racing up the path, shouting their own song of triumph.

"Lai, lai, lai, lai, lai!" the women sang, running to greet their lovers, fathers, and brothers in arms.

Overwhelmed with feeling, Yael dropped to her knees. Just before she fell to the ground, Edelira caught her and held her aloft.

"Help her!" she screamed as Yael faded into black.

CHAPTER TWENTY-ONE

G rasping the railing firmly, Yael placed her foot on the first step and smiled.

"Thank you, Charles. I can manage from here."

"Bless you," he whispered, kissing her on the cheek and jogging back to the golf cart.

Yael climbed the rest of the way up and walked onto the plane. She was later than she thought she'd be, but at least the job was done. Maybe tomorrow she would be proud of herself or at least happy for the islanders, but for now she just felt numb. Treading slowly to appease her aching muscles, she searched for Marge and Olivier, finding him seated with his back to her at the front of the plane.

"It's about *bloody* time," he slurred, swirling the ice in his drink without looking at her.

The table ahead had been converted into a bed. She felt terrible, wondering if Marge had been waiting to get some rest. They were supposed to be flying to England tonight, but Yael had no such plans. Groaning inwardly, she seriously considered taking the flight and heading home to Tampa in a few days. She was far too exhausted to argue with the man.

"The car was delayed, so I missed the ferry. We had to wait for some no-fly bullshit—"

Olivier put his glass in the cup holder calmly and tapped his fingers together. "Do not lie to me. Planes have been leaving all night. Couldn't drag yourself away?"

He still hadn't looked at her. Yael sighed. Was he really so mad? Of course she felt bad for leaving him hanging, but he was an adult. Why didn't he just watch a movie or something?

"I'm gonna get changed," she whispered. "Pick a movie, will ya?"

Olivier reached for her and grabbed the edge of the chenille throw she had draped over her shoulders. Still wearing the sheer golden dress, Yael yanked it from him and quickly backed away.

"I'll be right back," she assured him, her ire increasing with each passing second.

He stood and stumbled toward her. "What are you wearing, woman?"

"Stop!" she snapped, slapping his hand away from her chest. "What the hell is wrong with you?"

Olivier drew back and slapped her, knocking her head into the side of the plane. Yael collapsed, the pain of the headache she felt coming on exploding like a bomb in her mind. Suddenly, she felt cold.

"What's this?" Olivier asked. His hand slid along her calf as he murmured, "Why didn't you just say so, Peach?"

"No," she moaned, pushing herself off the floor. She slapped his hand as it slipped between her thighs. "No! Stop it!"

Olivier backhanded her. "Say it again! I dare you!"

Swallowing the blood in her mouth and wondering where it came from, Yael looked up at him in fear. Her luggage was all the way in the back of the plane. Could she make it to her go-bag in time?

He pulled her to her feet and squared her shoulders, trying to kiss her.

"No! Get off me!" she screamed, shoving him back. "Get off me, Olivier!"

"I don't mind a fight, Peach!" He dug his fingers into her shoulders and shook her. "Why don't you be a good girl and lie down."

Whipping her around, he pushed her back toward the bed behind them.

"Margie!" she screamed, kicking her legs wildly. Why had no one come to help her?"Margie, please!"

She tried to use her weight against him, but he was too strong. Lifting her limp body, he tossed her onto the bed and began to loosen his tie.

"This is going to be a very interesting flight," he sneered. "So, don't worry, I forgive you."

Confusion lit upon her face as she stared at him. Leaping from the bed, she shoved him and tried to make her way to the door.

"We're ready for takeoff!" he shouted toward the cockpit, lunging for her. He wrapped his arm around her neck and choked her, dragging her back with him. "I can see you want it rough. Oh, I can give you rough, darling. Yes, I can."

Blackness overtook her as he held her in place, whispering in her ear as she faded away. In her last effort to escape, she went limp. Olivier tossed her onto the bed and unbuttoned his shirt. When he moved to take it off, Yael jumped to her feet and pushed past him.

"Help!" she screamed, running to the door. She had to get off the plane before it left the ground. She had to get out of her before—

Olivier caught her by her dress and pulled her backward. She fell forward, hearing the fabric rip as he held it. Scrambling onto her hands and knees, she crawled for the door. But Olivier was there again, picking her up by her waist.

"Marge, the straps!"

Yael paled. "Help! Charles? Somebody help me!"

Olivier reached around to clamp her mouth shut. Biting down on his ring finger, Yael tried to take it off. He released his grip at her waist as he howled in pain at her ear. Slamming his knuckles into the side of her head, he pushed her into the cabinets beside them. "You stupid little twat!"

"Help!"

"Shut up!" he spat out. "Shut up, damn you!"

Wrestling from his grip, she stumbled into the cabin and searched for a weapon. The glass in the cup holder was the closest thing she could find, but just as she reached for it, Olivier tackled her to the ground.

"Oh my God, please!" she shouted. "Joe!"

"Bitch!" Olivier punched her. Punching her again, he said, "Look what you made me do!"

"Please, Joe," she sobbed, blinded by pain.

His hands closed around her throat, pushing her into the ground. He turned toward the cockpit and yelled down the hall. "Time to go!"

Yael slipped in and out of consciousness, vaguely wondering if it was all just a dream. She awakened briefly when he removed one hand from her throat to unbuckle his belt. If only she had thought to bring a change of clothes. Olivier switched hands, fumbling with his button as he leaned his weight onto her neck. Yael could feel her heartbeat in her ears. If only she had thought to keep her gun on her. Using his knees to open her legs, he pinned them wide open and unzipped his pants. She blacked out and came to, the sound of the plane door closing taking away her last ounce of hope.

Her final thought was a humorous one: he'd have to let his guard down someday. Yael smiled at the thought of shooting this man dead as she faded away. The door slammed shut just as Olivier collapsed on top of her.

CHAPTER TWENTY-TWO

Yael's head was pounding. She didn't want to open her eyes, didn't want to know what would be there waiting for her, so she kept them shut.

The last she could remember, she was on the floor of the jet. It was too quiet for them to be in the air. Were they in London already? Or had Olivier taken her straight to his country estate?

Her head wasn't the only thing that hurt. She felt achy all over. As far as she could tell, she was not restrained. But that wouldn't really matter if she'd been caged. Was she already trapped in some kind of sex dungeon? It didn't smell like a dungeon. In fact, the air was fresh and so were the sheets over her head.

What if she was still on the island? Had someone come to save her? Olivier might have let her go. Or maybe they were in Great Britain after all? She'd never seen him so drunk. Maybe he felt bad?

Enough of this!

Just get up already!

Wincing at the sound of the voices in her head, she pulled the sheet away from her face and bit back a groan. Her skin was so sensitive even the sheets hurt. This didn't look good.

Opening her eyes, she let out an involuntary grunt and closed them again. This time, opening only her left eye, she tried to focus on the ceiling above her. The wooden slats were painted white, though the paint was cracked and peeling. She was in a king-size bed in the corner of a house she'd never seen before. Rolling onto her side and pushing herself into a seated position, she breathed through the pain and waited for her head to stop spinning.

A few minutes later, she was able to stand with support. She held the nightstand, then the wall, and stopped at the door across from her. Turning the knob slowly, she peered inside and saw her and Olivier's luggage on the floor of the dark, narrow closet. Closing the door, she hugged the wall until she reached the window across from the foot of the bed. Pulling back the curtains, she saw the beach in what was either the early morning or late evening light. Judging by the colors of the sky, she determined it was morning and closed the curtains.

Ahead of her was a sofa and coffee table. Launching herself forward, she leaned over the back of the couch to catch her breath. The sofa was old and none of the furniture matched. If she was still on the island, she'd never seen this part before. Everything in Paradise said *luxury*, but so far, this appeared to be a simple cabin bungalow.

There were two doors, one to her left that would take her outside, and another to the right that probably led to the bathroom. Moving to hold the arm of the loveseat and then stumbling to the table behind it, she found a kitchen and open pantry in the other corner. Her legs were stronger than she expected, but the feeling of nausea that came each time she moved made it difficult to think straight, let alone walk. Pulling the chair from under the table with a loud scrape, she sat down with a thud.

The sound of a toilet flushing sent her reeling. Looking toward the door across from her, she saw a sign above it and lost her color.

Feeling irie?

"No," she whispered.

Dream Joe opened the door and smiled at her. "There she is."

She broke down immediately, her breathy sobs matching her slow movements. "I can't," she cried, her voice raspy. "Please, Joe. Not now."

Yael didn't have time for dreams—or nightmares, for that matter. She had to wake up. Surely Dream Joe would understand she needed her strength?

He approached her slowly and knelt before her.

"I can't stay with you today," she whispered, sucking the snot back into her nose. "He got me, Joe. He got me!"

"You're safe now," he said softly, reaching out to soothe her.

"No!" she screeched, pushing herself into the table. "Don't touch me!"

Dream Joe stopped and frowned, then held up his hands.

"I'm sorry, Joe." She wiped her face, forgetting her bruises. "Ahh! Fuck! That fucking bastard!"

Dream Joe stood and walked away.

Good! Yael thought, watching him fearfully. *Go away! I need to think!*

She'd been caught in numerous dreams and loops over the last month, but this was the first she remembered waking up *into* rather than *out of*. Maybe she was having trouble walking because she was restrained after all? In real life?

Yael moved her limbs and rotated her spine, trying to feel for the restraints through the dream. Pushing herself up from the table, she fell toward the sofa, catching herself at the last second.

"What are you doing?"

She turned and saw Joe standing by the window.

Glitchy, she thought anxiously.

"I have to get out of here," she groaned, launching toward the open door in front of her. "I have to wake up. I think he's killing me."

Yael fell into the bathroom and pushed herself onto her knees. Grabbing the counter, she pulled herself up and stared into the mirror.

Both of her eyes were black, the right one more than the left. A lump on the right side of her nose made her question if it would be broken when she awakened. The bruise on her cheekbone had a gash that had likely bled and clotted closed. Her lip was swollen; she lifted it and found the place where her teeth had split the skin wide open. Had she lost her teeth in real life? Would Olivier care enough about her appearance to get her the care she needed, or had he already discarded her somewhere?

Using her legs to force herself the rest of the way up, Yael stared at her clothes and frowned. Why was she still in this stupid dress?

"Change clothes," she told herself in the mirror. "Black shirt! Jeans!"

Nothing happened.

"Ugh!" she screamed.

"Maybe you should lie down?"

Yael fell down on the hardwood floor. Staring up at Joe, she scowled. "That's not funny!"

He frowned. "I'm sorry. I just thought maybe you might wake up in the right place if you went back to bed . . . "

She stared up at him, wondering if he was on to something. "Maybe you're right."

"Can I help you use the bathroom?"

She shook her head, squeezing her eyes shut when the room started spinning. "Never go to the bathroom in a dream."

Yael sighed. She did have to pee. It would be on Olivier to deal with it. She almost smiled, but then she realized it would be Marge cleaning the mess if they were still on the plane. Then again, maybe trying to go to the bathroom would help wake her up.

She sat up slowly and looked over at the toilet. Glancing back at her legs, she giggled.

"Wiggle your big toe," she imitated in a silly voice.

It only took a couple minutes, but she finally managed to get onto the toilet. Dream Joe watched her all the while, then he closed the door behind him. Yael knew she'd called to him for help, but this wasn't what she meant.

Closing her eyes as she felt herself going, she hoped to awaken before she finished. But she was still on the toilet by the time she was done, so she wiped and waited until she found the strength to rise.

When she stood before the mirror, her face seemed different. She didn't remember seeing the red marks along the side of her cheeks. Lifting her neck, she panicked when she saw the deep bruises on either side.

Fuck, he's killing me. I have to wake up now!

Yael slapped herself. Biting back the pain that flooded in, she felt a rush of adrenaline and smiled. She was getting closer. She took a deep breath and slapped herself again.

"Ahhh!" she cried, the pain becoming excruciating.

She fell to her knees, hard. The room was spinning again. She knew she was almost out, could feel the disorientation growing as she came to. Holding herself steady on the counter, she tried to bring her hand up again but lost her balance. Forcing herself into a seated position, she saw the cabinet before her and had an idea.

Opening it quickly, she whacked herself on the right side of her face.

"What are you doing?" Joe shouted, swinging open the door.

"Going home!" she screamed, hitting herself again. She fell, her head slamming against the bathroom floor.

"You are home!" Dream Joe dropped to his knees beside her. "You're home! I'm here!"

"I can't stay with you, Joe." The room went dark, though she could feel him there with her. "I don't have time to wait. Have to . . . save . . . myself."

"Yael!"

She opened her left eye and tried to focus on him.

"You can't fight him if you're hurt! Do you hear me?"

Yael flinched as his hand reached for hers and clasped it tightly, then she passed out.

CHAPTER TWENTY-THREE

Yael woke up and tried to open her eyes. Her face was on fire. It took several tries, but she finally got her left eye open and focused.

"Oh," she gasped softly. "I'm glad you're still here."

Dream Joe sat beside her in a chair, leaning forward with his elbows on his knees.

"I guess I'm stuck here?" she mused. "You're one of the nice ones, huh?"

Joe nodded.

She tried to sit up.

"Relax," he said, his voice firm yet gentle. "Nowhere to go."

Yael sighed. He was right. She was surprised to see him in the same setting, though his clothes and hair were different. Most of the time he looked angry, vengeful, and was usually wearing a dark suit. This version of him was intense, but at least he didn't seem so mad at her.

"Are you here to help me through *this*, too?"

He nodded again.

"Well, thank you. If this isn't . . . a trick. And thank you . . . for your help in Cuba. I never got to tell you I found her. I guess you already know, huh?"

He didn't move. Come to think of it, he hadn't moved since she'd awakened.

"This is weird," she said in frustration. "Does he have me tied up?"

Expression vacant, Dream Joe stared at her.

"Is that why I can't move?" Her eyes widened, thinking of Joe's ghostly figure in her waking moments. "Can you see him?"

He didn't answer.

She shook her head, then winced. "Are you . . . are you a ghost? Or is this just in my head?"

"What do *you* think?"

"I kind of wish you were a ghost. Then you could tell me what was happening out there." Closing her eyes, she tried to make sense of it. "But I saw Lira, and she wasn't a ghost, so I guess you're in my head. I don't know. Stupid powers."

"Powers?"

She looked at him. "What would you call them? Is dreaming a power?"

He gave her a blank look.

"Huh! Dreaming is my power, right?" She didn't wait for him to answer. "Why would I use my power against myself? Is that what this is?"

"What do *you* think?"

"Oh no," Yael groaned. "I remember you. You're the shrink version of him, aren't you? You're therapizing me!"

Smiling, he nodded.

"Okay," she said, trying to slow her thoughts. "I don't know how many times he hit me, but maybe I'm in a coma or something? My brain must be broken?"

"Is that what it feels like?"

She closed her eyes. "Yeah."

"You said I helped you before? Was your brain broken then?"

Yael's lip began to quiver. Her eyes burned with the sting of tears.

"What is it?"

"My brain has been broken for a long time, I think. But especially after you died." She choked back a sob as she faced him. "When you showed me the way in Cuba, I was ignoring my *calling*. If you hadn't called my name, who knows what would have happened to Maritza."

"You're okay," he said soothingly. "Breathe in. Now breathe out. Good."

She shook her head. "Your ghost gave me courage. Maybe that's why I called for you on the plane."

Tears formed in Dream Joe's eyes.

"I'm sorry," she told him, a grim look on her face. "It's my fault you aren't here to save me now."

"What else?"

Yael bit her lip, then released it. Exhaling through the pain, she tried to connect the dots. "I must be close to something big? Or . . . "

"What?"

She sighed. "Or I'm dying?"

Joe tilted his head, raising a brow in question.

"You know . . . if I'm dying there's nothing I can do. Right? No use focusing on *that* . . . So, the question is: if I'm not dying, what are we supposed to be doing here?"

A faint smile showed on his face. "Honeymoon?"

Yael's expression contorted as she fought off fresh tears. "Why would I look like this? Why would I be able to feel everything? If this was about rest and relaxation, why add a broken brain and body to a lovers' getaway?"

"So if it isn't about rest . . . "

Thinking about all they'd discussed, she sniffed. "I feel like my brain is trying to tell me something. Okay, brain? What is it? What's so important that I'd rather be in here than out there? Olivier could be doing—"

She stopped.

"What is it?"

"Shh," she commanded. "It's coming."

"What's—"

"Shh!" she said again, wincing. "He told me something. Something important."

"Who?"

"Olivier," she snapped. "He said . . . ugh! What was it? Something about sleeping?"

Yael laughed.

"Brain!" she giggled, throwing her hands up. "You genius!"

Joe stared at her, waiting for an explanation.

"He told me he wouldn't try to sleep with me if I wasn't awake," she said simply. "I think my brain put me in a fugue state!"

At her last words, his expression changed to disbelief.

"I know what I'm talking about," she said confidently. "I read this book—the lady forgot who she was because—oh, never mind."

"What do you think a fugue state is?"

"Well, in the book, the lady had amnesia because—wait . . . " she looked around. "What if I'm awake? What if I'm awake right now?"

He sat back, brows furrowed in thought.

"You," she whispered. "What if you're—"

Yael clamped her mouth shut. If she were awake, the man before her was certainly *not* Joe. Could her mind be projecting Joe's ghostly image onto Olivier?

She eyed him suspiciously. "How did we get here? Can I go outside?"

Standing with a sigh, Joe walked to the window and opened the curtains. The beach was real, but she'd spent the last month hopping from island to island. Her mind probably found it easy to create seaside images. That didn't help much with *this* conundrum. Eyeing Joe, she had an idea.

"Come here."

Mouth set in a firm, flat line, he approached her slowly. He sat in the chair and waited.

"Can I touch your hair?" she asked, eyes narrowed.

Leaning forward with a heavy sigh, he pulled his hair from its place atop his head and let his dreadlocks fall free. Yael reached for a lock and touched it, finding it to be real between her fingers. If this was Olivier, he'd have to be wearing a wig. She pulled on a lock, cringing slightly when Joe grunted in pain.

"Okay, maybe I'm not awake." When Dream Joe snorted, she rolled her left eye. An overlong moment of dizziness served as a reminder to stop moving so much. "Ouch, I get it brain. *Geez.*"

Sitting back in his chair, Joe crossed his arms and watched her. "You read one book and now you're a clinician?"

"Maybe it's not a fugue state," she retorted. "But I'm definitely hysterical . . . hey, don't look at me like that! This is serious!"

"You're right, you're hysterical."

Yael giggled, then clamped her mouth shut and dropped her eyes. Was it wise to fall in love with him all over again? Could Dream Joe ever be jealous of another version of himself?

"If this is a dream—and I'm the one who put me here—I think I'm the only one who can let me out. But if you're here . . . maybe I'm supposed to help you, too?"

"Help me what?"

"Cross over?" she wondered aloud. "But that's assuming you're a ghost."

"And if I'm only a ghost in your mind?"

She blinked. "Brilliant. That's absolutely brilliant, Joe!"

Dream Joe stared at her as if she'd lost her mind.

"If there was anything keeping you here, anything holding you back from moving on, what could it be?"

"What do *you* think it is?"

She groaned. "Even in death, you're like this."

Dream Joe grinned. "Well? Why am I here, Yaya?"

Yael had the strangest feeling of déjà vu. She looked around the room and then up at the ceiling, waiting for it to fade away. Nothing happened. She bit her lip, then winced.

"I think you're here to hear the truth."

"About what?"

She closed her eyes and sighed. "Me."

"You think that will help me move on?"

"No. I think it will help *me*." She looked at him and explained. "I ran away with Olivier because he was my only option. I think I'm in here because I have nowhere else to go. But there's another side to this. You've haunted me for a month and all I want, even now, is to tell you the truth. I hate that I never got the chance—I think it might be killing me. I think . . . I think you're here because my brain knows that deep down, I won't be able to fight him if I'm still worried about you."

"Then tell me."

"What do you want to know?" she asked, tears falling down her cheek. "I wouldn't even know where to start. I don't know how long we have."

He looked around the room and sighed. "Why don't we start with what happened to bring you here?"

"He hit me," she muttered.

"Maybe start a little further back? How about the night I . . . died?"

Lips forming a pout, she nodded tearfully. "I knew it was my fault, so I ran. He'd left me his number at the bar a while back, I must have left the card in my pocket? It was like it came out of nowhere."

He listened as she told him of her travels to Prince Edward Island, of how his ghost wouldn't let her sleep. She told him of her guilt, how she felt awful every time she laughed. She apologized for limiting her mourning time to the evenings, seeing how it had upset him so. She described her time in Cuba, how Lira's ghost came to her many times, including the afternoon he'd led her to Maritza. She tried to help him understand the feeling she had that night, how the story in her head had come from Maritza's tears. And then, she tried to explain how she ended up on the island in the first place and faltered.

"He told me I needed to get over you," she said delicately. "The nightmares were getting so bad I could barely sleep. I had no idea what Paradise was really like, and by the time I got there it was too late."

"How so?"

Yael told him about the frame room and cried when she described how they'd violated her, recording her and Edelira. She laughed bitterly when she recalled just how lucky she had been to be mistaken for Stacey prior to her arrival. Crying again when she told him about *the box* and the reason she decided to help the people, Yael accepted his touch of reassurance.

He moved his chair closer and held her hand. "Did Olivier get offered a membership?"

"No," she replied grudgingly. "If he had been, I wouldn't be here right now."

Dream Joe squeezed her hand tighter. "How did you manage to escape?"

She broke down their plan, explaining how Mama Cita always knew the day for freedom would come. The older woman had found a patch of poison fruit when she'd tried to run away during her first pregnancy with Lucia. Cita cultivated it for years, even working to become a chef in the hopes of one day taking her children back home to Dominica. When her youngest daughter was stationed in *the box*, Mama Cita had been beside herself. Yael's arrival had been an answered prayer, and Cita was willing to risk it all.

"In the end, it worked," she whispered, holding his hand in hers as she traced the lines on his palm. "But I don't know if it did anything. What if I missed someone? What if Mama came to take back the island already?"

"Do you think that's what happened?"

She looked at him, recalling Cita's fiercely powerful mien. "No. They'd have to bring an army."

"What happened on the plane, Yaya?"

"I was tired. So tired . . .," breathing through her tears, she choked back a sob. "He was drunk and I'd kept him waiting. I just wanted to go home, Joe. I have to get back—I have work to do."

"So you and Olivier . . . you were never together?"

She made a face of disgust. "I would never touch the man. And I swear, Joe, I swear I'll kill him. I know you didn't get to see Xavier brought to justice, but I promise you this: their line will come to a swift end. If I ever get out of this . . . I will make him hurt."

Dream Joe cocked his head. "What does Olivier have to do with Xavier?"

"That's how I met him." She blinked. "They're cousins, remember?"

CHAPTER TWENTY-FOUR

Yael watched a fluffy cloud speed by and smirked, wondering how many more glitches she would experience in her dreamscape now that she was more aware. When Yael awakened that morning, her brain seemed to have reset itself. Arising before Joe following a strong urge to empty her bladder, she found the colors on the horizon were identical to yesterday's painting in the sky.

She tested her body in the bathroom, craving nothing more than to stretch her legs. But when she found the tampon wrapped in plastic lodged inside her, she opted to shower instead. It was a bitch getting the damn thing out; there was no string, and pulling the plastic wrap led it to rip. By the time she got it out, the exposed cotton was tinged with pink blood. The good news? There were *two* chips inside and they were perfectly dry. The bad news? She had no way of knowing if any of it was real.

Her anxieties were overwhelming her. Yael needed to know what data had been uploaded before they wiped the island security system clean, but she knew her mind could not go so far. Even if Dream Joe could procure a computer and the right connector, anything she saw would be pure conjecture and speculation.

Why had it taken a full day for her to notice the odd sensation within? And if Olivier had been lying about taking her while she was unconscious, would he have removed the tampon and thrown it away? There was a chance the plastic wrap would tip him off . . . but would he think to check inside or assume she was up to something else entirely?

A ray of sunlight shone upon her, warming her from the inside out. She relaxed more deeply into the sand and closed her eyes against the bright sky. Unwilling to ruin the fantasy of this dream reality, she kept her distance from the water. It had been beckoning, calling her name, but something about it didn't feel right.

After her shower, Dream Joe had still been sound asleep in bed. She thought it was strange that he would sleep at all, but the nature of this fever dream was distorted and very . . . *glitchy*. At various times throughout the day, she questioned whether or not she was alive. This morning, she wondered if Dream Joe would be different. Would he return to his suit and tie, to his vengeful anger and rage now that he knew the truth about her?

A part of her was happy to find him next to her this morning. She was glad she hadn't come here alone. Dream Joe was simple, and this caring psychologist version of him provided exactly what she needed to heal in this space. He'd responded to her exactly the way she thought he would, especially when she told him about Xavier, though that was to be expected. Though it was strange to know it was all in her head, talking through one of the worst times in her life had been therapeutic.

Unfortunately, the fact that he was still here proved she wasn't finished yet. Dream Joe was supposed to have received his closure last night. He was supposed to have moved on.

Doing her best to listen to her deeper self, she'd followed the call and left the cabin to explore what she'd dubbed Irie Island. The cabin was situated close to the white sand beach and was otherwise surrounded by lush palm trees, ferns, and mangroves. Two trees with pink flowers were planted at the corners of the small house, their winding branches growing like vines up the wall and hanging over the roof. It was simple enough for her brain to maintain, but something about it was too perfect.

She'd decided to venture to the right, wondering what she would find when she reached the end. Yael pictured the islands often drawn in cartoons, imagining herself on a small circular island in the middle of the sea of her mind. She set off with the intention of proving she had been dreaming somehow. At worst, she assumed she would end up back at the cabin. Less than an hour later, a wave of nausea threw her for a loop.

Picking up the sand and letting it slip through her fingers, she mused at how fortunate it had been that she'd picked the summertime to run away. Had it been winter, she might have imprisoned herself in a cabin in the woods and snowed herself in. At least here, she had the beach.

Yael clumsily rolled onto her knees and pushed herself up off the ground. She didn't feel as wobbly, so she decided to return to the cabin to see what Joe thought about trying to access the data on the computer chips. Last night, he pulled out one of her suitcases so she could find a change of clothes. Hopefully he would agree to go through Olivier's bags today; when she asked before bed, he had refused. Yael knew it didn't matter what she found, that none of it was real. Still, she wanted to believe it wasn't a waste of her time and decided that she was willing to try anything to snap out of this fugue.

She made it halfway to the cabin before the nausea once again reared its ugly head. Collapsing into the sand, Yael remembered that she hadn't eaten or drunk anything since yesterday. Assuming she was dehydrated, she told herself she'd have a cool glass of water upon her return. But when a sick thought crept into her mind, all she could do was lie still and close her eyes.

How would they feed her if she wasn't awake? If she really had been here for only one or two nights, she could probably survive a little longer. But what if her perception of time was skewed in this place? A day could be a week. A week could be an hour.

You've got to stop.

Yael opened her eyes. The voice inside her head was quiet, calm. It spoke like the others, but it didn't sound like them.

"Joe?" she whispered, her lips feeling dry. She licked them and closed her eyes, trying to hear the voice again.

Silence.

She took a deep breath, then another. Yael realized she was burning up, so she set her mind on the water and willed it to come to her. When it didn't happen, she lifted herself up onto her elbows with a groan and gazed out at the horizon.

The water wasn't too far. If she could make it the few steps, she could lie in the water and let it soothe her. Ignoring the nausea creeping in, she rolled, flipped, and crawled until she felt the warm, damp sand sink under the weight of her hand. Seconds later, a wave washed over her fingertips. When it receded, a breeze chased the water, caressing her with cool air.

It was nice to find that her mind had such a perfect memory of her favorite thing. For Yael, there was nothing like the first touch of the ocean upon her skin. She smiled in satisfaction, her anxieties melting away. Fifteen minutes later, she was completely calm. Her body temperature had cooled and she felt strong.

She made her way toward the cabin, happy she could see the bright pink flowers more clearly than before, now that she was rounding the bend. Each time the nausea returned, she focused on her breathing and reminded herself she was in control. Walking through the water made the trip slower, and she was glad to have the reminder that slowing down was part of the reason she was here.

As she made her final approach to the cabin, a big, dark cloud covered the sun. The entire island went dark. She looked behind her and gasped.

The ominous cloud blackened the sky as far as her eyes could see. A breeze whirled about her as she saw a tiny flash of light; the lightning was followed by a low tremble of thunder in the distance. For a few seconds, Yael felt cold. Then, a flash of heat slapped her in the face.

"Ugh," she moaned, going pale.

A sharp pain in her gut did her in. Doubling over and applying pressure just below her belly button, she fell head first into the sea. A wave crashed into her face, filling her mouth and nose with water.

You're drowning!

Get up!

Bursting from the water with a deep, guttural sound, she sputtered and coughed up the liquid from her lungs. The clouds were moving in quickly above her, but she couldn't move. She was paralyzed.

There hadn't been a single storm in the last month. Why was her mind creating this terrifying situation? What might be happening in real life?

Swallowing the bile rising in her throat, she closed her eyes and tried to focus. The clouds in the sky had made it dark—was it dark wherever Olivier had taken her? What if he put something over her eyes? She might be blindfolded. The water rushed over her and she froze again. Someone had covered her face and poured water over her.

I'm being waterboarded.

Panic struck her. If she were connecting with the outside world, her dream would likely end here. It was her choice, wasn't it? Would she rather die or live?

"Yael!"

Her heart sank. Olivier's voice rang through her head.

"Yael!"

She closed her eyes, tears falling as she tried to decide. A crack of lightning out at sea brought her back.

Climbing to her feet and stumbling forward, she told herself it was time to fight. She would do whatever she had to do, but staying here was no longer an option. If Olivier was willing to torture her to wake her, she would give him what he wanted. Just long enough to get to a weapon.

"Yael!"

Gritting her teeth, she turned toward the fading light to say goodbye to the cabin. Dream Joe had found his closure after all. She hoped she would remember the Irie paradise when she awakened.

A wave of heat caused her stomach to roil and another sharp pang knocked the wind out of her. Was Olivier beating her? She grabbed her belly, overwhelmed by the looming sense of doom. When she opened her eyes, she saw it.

Blood.

"Oh God," she whispered fearfully, the strength she'd been relying on fading quickly.

"Yael!"

She turned toward the sound, expecting to awaken and meet her fate. But it was so much worse.

Olivier was running toward her, sprinting down the beach and screaming her name.

"No!" she howled.

He had come from the cabin.

"You killed him," she screamed, the half-healed wound of Joe's death torn asunder.

Running into the water, Yael dove in and tried to swim. Olivier was screaming at her, telling her to turn back. Going against the flow as she was, exhaustion came quickly. Too tired to hold her breath, her lungs filled with water. And it was there Yael gave up, drifting deeper into the choppy sea as she embraced death with an openmouthed kiss. It was time for the nightmare of her life to end.

DROPS OF WATER stung Yael's skin. She coughed, fluid pouring from her lungs. A strong arm gripped her firmly, swimming them toward the shore. She jerked and tried to kick herself free.

"Cease, woman!"

Craning her neck, she turned to see it was Dream Joe carrying her, a look of worry on his face.

"He killed us," she coughed out. "I'm bleeding, Joe. He's torturing me."

"Where?" he shouted, taking a step onto the sand bar as he approached the shore. "Where are you hurt?"

Yael's head drooped as the dull ache intensified. She slurred her words, explaining, "I think I'm dying. My body is trying to tell me, but I can't fight anymore."

"Where are you hurt, Yael!"

She sobbed. "He's raping me, Joe! It hurts so bad."

Joe knelt onto the sand and lay her down gently. "Tell me where?"

"My stomach," she moaned.

Turning onto her side, she retched. Only bile came out, but she couldn't stop.

"What do I do?" she begged, choking. "Just tell me what to do?"

He touched her belly here and there, then rubbed it side to side. "There's nothing here."

"I saw it," she gasped. "On my legs. It was there!"

Dream Joe slid his hand along her hip, scrambling in the sand as he worked his way down to her ankle. "I've got to turn you over!"

Quickly and carefully, he wedged his hands under her bent knees and lifted, rotating her onto her other side. He wiped the sand from her leg and examined her again. When he reached her ankle, he stopped.

Yael lifted her head and saw his look of shock. Dread flooded her senses. "What is it?"

Dream Joe's face contorted as if he were in pain. He bit his lower lip to keep it from trembling, staring into her eyes as his filled with tears.

"Oh, God, no!" she screamed, dropping her head into the sand.

Crawling toward her as the rain picked up, he scooped her into his arms and held her tightly. When she felt him shaking, heard his cry, she knew it was the end. She was thankful she didn't have to die alone.

"When was your last cycle?"

His question didn't register at first. She stared at him through her tears uncomprehending, her breathing ragged.

Dream Joe smoothed her hair out of her face. "I think you're on your period, Yael. Do you understand me? When did you have it last? Think!"

She blinked.

Thunder sounded above them, as if to snap her out of her hysteria. The heavy rain drops splashed loudly off their skin. Closing her eyes to focus on the sound, she reflected on her trip. It had been just over a month since she called Olivier. She remembered waking up in Cuba, having to clean herself up. Yes, it was about that time. The dark clouds, the pain, the nausea . . . her brain had done its best to signal to her, to prepare her. Once in a blue moon when she was especially stressed, the pain was worse than usual. It was . . . a lot like this.

"Shit," she muttered. "Shit, shit, shit."

"It's okay," he told her, stroking her brow with his thumb. "We have to get inside."

Yael frowned. "I'm gonna die in here, aren't I?"

Dream Joe didn't answer her.

"I can't! I can't do this! I don't want to die, Joe. I want to go home."

His lips tightened, then trembled. Drawing her close, he hugged her and rocked her back and forth as she whimpered in despair.

"I wanna go home, Joe. I wanna go home!"

CHAPTER TWENTY-FIVE

Though the days passed by and time seemed to tick on, Yael had trouble believing she was alive anymore.

Dream Joe had magically procured a stock of food and spent much of each day trying to get her to eat. In the week since the bleeding started, she could barely keep anything down. Food and drink were taken in only when she felt faint or dehydrated. Even as Joe prepared meals that smelled so delicious her mouth watered, when the plate was set before her, the nausea returned.

When Yael awakened on this morning, she was irritated with herself. For the last week, storm clouds darkened the skies above. Now that her cycle was over, the sun was shining and there wasn't a cloud in the sky. She felt betrayed. It was as if her own mind was trying to destroy her.

For a few days after the incident on the beach, she anxiously awaited another torture session. Olivier was no doubt furious that she was still unconscious, especially if the time in this dream world matched his waking life outside. Would he grow tired of waiting for her and dump her body? Would he kill her first?

The water torture never came and neither did any other pain. She watched as her bruises got worse and then better, and laughed when Dream Joe tended to her cuts. It was likely all in vain. While there was a chance that someone at Olivier's estate might be caring for her, she was becoming more sure she was no longer on the earthly plane.

Dream Joe had been quiet for most of the week, seemingly happy to hold her in the silence. Each day, they would sit on the couch or relax in bed and watch the clouds roll by. Though she couldn't say she was happy, she found it easier to be at peace in those moments.

Yael felt her awareness slipping away. When she closed her eyes at night, she didn't dream. She was now somewhat convinced that these moments of wakefulness *were* her dreams. Another part of her was also certain that she wasn't sleeping when she shut her eyes, but rather shifting from one scene to another. This left Yael in a quandary. If she was stuck in a perpetual dream state, there was a chance she was never going to wake up—assuming she wasn't already dead.

And so it was. This was the hamster wheel she'd created, the cage she chose to lock herself inside of rather than facing Olivier directly. Either she was fully awake and having a psychotic break, in a comatose state, or already dead and unable to move on.

Though she could not fathom the possibility of the first option, she had just as much trouble believing she could really be in a coma. She'd been through this before, when she first moved in with Frederico after killing Lilith. When the nightmares intensified, Yael spent a month believing Lilith had gotten to her first; the idea of living inside a coma dream had rocked her world. Now she knew it was all wishful thinking.

Ultimately, the third option was the most likely. It explained why Joe's ghost had haunted her. It explained why she saw Edelira glowing the day they met. Meeting Joe had set off a chain of events that led her to save hundreds of lives on Paradise Island. She had fulfilled her *destiny*.

It was never Joe who couldn't move on. It had always been *her*. The question was, what would it take for her to cross over?

She turned to face Joe on the bed beside her. "It's a beautiful day out."

Dream Joe nodded and gave her a half smile.

"We shouldn't waste it."

He raised his eyebrows in question.

Yael felt tears well up in her eyes. Crawling toward him on her knees, she cradled his face and kissed his forehead.

Dream Joe closed his eyes and shivered under her touch.

"Get dressed," she whispered. "Let's go for a swim."

His eyes bore into hers, speaking to her soul in words she could not comprehend. She understood the meaning—she felt the same way. If she had already crossed over—if this was heaven—she was happy to spend it with the love of her life. For even in this cage, Joe was still the man of her dreams.

CHAPTER TWENTY-SIX

Yael took the twin braids out of her hair, working her fingers through the strands as she studied herself in the mirror. If her timing was correct, it had been almost two weeks since she left Paradise. The bruises on her face had turned yellow, making them invisible on her sun-kissed skin.

Exiting the bathroom, she scanned the room for Joe and found him opening the windows to let the evening breeze flow through the cabin. It had become their nightly routine, leading Yael to wonder if someone might be taking her out for fresh air each day. Then again, it was a heavenly wind; there was also a chance this would be her evening routine for all eternity.

Ever since she accepted her fate and acknowledged the likelihood of surviving weeks without sustenance, she had found it easier to enjoy the peace of Irie Island. But today she was feeling anxious, knowing there was still much she needed to share with Joe before whatever happened next happened.

Joining him on the loveseat, she sat in his lap and rested her head on his shoulder. She couldn't understand why she was having this urge, but she wouldn't fight it anymore. If Dream Joe could handle hearing about her actions in Paradise and her training with Xavier, he could certainly handle the rest of her story.

"Joe?"

"Hmm?"

She sat up. "I think we should talk about something."

Dream Joe smiled at her.

"Thanks for making this so much easier," she said quietly, giving him a weak smile. "If anything were to happen without me telling you *this* . . . "

She shook her head, trying to find the right words.

"I already know what it's like to lose you. To miss out on all the time I told myself we still had. I put it off for so long because I knew you wouldn't believe me. And now it's my biggest regret." She gazed up at him tearfully. "I wish I would have told you the truth. I'm pretty sure you would have just arrested me, but at least you'd still be . . . "

Yael cleared her throat. Wiping her eyes, she sat back and stared at the ceiling.

"I never dreamed. Not my whole life. I didn't even know what dreams were! After my mom died, I started having a lot of issues. I was probably just grieving," she admitted. "My father didn't see any good in focusing on the past, so to appease him, I threw myself into my schoolwork and set my sights on getting out as soon as I graduated. It kept me going, but when the nightmares started . . . something in me knew I didn't have much time.

"From the moment my dad remarried, his wife, Lilith, was obsessed with getting pregnant. Only, that didn't happen, so my parents fought a lot. I don't know why they stayed together, but it got to a point where they were having shouting matches every night." She bit her lip. "That's what I kept seeing when I slept. My dream—it was scary—but it made perfect sense. I started tracking my dreams, and with the help of my guidance counselor, I was able to function and get good grades."

She looked at him, wondering if he would believe what she had to say next.

"It was my senior year and I had been accepted at the University of Florida. It was like I could finally see the light at the end of the tunnel! I was so close, you know? But I started having this one dream, this nightmare that was so scary I refused to see it no matter how many times it recurred.

"I woke up one night from the nightmare. They were fighting—nothing new. But then I heard something familiar . . . it was like I'd already lived that fight, that whole night. I told myself it wasn't real, but when I went to see for myself everything played out exactly as I knew it would. She had a gun on my father. She told him she was going to kill me next. So . . . I killed her first."

Yael gazed up at him slowly, waiting for a response.

Joe searched her eyes, but said nothing.

"I ran away that night. I called the only number I had memorized —I called Fred. He helped me get rid of the car and that's how I ended up in Ybor. I thought that was it. I hid in the shadows, even when I found out I was a missing person, not a fugitive.

"My father was obsessed with keeping up with Jones' and I had ruined his life. So, as you can probably imagine, I stuck to myself. I didn't leave the house for a while, then I spent all of my time and energy helping my cousin turn it into a home. Eventually, I started working on the strip in Ybor, just to stay busy. But something was . . . off?"

"How so?" Joe asked.

"I was still having nightmares, but they were hard for me to understand. I thought I was just traumatized, you know what I mean? It's another reason I wanted to keep myself occupied; I needed the escape. My mind had become a prison. Maybe not this bad, but still . . . ."

"Seems like you found a way to emancipate yourself."

Nodding, Yael took a deep breath and exhaled. "I did. I started to notice a pattern in my dream journals. And one day, there was a man on the front of the paper. I recognized him instantly! He was . . . dead.

"The crazy thing about it was, I never read the paper! I never watched the news! And I was in my zone at work. Even if I wasn't, people didn't talk about that kind of stuff. Deep down, I knew what was happening. Joe, I didn't have to read the paper or watch the news or anything. I was dreaming about these people. Innocent people were dying all around me, and I knew they were dead because of me."

Dream Joe shook his head. "I don't think I'm understanding."

"In my dreams? I would see everything exactly as they described it in the news—except, I killed the killer before they could take out the victim. Every time I ignored a dream, every time I decided not to follow instructions, someone died. So one night, I changed my mind. I got up at the time I remembered from the dream, I went to the place I remembered from the dream, and I killed the person exactly how I killed them in the dream. After that, they were always there, as if they were waiting for me. As if they were just being handed to me. Somehow, even without a plan or any special skills, I was taking out the bad guys."

"How do you know they were bad guys?" Joe asked softly. "Did you see them commit the crime? Did you talk to the victims?"

"Sometimes," she said.

"Explain."

Yael thought about the girls she freed from a sex trailer last year. "There were these brothers I took out—the Rizzoli's. They were trying to start some kind of sex trafficking ring in Tampa Bay. The middle brother was *sick*. When I found him and his girlfriend in Lakeland, they had two young girls naked, bound, and gagged. Oh and *drugged*! I killed the bastards and I helped the girls escape."

Yael watched in fascination as Dream Joe's eyes darted back and forth. She knew if Joe was alive, he'd be responding the same way. Well, he'd probably have a lot more questions, but . . .

"By then, I'd been recruited by the mob. Actually, the Rizolli's were my first official job."

"How did you get caught up in that?"

She blanched. "Xavier."

Joe frowned. "What mafia was Xavier a part of? Do you mean a gang?"

"I think Xavier was his own gang," she snapped. "Son of a bitch was only loyal to himself. But he had money and power. And connections! I don't know why the Don did business with him; he didn't seem to like him much."

"You know the mafia Don?"

Yael cocked her head.

"What?"

She frowned. "Don't you technically know all this?"

"What's the point in telling me?"

Yael gave him a look, then softened. There was a lot she should have said to Joe when he was alive. Getting frustrated was pointless.

"I met the Don when my handler, Johhny, brought me in for an interview. He had a meeting with Xavier at the dojo and he said he recognized me. Turns out, the Family has surveillance all over Ybor. When I turned up for my 'bartending interview', I was taken into the tunnels underneath the city. The Don showed me a tape in his office of me slitting Antoni Rizzoli's throat."

"The tunnels are real?"

"Very." She smiled. "It's amazing to think that they've been there since Ybor was first being developed. The Don's office is in an old factory storage room. I used to run the bar down there. But Vitto ruined that."

Joe's brows furrowed in thought.

"I can't believe it," she mused, saddened by the thought of Joe's killer. "I can't believe I haven't thought about him in so long. For months, he was all I could focus on. I don't know why I didn't think to warn you."

"Don't worry about that," he said. "I am slightly confused here. How did . . . er . . . following your dreams get you a job with the mob?"

"They thought there was a mole!" she recalled. "They were hiring their enforcers to take people out, only I kept getting to them first. By the time the Don realized it was me, I was days or even hours ahead of the call."

"You killed the men before they ordered the hit?"

"Exactly!" She shook her head. "I thought I was a goner. But in the end, they gave me freaking back-pay! Told me I was sloppy. Offered to bring me in so I could do it right. Suddenly, I had backup. I wasn't so alone anymore."

"You must have been training. Taking on paid hits must have changed things."

Yael shrugged. "I only took the job if it was one of *mine*. No dream, no interest. Drove Johhny crazy, I think. But Vitto must have been watching the whole time because, after a while, it was like I became the target.

"All those hits I stole? They still sent him in to do cleanup. Only, he did the opposite. I'm guessing he saw me at some point and was trying to figure out who I was working for. Johhny seemed suspicious of that as time went on. I think Vitto seeing me on the official payroll was the last straw. It wasn't long before he was hunting me . . . or maybe, hunting us."

"Why did he . . . want me?"

"You were the only thing I had to lose. The only person I really cared about."

Dream Joe blinked. "What about your cousin?"

"Frederico kicked me out when Vitto became a threat—"

"He knew about all this?" Joe asked, incredulous. "I can't believe he let you do it."

"I don't think it was ever a matter of *letting me*. But he only found out last year—he caught me red handed, so to speak. I probably wouldn't have told him, or anyone for that matter. Seemed like the smart thing to do." Yael bit the inside of her lip. "For a long time, I've wanted to talk to you about this. I know it's a long shot but . . . is there any chance you could tell me what Joe would have thought?"

Eyes darting side to side, Dream Joe anxiously stroked his beard. "I think it's a good thing you didn't tell me."

"You don't have to say that," she sighed. "I don't want to hear what I want to hear—I need to hear what I need to hear. Do you understand me, brain?"

Smirking at her, Dream Joe relaxed into the sofa and dropped his head back to look at the ceiling. "I would have arrested you on the spot. You've just admitted to being a serial killer, and a hitman. At the very least, you're a vigilante acting out some sort of trauma response. The state of your mental health indicates the likelihood of acute sociopathy, likely set off when you were forced to save your father's life after years of abuse."

Yael stared at the wall. "Well then . . . "

"How do you know you've never killed an innocent person? How do you know that the people you took out weren't supposed to see trial, to have a chance for justice to prevail?"

"Not everyone gets that lucky. I think you know that."

Dream Joe frowned as he faced her. "What's that supposed to mean?"

"Look how long it took the cops to close your case! You told me that you would have preferred that Xavier go to trial. That didn't happen."

"How is that—"

She placed a hand up. "I never sought these people out, Joe. I didn't research them: I almost never knew them. If I did it was in passing. Somehow, I showed up and took out men bigger and stronger than me—most of the time, without a fight."

"Maybe you dissociated? Maybe you have another personality that chooses the victims? Maybe the dreams were daydreams—you imagining your plan ahead of time?"

Yael met his eyes, nodding along as he spoke. "I know, Joe. I know. I didn't want to believe. But when the visions started, I knew it was real. How do you think I found out what Vitto was up to? I saw it in a vision on your couch last August. How do you think I found Maritza? Even when I was completely broken, my powers saved a life. How do you think I took out a hundred men in Paradise? Joe, how do you think I found *you*?"

His mouth dropped open, then shut. Shaking his head, his mouth opened again.

"Joe," she continued, clasping his hand. "The night I came to your house, I thought I was there to kill you. I thought you were a criminal. Only, I couldn't figure out why I was there or what I was supposed to do once I found you. I didn't have a single entry in my dream journal about you; I had hundreds."

"I don't understand?"

"The night we met? I had been dreaming of you for *years*. Didn't I mention that? It was the only time I dreamed a dream I couldn't remember. I tried everything to crack the code, eventually discovering what you would smell like, what you would taste like. When you kissed me—"

Dream Joe's hands were on her in an instant. He combed his fingers into her hair and pulled her close. Forehead to forehead, then nose to nose, he brought his lips to hers.

The electricity between them was always explosive, but for the first time, the energy seemed to explode *in* rather than *out*. Where they had previously been driven apart, zapped by the static shock, Yael felt as if she were being sucked into his soul. She devoured his, the white, hot light between them glowing bright until—

Yael came to, in a daze.

"Joe!"

He blinked and shook his head. Watching her, mouth agape, his eyes drifted behind her and widened.

Yael felt a chill. She turned to look out the window and saw daylight.

"What happened?"

She interlocked her fingers with his and gazed into his eyes. "I think it's working."

"What?"

Yael shrugged. "Taking back my regrets. Doing something I should have done a long time ago. Doing the one thing I've been thinking about all month."

When she leaned in to kiss him again, Joe stood up.

"Ow!" she snapped, rubbing her elbow where she hit it against the coffee table. "What's wrong with you?"

"The sun was just setting." He spun around from his place at the window and gawked at her. "How long was I out?"

"It only felt like a second." She giggled and stood up. Stretching her limbs, she said, "No soreness. You?"

Dream Joe stalked to the front door and opened it, staring directly up at the sky.

"Alright, alright," she said with a laugh. "You win."

Pulling him back inside, she held his hands and smiled. "This is very sweet of you. You don't have to play it up for me. I think I got what I needed."

He looked at her hands as if they were made of solid gold.

"For so long, I have been disgusted with my life. Embarrassed and ashamed that this was the woman I was born to be. And now, as I come to terms with all of it, I thank you." She shook her head and smiled. "I thought I had more to do. I thought it was up to me to take Mama down—to somehow end human trafficking once and for all."

Yael chuckled.

"I always was an overachiever. An over-giver." She hugged him. "But having you here with me, it helped me see the truth. I may not have been able to change the world, but I believe I changed a few people's worlds. Maybe one of those people will be the one to do it all? Maybe I was just a catalyst. And if that was the case, then I gave exactly what I should have. I gave my life. I gave my all.

"I wish that hadn't have included you. I wish I had more control, that I had been given more than just a part to play. If I had known what would happen to you, I would have made damn sure it didn't happen. But since it did, I have to believe you must have left a legacy, too.

"So, thank you. I hated my past. I hated how naive, how foolish I was. I hated Xavier for his lies, but without him being exactly who he was, I never would have met Olivier. Without Olivier, I would have never of met Edelira. I might not think it was enough, but there is a new generation of children out there who will live free because of what I did. Even in death, you show me the truth, Joe. You were the only mirror I ever saw my reflection in."

They gazed into each other's eyes for a long while.

Joe sighed. Cupping her face in his hands, he said, "I don't know how it's possible, but I think I might believe you."

"I'm sorry I lied to you. I would have loved to save the world together."

He shook his head. "If you had told me the truth then, I wouldn't have listened. I would have locked you up. So I'm glad you didn't. You're a hero, Yael."

Scooping her into his arms, he carried her to bed and kissed her to sleep.

CHAPTER TWENTY-SEVEN

Yael was ready to die. She didn't *want* to die, but she was ready.

In the days following the reset, she had been seeing things. It started with pinpricks of light and strange shapes that reminded her of eye floaters. Last night, the white haze that enveloped all she could see had been accompanied by a dull pain between her eyes. Today, she had a full on headache. The cabin was aglow. She no longer questioned her plight, for it was clear. Heaven wouldn't wait much longer.

Dream Joe had been unwavering in his support of her divine calling, loving on her and encouraging her to share anything she needed to. She knew her mind was compensating for giving out on her, bringing her into a mental prison to ease her into death. But she had forgiven herself when Joe had. Even though she knew the real Joe would never have accepted her, she appreciated her brain giving her this one final gift.

Yael crossed the cabin and climbed into bed, wincing as the room grew even brighter. She could barely make anything out now, but that didn't matter. She could see Joe.

"I think it's time," she whispered, entranced by the halo of light around his face. "Please don't take this the wrong way. I appreciate everything you've done for me, I do. But I think we should make our peace. I-I don't want you here when . . . when I go. I might not be able to let go if you stay."

"Yael?"

"Hmm?"

Joe's lips were moving, but they were out of synch with the sound of his voice. A high pitched ringing reverberated through her mind. She rubbed the bridge of her nose and shook her head.

"Yael? Look at me."

Focusing her eyes on his, she squinted and tried to listen.

"I don't know why you're giving up on us. We can still be happy."

She smiled weakly. "Don't cry, Joe."

"Marry me. Be my wife!"

"Oh, Joe." Yael sighed. "You've made me the happiest woman on the ghostly plane. But you and I know this isn't necessary. I told you, this isn't what I wanted. I would have been able to move on whether you accepted me or not. Even if you had lashed out or left me here, I would have been at peace. I don't have to lie to myself, so you don't either."

"Yael, please. You aren't listening to me."

She straddled his lap and wrapped herself about him. "Before you go, I need one last thing."

Sighing in relief when she closed her eyes, she kissed Joe with everything she had. The inside of her eyelids was bright gold. When she opened them, she was completely blind.

"We don't have much time," she whispered against his lips. "I need you to make love to me, Joe. I need you more than you could possibly understand."

Yael felt for him, gripping his arms, his chest, sliding her fingers up his neck and into his dreadlocks. She moaned when he kissed her, the ecstasy of their final climax overwhelming her from its moment in the future. She could feel it coming in the air she breathed. She could taste it on his lips. It was a holy presence that held her safe as all her senses faded away.

"Say yes."

She heard his voice—his whisper in her ear—deep within her heart. And she knew in that moment that it could have been real. If Joe had lived, if she had been honest . . . oh, what might have been.

Clamoring for the pleasure of his mouth on hers, she pulled him to her and searched for his lips. Finding them warm, ready, waiting for her, she moaned into him with abandon.

Yael traced her fingertips down his chest and torso, slipping them into his waistband as she sought treasure. She found him, harder than she had ever felt, and gave him a squeeze.

"Now! Take me, Joe! Please."

She didn't feel him place her on her back, only noticing they'd moved when he lowered himself onto her and pushed his way inside. Yael saw only pure white, felt only Joe moving back and forth within.

"You are mine."

When he growled and kissed her again, she could no longer sense the bed beneath her. She reached out, her hands searching until he grabbed them both and interlocked his fingers with hers. They moved in unison, forehead to forehead.

"I love you," Joe said against her lips. "Forever and always. You are mine."

"I love you, Joe," she whispered, though she couldn't hear her voice.

Her world imploded and collapsed onto itself again and again. Yael lay perfectly still, floating naked in a haze of white. Two golden lights whirled and swirled above her, around her, and through her.

When she returned to the bed in the cabin, everything around her had turned stark white. Even Joe, who lay next to her asleep, appeared to be a statue of the purest porcelain. Yael held out her hand and saw she had turned to gold.

She smiled.

"Forever and always."

Yael didn't want to go. But she was ready.

She never expected to find peace, but she had. She didn't deserve his love, but he had given it freely. Perhaps in some other lifetime, she and Joe were married and happy together. Here in this life, she had learned a valuable lesson far too late: that love was the greatest of all.

A bell rang behind her, the tone unending, growing louder instead of quieter. She turned around slowly and saw a small, black dot floating beside her. As it expanded, watery ribbons of light burst forth and encircled it.

Yael cocked her head, enraptured by the gold, silver, and white ribbons, watching as they ebbed and flowed in size and shape until they connected around the growing black sphere.

She gasped when she heard the crack in the sky. Turning to take one last look at Joe, she disappeared from space and time with a loud pop.

CHAPTER TWENTY-EIGHT

Yael could hear before she could see. The bell tone seemed to carry her through the empty, the sound growing louder and louder until it no longer sounded like a bell at all. If a gong could scream, this would be the sound.

She opened her eyes when they came into existence, blinking gold, then silver, then white and finally in color. There was only one color here in the white space. A small black dot.

Her mind screamed over the raging resonance, telling her she had seen it before. Just before the *now*, in the *then*. Yael's mind felt like music. The only way to understand was to sway along the melody of thought.

"Oh, so you're a funny one? I can do funny."

"What?" Yael heard herself scream.

The sound was delayed, choppy; her voice seemed to decay the moment she heard the first whisper of the word. The black dot appeared to be moving. Her brain told her the figure was a human mouth. She knew *mouth*. That was where her words came from.

"*Welcome, we've been expecting you.*"

Yael gasped into fullness. She looked around for an intercom, recognizing the man's voice from the *Moviefone* commercials.

"Am I in heaven?"

"Or is this hell?"

She gasped at the sound of her own voice. Yael had spoken the first statement, but she *thought* the second.

"Okay, he'll do."

She spun around. She could see nothing, yet everything. The space around her was full, as if packed with the densest fog on earth. And yet, there was nothing here at all . . . billions and billions of tiny *nothings*.

"There we go."

Yael turned back and saw the mouth now had a man. She knew this man. Elation spread through her like twinkle lights.

"I knew this was a good choice. Here, let me help you."

The man approached her and reached his hand toward her face, pressing and dragging his thumb down the center of her forehead.

"And . . . there. Hello, Philomena."

She stared at him mouth agape. "Are you—"

"No, no! Don't get too excited, kid," he said, holding his hands up in apology. "I take on the form you are most comfortable with. You really love this guy, huh?"

She blinked and nodded.

"Santamaria Philomena Piccirillo," he read, a flat image appearing in his palm. "*The holy mother, lover, and friend, the pillar of strength, she courageously defends.* Why alter the energy of your divine name?"

"I—"

"Yael Philomena Clarke," he said flatly. "Hmmm . . . mountain goat? Fertile moor? Oh, okay . . . this is interesting: she drove a tent peg through his head while he slept. Did you know that?"

She raised a brow.

"Courageous defender, strength of God . . . ah, *to ascend*? Look at that goat." He put his palm in her face and showed her a goat walking sideways on a vertical wall. "That is one crazy goat. Alright, scholar . . . *cleric*? Hmm . . ."

"Yael Philomena Clarke," he repeated, his inflection curious. "*Leading the tribe in great courage through service, the strength of God ascends to her purpose.* You know, it works."

Utterly baffled, she made a face of confusion and held up her palms.

"Perfect," he said, clapping his hands together and holding them at his chest. "I've submitted your request."

"But I—"

He held up a hand and then a finger.

Yael crossed her arms and stomped her foot angrily. Not a sound. She looked down and saw nothing beneath her feet. She jumped. Though she felt her body move, the space around her did not change. Waving her arms around, she grasped at the air trying to touch the molecules.

"The appointed time has come. You—" He stared at her. "What are you doing?"

Flailing her arms beneath her feet in search of the floor, she froze and looked up at him. "There's no floor?"

"There's no *anything*." He sighed. "Give me a second."

Yael watched in horror as his eyes rolled back so fast they disappeared, leaving empty sockets. She heard a loud pop and found herself standing in the middle of a room she couldn't quite remember.

"This should work. You've missed this place."

"*The Lieu*," she whispered. Searching the bar, she found him up front on the small stage. "Is this . . . real?"

Holding the mic up to his lips, he shook his head. "Santamaria

Philomena Piccirillo, pay attention. It is the appointed time of appointed times."

Yael felt something push against her knees, looking back to see the chair just as she fell onto it.

"You have been assigned an important mission. Do you accept it?"

"Sure," she shrugged. "Why not?"

He narrowed his eyes, recovered, then bowed his head. "Let's get started."

"You aren't surprised or anything?" she ventured. "And why'd you look at me like that?"

"At the appointed time of appointed times, the anointed one *always* accepts. Why weren't *you* surprised?"

"You guys give me magic powers and expect me not to notice?"

Sighing loudly into the microphone, he asked, "Have you finished? We have a lot to do before you go home."

She stood and threw her hands up. "Alright, alright. What happens now?"

"*Book update approved.*"

Yael stared at the ceiling. "Who is that guy?"

"Your name is now officially changed. I wouldn't do that again if I were you. The words you speak carry greater meaning than most of you humans would ever know. By changing your name, you've changed your destiny."

"Really?"

"No, not really," he laughed. "Now, come over here. We need to correct that cognitive dissonance before you hurt yourself."

Stepping down off the stage, he met Yael halfway and placed his thumb on her forehead. Rather than the smooth motion she was expecting, he wiggled it fast as if scrubbing off dirt.

"Hey!" she yelped, grabbing her forehead as she winced. "What's wrong with you?"

Squeezing her eyes shut against the dull ache between them, she fell sideways and lay down on unexpected softness. After a few seconds of fighting, she took a deep breath and exhaled. The pain subsided immediately and she felt . . . free.

"You're going to have to learn faster than that. You've got a fighting spirit, but for years you've seen everything as a battle."

Opening her eyes, Yael found herself on a red chaise. He was sitting across from her on an oversized leather chair from the cigar lounge.

"You better put this stuff back," she warned.

"We're not actually *here*," he replied tiredly. "Your precious bar is safe. As I was saying . . . when your first instinct is to fight, we have to explore the cause. You are shockingly resilient. Unfortunately, your body isn't as strong as you think. Your adrenal glands are *fried*."

Brow furrowed, she looked around wondering what she was supposed to glean from that statement.

"Your trauma and subsequent lack of healing have created a condition inside you that causes you to choose one of four responses to any situation you can't handle. Your favorite move?" He tilted his head. "Fight it off. If you think you can overpower it, you will. When you feel overwhelmed and you let your anxiety turn to panic, you run. I'm sure you've heard of this. Fight or flight?"

She nodded.

"Long before you became the fighter you are today, you relied on the other two responses. Before your mother died, she taught you to fawn. That was her favorite move. Stefano completely overpowered her identity when he married her. He had no boundaries and his explosive behavior forced your mother to remain compliant and codependent. When you feel powerless, you follow the same patterns.

"And of course, there is your last resort: the great escape. Your numbness is the result of years of enduring. It's why you struggle to make decisions. It's why you continue to choose isolation. It's why you are so good at dissociating. You have a lot of mental health issues, but most of them are by design. This particular set of . . . strategies . . . will most likely get you killed."

She frowned. "What do I do?"

"I can heal you of this, but only if you want me to. And you don't just have to want it, you have to believe you've been healed. You have to know that there was a specific set of circumstances that created these traits. You have to understand that human nature responds to life in ways we can easily anticipate. If not, you'll turn on yourself again and again."

"I do," she cried. "Everything you've said is everything I hate about myself. It's like no matter how hard I try to see the light, I'm stuck in the shadows."

"Or you freeze in front of a Mack truck."

Sucking her lips into a pout, she stared at the carpet.

"Would you like to see yourself up close and personal?" he asked quietly.

"Mmm . . . nah."

"It might help you gain some perspective."

Sighing, Yael nodded hesitantly.

"Come here," he said, taking her hand and leading her to the middle of the room. "Okay, hold very still."

Swallowing nervously, she watched as he raised his hand to her face. Using his first two fingers, he pressed down on her nose.

"Boop."

"H—achoo!"

Yael sniffed and blinked.

"Where am I?"

Turning to her right, Yael saw *herself* standing there beside her, gun drawn.

"What is this place?" another voice growled.

To her left, Yael saw . . . another *her*?

"Oh my—"

Both *hers* drew their weapons and fired in her direction.

"Whoops." He snapped his fingers and the two new *hers* froze in place. Plucking the bullets from the air, he handed them to her and grinned. "Sorry about that. Shoulda known you were gonna be feisty."

Staring at the hot bullets in her palm, she exhaled sharply and slid them into her pocket. Yael turned from side to side, unable to choose which *her* to focus on first.

Opting for the *her* to the right, she walked around the living statue in awestruck wonder. Unlike the *her* to the left, this version of *her* appeared to be almost identical to her true self. She was the same size, shape, and build, and even wore the usual outfit of a black V-neck and jeans. Yael circled *her* several times, but it wasn't until she stood directly before *her* that she saw it.

"It's all in the eyes," he said from behind her. "You know that."

Yael nodded. "She's a killer?"

"Straight up. No holds barred—no limits. Specializes in erasure and family eliminations. Once your name is on *her* list, you might as well do it yourself."

She swallowed, a sick feeling rising from her gut.

"She really only has one major issue: she's a narcissistic psychopath." He pushed *her* arm down to lower the gun, then examined *her* cold expression. "In *her* story, she kills Stefano and never looks back. She lost *her* soul long before, though. It was Stefano's fault for teaching *her* how to lie. After a while, doing wrong became second nature. What might have been an antisocial personality evolved into a full-fledged monster thanks to him."

Yael looked at the other *her* and scrunched up her face. "Do I even want to know what this is all about?"

Clearing his throat, he tilted his head back and forth. "Personally, I'd rather have that one on my side. She's nuts, but she's loyal."

The *her* to the left looked . . . less like her. *Her* hair was a matted mess of different sized dreadlocks and braids. She was wearing an eye patch on one eye and it appeared the *good* one was lazy. *Her* outfit was all black leather, including a vest she wore over a black tube top; *her* pants were skin tight and bright purple.

"Did she get a boob job?"

"Yeah," he said with a chuckle. "*Her* first husband recommended it. Said she'd look badass."

Yael made a choking sound. "First husband?"

"She'll have eight by the time she dies. This one isn't right anymore; *her* mind is gone. She's a great boss and a wonderful friend, but the trauma was just too much for *her*."

"So I'm the good one?" she asked, not sure what she was supposed to get out of all this.

He shook his head. "There isn't a good or bad. She's off *her* rocker, but she's got a heart of gold. Truth is, although you might look and dress like silent but deadly over here, you are well on your way to your own eye patch and matching vest."

Yael eyed him warily, wondering how he knew.

He snapped his fingers. The other *hers* disappeared and the vest reappeared over her own clothing.

"Just go with it," he said with a wink. "Well? What's on your mind?"

Yael played with the zipper of her new vest. "I still don't get it? What was the point of all that?"

"Without your trauma experiences, you wouldn't have developed your impulsivity, nyctophobia, hyper vigilance, paranoia, or any of the other issues that served to keep you alive. I can fix what you want fixed; I intend on resetting you when we finish tonight. But you have to know exactly what you want and why, or else it won't stick."

"I just want to trust myself," she whispered. "Everyone sees me as some kind of hero, but I can't seem to find the same confidence."

"You're not a hero because you're confident. You're a hero because you refuse to give up, no matter the cost. You endure so others won't have to." He put his hand on her shoulder. "Your strength comes from the weakness of others—the moment you believe you are the only hope, all your doubts slip away. Where you might fall apart for yourself, as soon as someone else needs saving, you fill in the gaps and knock down the obstacles like they never existed. Take it from me, kid. You never needed confidence. You had love."

She studied him for a second, then sighed. "I feel like you're telling me all the things that are wrong with me while simultaneously telling me there's nothing wrong at all."

"Now you're getting it."

"Sure," she muttered. "Totally . . ."

"You know we're not finished yet, right?"

Hands on hips, Yael asked, "What else is there?"

"Now that you're up to speed on *you*, there's still a matter of your mission . . . and your benefits package."

Perking up, she smiled. "That's more like it."

"Why don't we sit down over here?" he said, walking toward *The Lieu's* makeshift cigar lounge. "You're going to have to see this to believe it."

Joining him in the semicircle of plush leather chairs, she looked up at the projector screen and watched the countdown.

"You will remember this day clearly. Joseph Thompson Clarke —*blessed is the holy man joined with the same, for he shall father the apostles of name*."

"Next," Yael said coldly. "Why would I want to see this?"

"On Sunday, May 22nd, Joe is seen here preparing for your engagement dinner. Would you like to see him practicing his speech in the mirror? No?" He shrugged. "He receives a call from a friend, Seal, who provides him with a mostly full—though somewhat incorrect—dossier on one Yael Phillips.

"That evening, Joe returns home after bad weather delays his flight. He hopes to run into you before he leaves and stands here by the garden, pretending to water plants while you fall into your usual trauma response behaviors. Vittorio Pelaratti Pecatti . . . do you want to know what his name meant?"

"No thanks," she grumbled.

"Vitto was waiting for you to return, but he was unable to resist changing his plans when he saw Joe waiting and watching for you, too. Giving into his anger, he intends to shoot Joe twice in the chest. Fortunately, he is unaware Joe has already donned his vest for his trip. One bullet hits a weak point in his vest, knocking him backward just as the second bullet grazes his arm. He hits his head on the way down and is knocked unconscious in the dirt."

"Oh my God," Yael cried. "I really did kill him. I . . . I just left him there!"

"An hour later, Joe comes to just as his team arrives to search for him. He collects his gun and finds Vitto's body right as they enter the driveway. No one questions his story—that he killed him in self-defense. He asks for time off, contacts Seal, and begins his search for you."

"What are you saying?"

He looked at the screen. "Though he is unable to trace your location, he and Seal use every resource available to them and follow the pings from your cell. They finally catch up with you on the third island, but they are denied entry by air traffic control. Joe cannot shake the feeling that you are still there. In fact, *this* tearful moment is the only reason Seal was willing to return."

Yael choked back a sob as she watched Joe through Seal's eyes, listened as he begged him to fly back.

"Stop it," she cried, closing her eyes against the pain.

"The night they return, Seal plans to barter his way onto the tarmac. To his surprise, the tower is silent and the highway in the sky above the island is empty. They land and search the small airport, finding no one. Just as they are about to leave, they meet a man named Charles."

Watching the screen with fascination, Yael took in the scene before her. It couldn't have been more than a few minutes after she boarded the plane. As far as she could tell, just as Charles extended his hand to Joe and said his name, she had screamed it from plane on the tarmac.

"Is this real?" she asked, unable to face the reality of what she saw.

"Together, the three men ride across the tarmac and enter the plane. Joe shoots Lord Olivier Maxwell Hulley, the third, 15th Earl of Ravenscar in the temple; he dies instantly."

Mouth wide, Yael gawked at Joe as he threw Olivier into the wall of the plane and tried desperately to wake her. She covered her mouth, but it didn't stop the sound, couldn't stop the tears. Joe held her as if she were dead, mourned her as if she were already gone.

Patting her hand, he motioned toward the screen to advance the picture. "Seal is kind enough to remind Joe to check your pulse. It's weak, but it's enough to snap him out of it. Seal asks Charles for your luggage, but Marge has finally found her nerve."

"Oh, no!"

"I think you'll like this part." He put his hand up again and the volume increased. "Margaret Elizabeth O'Neill—*From an oath descended, she champions the earl, but beneath the surface you'll find the pearl*."

Yael shook her head in confusion.

"Leave the body!"

She jumped and gasped when she saw Marge on the screen, the shotgun in her hand aimed directly at Joe.

"Marge, unaware that Joe had come only for you, believed someone had finally caught up with her Master for his numerous misdeeds. She never gave a damn about Olivier—he took advantage of both of her daughters many times. However, she feared for her own life and safety should she return to England without a body to bury."

"We don't want the damn body," Joe screamed on the screen. "I'm taking my woman!"

Marge lowered the gun barrel. "You the one she's been crying over, then?"

Yael watched as Joe nodded in surprise, unsure but hopeful. She melted.

"Marge is kind enough to give up all the luggage—aside from her own—unwittingly including a briefcase containing Olivier's membership dues and initiation fee." He turned to whisper, "It's the heavy one. It's gonna come in handy soon, I promise.

"While Charles loads the bags onto the cart, Marge is also kind enough to pack a dinner for Joe and Seal. She then helps get you cleaned up with their first aid kit. She enjoyed your company, you know. You were as much as a savior for her as she was for you."

"What happened to her?" Yael wondered aloud. She bit her lip as she faced him. "Is she okay?"

"She will be offered a medal of honor, and eventually, her royal lineage will be uncovered. Marge's family has been offered a new beginning; Lord Hulley's family line has ended. With no heir and no other relatives, his estate will be divided according to the usual customs of British noblemen." He leaned in again. "There is a black portfolio in the large suitcase. Give it to Sampson at the appointed time."

"I thought this—"

"Our final scene ends here, in Ocho Rios, Jamaica. Joe's uncle has offered him a month at the family cabin as an engagement gift. Seal drops you off and gives Joe a satellite phone in case of emergency. You convince yourself to disassociate, unable to process the grief—and unable to understand the messages we've been sending you for weeks."

"No," Yael snapped. "I know what I saw!"

"Then why wouldn't you check your phone? Joe texted and called, all you had to do was look at the messages." He snapped his fingers when she glazed over, deep in thought. "Your connection is sacred, Yael! His soul cried out to you for weeks and you called him a ghost."

"Stop it!" she screamed, holding her hands to her ears. "Why are you telling me this?"

"Because you're too smart for your own good," he replied simply. "And when all else fails, you rely on your trauma rather than your intuition. For anyone else, miracles are possible. You believe you might even be the one to make it happen. But in your own life? You're convinced that you deserve the worst—that you deserve and attract bad things."

"How dare you?" Yael slammed her fist onto the arm rest. Rising from the seat in a fury, she turned on him. "You did this to me and now you blame me? Fuck you! Why give me a mission, then wait til it's halfway through to tell me about it? Why make me go through any of it if this is the end result. I mean, look at me! You said it yourself! Give me my eye patch; crazy girl's home!"

Expressionless, he stood and handed her a remote from nowhere. "You already answered all these questions. Take this and watch it again; think of a moment and it will play. You only get one chance at this, so don't waste it. When you're ready, just holler."

She sniffed. "Do I call you—"

"No," he barked. "Don't confuse yourself. Just call me Scribe."

Two and a half hours later, Yael was spent. She had rehashed every moment from the movie of the time she missed and then some. Worse still, she watched several moments from the cabin from Joe's perspective. She was embarrassed, ashamed, and confused . . . but she was hopeful.

"Scribe?" she called out. "I have a question."

Yael jumped when he appeared in the seat next to her.

"So Joe is really alive?"

He gave her a knowing look.

"Oh, God." She buried her face in her hands. "This is bad, Scribe. Really bad."

"Look at me," he said softly. "Joe has his own issues and his own cross to bear. His healing won't be as instantaneous as yours, so make sure you give him some grace. I can promise you this: he is your match. Nothing can separate you, not even me."

"I told him everything," she whispered. "*Everything*."

"Good! You're lucky to have him. Plus, your mission won't be possible without him." He swiped at the screen and it faded to black. "If your mother had your father by her side, she might still be here today."

"My mom?" She stood and faced him. "My mom had powers, too?"

CHAPTER TWENTY-NINE

The scribe opened his palm and scrolled through until he found what he was looking for. A pair of glasses appeared as he zoomed in, then disappeared.

"First of all, you don't have powers. You have *gifts*."

He held up his palm and showed her an image that made her head feel like it was going to explode out of the base of her neck.

"This is the mathematical representation of your *endowment*." Closing his hand and reopening it to reveal an empty palm, he bowed his head. "Your *gifting* has been recalibrated."

She rubbed her neck and rotated her shoulders. "I don't feel any different."

"You'll see."

Yael sighed. "My mother?"

"The *endowment* is genetic, meaning the *gifting* is transferable through blood and spirit. Your soul is like any other human soul, except it's been *activated*. As you know, the activation does not mean you have control of the *gifting*. It only brings the *awareness*.

"When you were born, you held the necessary genes for activation. Your mother, like her mother before her and so on, was offered her mission at the moment of conception. When she refused, her soul was scheduled for deactivation. In some rare cases, the body is able to survive the loss.

"Your grandmother lived a long life because she was able to maintain her passion: caring for her community. Stefano stole that from your mother when he took her from the only place she ever loved. Your light kept her alive for a long time, but without her own identity and good work to apply her hands to . . . she died of despair and a broken heart."

Yael had done her best to be strong, but her heart broke with every word he spoke. To know her mother died with this very feeling tearing her apart from the inside? She cried for a long, long while.

When she finally caught her breath, she heard his words echoing in her head.

"Scribe?"

He appeared before her with a pop. "Yes?"

"My mother," she said, choosing her words carefully. "Did I hear you right? You said . . . *conception*?"

Scribe smiled and nodded.

Yael touched her belly. "The lights?"

He winked.

She didn't understand. "Why did my mom say no?"

"At first, she said yes," he admitted. "But once I told her about you, she refused. She knew she couldn't protect you from Stefano if she was out saving the world."

"Should I say no?" she asked herself, looking at her stomach as if she had x-ray vision. "No! Joe would never accept that."

Scribe smiled. "Yael Philomena Clarke, it is the appointed time of appointed times. Within you are a pair of apostles, designed for such a time as this. Though you have been endowed with gifts, their mission will require power. It is up to you to prepare them both for the darkness that will come upon the earth.

"In the meantime, you will blot out evil and put out fires. Without you, the world will perish. With you, your children will have a world to save. You have been assigned an important mission. Do you accept it?"

When he extended his hand, she took it firmly and shook it three times.

"I will do whatever I have to do."

Clasping her hand in both of his, he said, "Congratulations. You are officially one of the most powerful beings on the planet."

Eyes darting side to side, her face read doubt. "I thought I didn't have powers?"

"You don't." He held her hand steady, still staring into her eyes. "However, choosing to use your gifts for the good of mankind makes you powerful. There's no way around it."

"Oh . . . "

"Don't worry, that won't last long. Your family will help raise the next generation, the gifted ones. At birth, they are *activated*. But unlike you, they won't have to wait until puberty for their awakening. And because of you, they will be able to take purposeful, intentional action with regard to their shared and individual missions. You and your generation have broken the curse."

"My generation?" Yael shook her head. "You keep saying that, but it's just me. Are you talking about Fred or—"

"The final battle is closer than you think. Your mission is not the only mission, and you are not the only . . . just the first."

She sighed. "You're not going to tell me what that means, are you?"

"No. But when you decide you're ready to explore your real family tree, it won't take you long to figure it out." He pointed to his temple. "Trust the recalibration. And trust me."

"Will you be here to help me?" she asked nervously.

"In a way, I've always been there. Now that you've heard my voice, you'll be able to tell the difference."

"So I get to hear this voic—"

He rolled his eyes. "Not *this* voice, this voice."

Yael gasped when she heard the sound of the screaming gong in the distance. Even at a low decibel, it was unnerving.

"A word of warning," he said quietly, crossing his arms. "Though Joe is *activated*, he is not *aware*. Not fully. He is a pure soul, so it won't take much, but his trauma has created a blockage."

"Can't you heal him, too?"

"Negative."

"What do I do?" she asked, desperate for the answer. "I've already got two kids to worry about. How do you expect me to do my job if I can't help my husband?"

He studied her for a moment. "Have you decided which parts of your mind you would like me to heal?"

She thought about it. "Yeah, I think so."

"I'm assuming you're leaving the anxiety?"

Yael held up her fingers. "Just a bit."

"Good, you'll need it." He sighed. "I'm going to tell you something, and you'll do well to remember it. Joe is your future. You will share a lifetime with him, and a full life at that. Your children will outlive you. There will be much to fear, but you must trust the divine destiny presently unfolding. Believe me when I say, the four of you are too valuable to lose. Do you believe?"

"Yes."

"Don't worry about the block. Just as your life was designed to provide you with everything you need in the exact time of requirement, his steps have been ordered. Though he will have varying levels of unbelief over the next year, everything will change when he looks into his son's eyes again."

"Again? His son is alive?"

He held up a hand and then a finger. "You're going to confuse yourself. Go with the flow, you can trust what comes next."

Crossing her arms with a pout, she said, "Fine."

He opened his palm and scrolled down, reading. "Yael Philomena Clarke, you are hereby ordered to return home and begin nesting. You may not stop your work for any reason. You will accept the resources offered to you and utilize the human resources in a way befitting your new name. You will not see a doctor and you will give birth at home—only your husband may be present.

"We will meet again, when the appointed time comes. Until then, if you need anything, you will think of me and trust the first answer you receive. You will remember this time outside of time vividly, and you may draw on it for inspiration whenever you need to. If you hear my true voice instead of your own, you will acknowledge that your *gifting* is waning and seek immediate restoration. This is the decree. Do you accept?"

"No."

"Good . . . wait, what?"

She held out her hand and tapped her index finger. "You're telling me I'm about to go home and get back to work?"

"Yes."

She tapped her middle finger, then her ring finger. "And prepare my house for two babies?"

"Uh huh."

"And my man—who just watched me lose my ever-loving mind—isn't even going to believe me yet?"

"Right."

She waved her fingers. "Uh uh. No way. I'm not doing anything without a montage."

"Oh," he said in relief. "You want the Rocky or what?"

"I don't know what that means," she replied with a smirk. "But I want something I'll remember—something to look back on when the bad days come."

"I know exactly what you need." He walked toward her and zipped up her vest. "But once we're done, I'm healing you and sending you home. You're going to need a full night of rest to recover from the transition."

CHAPTER THIRTY

OCHO RIOS, JAMAICA

J oe was groggy. He felt as if he'd had too much to drink the night before, but there wasn't an ounce of liquor in the cabin. Opening his eyes was a challenging task. They felt like they'd been weighted down by tiny gold bricks. The light shining through the cracks in his lids was too bright.

It's morning already?

He heard a rap on the door. So he wasn't dreaming? Rubbing his eyes, he sat up and checked the bed for Yael. She was bundled up in the sheets beside him, meaning it had to be Seal knocking. He was a few days early.

Forcing himself from the bed and noting the soreness all over, he squinted at the window and wondered if Seal was actually right on time. Last week, he had somehow lost a whole night. What if it had happened again? Glancing at the mound in the bed suspiciously, he stumbled toward the door.

"Yeah man?"

Seal's expression was a mixture of confusion and relief. He looked over Joe's head into the cabin. "I came as fast as I could! How'd she do it? Why didn't you call me? Did she take the sat phone?"

Joe stepped onto the sandy mat and shut the door behind him. "What the hell are you talking about?"

"Wake up, Joe!" Seal snapped. He slid his pack from his shoulder and knelt to unzip it, leaving it in the sand when he retrieved a tablet. "Your woman is on the run again. And you're not going to believe this! She must be part of some kind of operation or something I can't even begin to understand.

"I've got a grainy shot of her here, but it's definitely her. This was taken outside of a nightclub. Get this, they got paninis at a food truck and then vanished. Mind you, the timestamp says it was midnight in Italy. Now, look at this. This footage is from O'Hare—it seems she also went to a popcorn shop last night. She was seen in this corridor here, then they go around the corner into the bathrooms and . . . poof."

"Is that—"

"Yeah!" Seal's face read confusion. "Well, no? I don't know, brother! Facial recognition says it's a hundred percent match. There's something going on here man! He's performing at a comedy festival all weekend, there's no way it could really be him. But what technology have you heard of that could do this?"

"Stay here!" Joe said, his adrenaline pumping.

Rushing inside to check the bed, he sprinted across the cabin. His mind was flooded with anger, considering the horrible possibilities.

When did she drug me? How long have I been out?

Diving onto the bed, he reached for the comforter just as Yael threw it off with a gasp. They stared at each other in shock, breathless in the silence. Then, she leaped for him, throwing her arms around his neck and pulling him down with her.

"Oh my God!" She kissed him all over his face and neck, choking back small, broken sobs as tears poured from her eyes. "I thought you were dead! I'm so sorry. I'm so sorry, Joe!"

"Yael, what—"

She gasped for breath, kissing him again. "The angel, he fixed my mind. I mean, not all the way—he said a little crazy wouldn't hurt—but he showed me everything! Could you believe Marge? We've gotta send her a card or something!"

"Cease, woman!" he said in exasperation, pulling his face from hers. "I can't concentrate when you . . . did you say angel?"

Yael kissed the tip of his nose and grinned when he shivered with pleasure.

"I missed you so much," she whispered.

"What happened last—"

She ignored him. "I want to be your wife, Joe. I want to love you for the rest of my life. Take me home."

Joe sat back on his heels and stared at her. As far as he could remember, they had gone to sleep naked last night. Not only was she fully clothed, but she was wearing the same outfit and leather vest from the footage.

"Where did you get these clothes?"

Lifting herself onto her elbows, she glanced down at her vest and grinned sheepishly. "I'm pretty sure these are from my closet at home. The vest . . . it's a long story."

"One you intend to tell me?"

A brilliant smile formed on her face. Joe's heart melted and the whole room seemed to get brighter.

"Yes. All of it. Everything."

Joe exhaled and looked at the ceiling. He knew they had a long battle ahead of them. Yael's story was . . . unbelievable. But he wanted to understand. And he should have expected things to be a little weird as she worked to reconstruct her memories.

Though if he were being honest, this new evidence from Seal was giving his logic a run for its money. What if it were all true? What if everything she told him had happened exactly as she said it?

He'd assumed Olivier had been attempting to sell Yael or otherwise traffic her on that island, but what if Yael really was a woman of means? What if she had saved the women she had met while she visited, not just left them behind? What if she really was some sort of angelic avenger?

The knock at the door interrupted his musings.

"I'll be right back." He gave her a smile. "And pack up, we're leaving."

He would have to investigate everything when they returned to Tampa. Until he could connect the dots, he was willing to hide Yael's history from the Bureau. As far as he could tell, her vigilante activities were not far from those Seal had participated in during his early years as a government contractor. There was a strong likelihood she was no more a murderer or killer than he.

Stepping into the light, he closed the door behind him. Seal appeared to have been pacing all the while, digging a short trench a few feet away.

"What else can you tell me about last night?"

Seal shook his head. "I've never seen anything like it. She zigzagged across four continents in a span of only a few hours, accompanied by a man with a damn good alibi and hundreds of credible witnesses. I don't know how she pulled this off, but . . . I'm sorry to say, I don't think she wants to be found, brother."

"She's inside," Joe offered. "Packing."

Frowning, Seal looked at the sand. "But . . . how?"

"How many people have seen this footage?"

Seal eyed him curiously. "Me and a couple trackers. Why?"

"If anybody asks, tell them it was a publicity stunt." Joe stretched and took a long, deep breath. "You ready for us?"

"Seriously, brother? You aren't going to explain this?"

"I don't think I can. Don't really understand it myself, and even if I did," Joe turned to head inside and shrugged. "You wouldn't believe me if I tried."

YAEL TOOK Joe's hand and climbed from the tender onto the aft deck of the yacht. He watched as she walked to the corner and gazed longingly toward the cabin on the shore. For him, this would be his last look. For Yael, it was the first time she'd seen it like this. Perhaps they would return here one day, when she healed.

"Help me tie this on," Seal told him, operating the mechanized lever that would reveal the mini garage for the smaller craft. "We're all clear and the weather's right. It's a good thing I came early, a new tropical depression just formed and it's headed straight for us."

They finished up and prepared to set sail for the coastal airport where Seal's copter was waiting. By the end of the day, they would be home, safe and sound.

Joe found Yael in the same spot, hair blowing in the wind. His woman was always lovely, but when he caught her in moments like this, she took his breath away.

"Come," he said as he clasped her hand. "You haven't met Seal."

"Hmm?" She tore her eyes away from the cabin and stood. "Didn't expect to feel like this."

Wiping the tears from her cheeks, he kissed her forehead. "What's wrong?"

"Nothing," she shrugged. "I wish I hadn't been so . . . I mean, I wish I had a real chance to enjoy it, you know?"

"We will."

She hugged him. "Do we have a long way to go? I think I might need some seasickness pills . . . are those safe for pregnant women?"

"Do you normally get seasick?" Joe blinked and grabbed her shoulders. "Pregnant?"

"Twins." Yael smiled, new tears forming in her eyes. "The angel told me."

"Ah," Joe said, returning her smile knowingly. Following through on his decision to appease her for the time being, he nodded. "We'll see what he has."

Seal started the engine just as they climbed the steps to the upper helm of the flybridge. Engrossed in his work at the control panel, Seal hadn't heard them approaching. Yael gasped when she looked back at the island, the increased height providing an even better view of the cabin. She squeezed Joe's hand, then went to kneel on the leather seat to scan the shoreline.

"Seal!" Joe shouted, hoping to scare him.

Scowling, Seal turned to face him and shook his head. "Nice try."

Shrugging, Joe thumbed over his shoulder. "Sleeping Beauty is awake. Thought you'd like to meet her. Yael?"

He and Seal approached her and Seal offered her his hand. Smiling as she reached forward to take it, her smile faded when she met his eyes. Turning slowly to squint at Joe, she stared at him as her mouth tightened around her teeth.

Joe's mouth dropped open, then he cringed. He had forgotten about this.

"Quite a grip," Seal said uncomfortably, trying to pull his hand away.

Yael didn't release him. She just stared at Joe, shooting daggers into his soul. In all their time together, in the rare moments they had fought, he'd never seen that *look* on his woman's face. When she turned back toward Seal, he felt instant relief.

"You." She exhaled, took a step forward and flipped Seal onto his back.

Grunting as he hit the hard deck, Seal didn't move.

"I don't like being followed," she told them both, her arms crossed defensively.

Joe stared at Seal, waiting for the explosion. He'd never seen his old friend hit a woman. Then again, he'd never seen a woman look at Seal without instantly falling in love. To his surprise, Seal sat up and laughed it off.

"I promise you this," he said as he grinned and cracked his neck, "I'll never follow you again, no matter how much they pay me."

CHAPTER THIRTY-ONE

YBOR CITY, FLORIDA

Frederico grabbed his phone from the nightstand, frowning when he saw it was dark out. He'd gone to bed just after sunset, having spent the day at the beach with Tres and his best friend, Deon. His phone almost never rang anymore, and definitely not this late at night. Worst of all, he'd been having another dream about Mystique that had just been rudely cut short.

Better not be no wrong number, he thought, his mood blackening with every second.

"Shit!" He fell out of bed. "Hello?"

"Hey, Fred."

Sighing in relief, he rested his head on the hardwood floor. "Hey, cuz."

"Sorry for disappearing," Yael muttered. "I got a lot of messages, figured I might as well call."

"Bout damn time," he replied irritably. He rose and sat on the edge of his bed. "Where have you been? What happened to you?"

"I had to run again," she said softly. "I took out Vitto, but not before he got to Joe. It's a long story, but I'll explain everything. What about you? What happened with Tres?"

"That's it?"

She didn't answer him.

"Cuz, you fucking dipped on me! I thought you was dead! Where you at now?"

"I'm in bed, at Joe's." Pausing for a beat, her tone shifted. "I'm sorry, cuz. I really am. But everything's different now. I have a new lead on a major trafficking ring. We have work to do. Can we meet up this week?"

Frederico relaxed his shoulders and took a deep breath. He wished he could make her understand, but there was no use. Besides, he didn't want to make her feel worse. He could hear it in her voice, she had a lot going on.

"Yeah, just let me know when you tryna come through." Standing up and turning on the speaker, he held the phone aloft and paced. "Tres doing real good, they brought him back the night I was released. Fi in jail—unrelated charges."

"What?"

"Yeah, she'd been fucking around with some dude, and he called *twelve*. They got her ass on domestic violence charges, resisting arrest, *and* assault on an officer." He scowled. "I been worried about you, but now I'm finna get a lawyer and take that bitch to court myself. It's like they don't even care what she did to me."

"I know, cuz. I know," Yael said quickly. "Don't worry about that, I already got it set in motion. My team is ready to go after the county *and* the state. I'm sure they can build an easy case against your baby momma. You know how she's been livin' . . ."

Fred blanched, thinking about how he was living before his son moved in. That life was behind him, but there was no doubt Serafina would try to use it against him. Still, that didn't faze him. He would cross that bridge when he came to it.

"Cuzzo?"

He looked at the phone. "Yeah?"

"You're gonna be an uncle."

Dropping the phone in surprise, he scooped it up and brought it to his ear. "You for real?"

"Yes!" she shouted happily.

Fred winced, having forgotten he was using speakerphone. "Who the daddy?"

"Fred!" Yael shouted again. "I'm gonna kick your ass when I see you."

"You prolly too fat already. Can't catch me if you can't run."

Laughing heartily into the receiver, she snorted and cried, "It's only been a month you ass!"

"Congrats, cuz."

"Yeah, Joe and I are excited. We're moving in together—building our life together. He wants me to quit the job, but that's not possible. Not yet at least."

"You told him?" Frederico asked, incredulous.

"Mmm hmm."

"Well? What does he think about all this?"

Yael giggled. "I think he thinks I'm crazy. Or maybe he thinks I'm an angel after all. Either way, it's cute. He's sweet."

Fred had trouble seeing Joe in that light. But he seemed like a good dude, and he was definitely sweet on Yaya.

"I got your other messages," she continued. "You never really explained what happened. How did you get mixed up with Johhny?"

"You need to call him ASAP," he retorted quickly. "If he hadn't of come by a couple months ago, I wouldn't have known anything. No one had seen or heard from Vitto since May, they prolly still think he has you."

"The feds probably buried him," she explained. "I'll see what Joe will tell me. I hope there wasn't any trouble? Sorry to have them poppin' up on you like that."

"We were on the same side," he countered. "We had the same mission. Seems like they really care about you."

"Joe's about to get out the shower," she whispered. "You wanna have lunch on Wednesday?"

"Sounds good, hit me up." He started to hang up, but then remembered something. "Cuz!"

"Yeah?"

"Two old biddies from the bar keep showing up looking for you," he said, annoyed at the very thought of Tweedle Dee and Tweedle Dum. Bringing the receiver to his mouth, he snapped. "Call yo friends —and tell them stop coming over here!"

EPILOGUE

Joe held open the door for Yael, doing his best to hide the look of disgust on his face.

They had been home for a few weeks and, in many ways, his woman had shown a marked improvement. Her mental health was generally the same. Though he had to admit her highs were much higher, the lows were typically accompanied by her usual anxiety. The difference now? Her new psychosis—a nonexistent pregnancy—was at the forefront of her mind at all times. If she became anxious, she blamed it on her changing body and then quickly found her center.

He wasn't exactly happy she was using such an unusual strategy to ease herself back into her normal life. She refused to take a pregnancy test but had already purchased a number of books about what to expect. The room next to theirs was in the process of being cleared so she could begin the nesting phase. And all this time, she had refused to go to the doctor, citing the *angel's* instructions as reason enough.

What was going to happen today, when the doctor told her she was experiencing a phantom pregnancy? It hadn't helped when she missed her period a few weeks ago. When he tried to show her the studies about how trauma could bring on the condition, she seemed to pity *him*. Was it too late to prove her symptoms were obviously psychosomatic? Would she be willing to start therapy or would she spiral out of control?

"Mr. and Mrs. Smith?" An older gentleman came into the shabby living room and shook both their hands. "Nice to see you, I'm Dr. Abate. We're all set up in back, come along."

Joe wiped his hand on his pants and leaned toward Yael. "Are you sure you don't want to go somewhere else?"

"Stop it," she said, poking his belly. "You're being ridiculous."

Am not, he thought, rolling his eyes.

"Johhny says you think you're about two months along?"

Yael touched her flat belly. "Almost. We conceived in the middle of July."

Dr. Abate nodded. "We might be able to get a heartbeat today. But first, let's make sure your little fetus is in the right place."

He took them down a short, smelly hallway and through another door. Joe marveled at the sterile space, surprised to find himself in what appeared to be a full service clinic.

"Right over here," Dr. Abate called to him, pointing into a room off to the side. "Relax, Papa. Mama looks great."

Joe watched as Yael climbed onto the long chair and reclined, folding her shirt up and over to expose her belly. A short woman came to stand beside her, letting her know the sonogram gel might be a little cold.

"Are you sure you want to do this?" Yael asked pointedly.

Nodding, Joe forced a small smile and came to hold her hand.

She'd done her best to warn him off, claiming the angel had told her not to visit any doctors. He was surprised that she agreed to an appointment, though he was now questioning whether or not he should trust a mafia doctor anyway.

"A bit of cold gel here . . . and some pressure," the doctor told them, sliding the handheld wand along her abdomen as he stared at the screen. "And there's your little baby!"

Yael lit up.

Mouth open, Joe stared at the screen. Tears sprang into his eyes.

"Where's the other one?" Yael asked in excitement.

Dr. Abate moved the wand. "Hold on . . . my screen just went black."

Joe stared at Yael's belly, overwhelmed by what this meant. He heard a loud hum, then a crack of thunder. The building's electrical sputtered and went black.

"I'll be damned," Dr. Abate said in the darkness.

The lights flickered and flashed back on.

"We'll have to wait for the machine to reboot," the technician explained. "Doctor, I'm going to go check and make sure everything is okay."

"Thank you, Denise." Dr. Abate put the ultrasound wand onto the rolling tray beside him. "It will just be a few minutes."

"Actually," Yael said quickly, "I think I need go home and lie down."

"Okay, no problem at all." Dr. Abate moved to grab a towel and wiped the gel from her belly. "From what I could see, everything is going very well in here. Looks like you're due first or second week of April."

Speechless, Joe met Yael's eyes, hoping she could feel his apology. But all he saw there was love.

Read on for an exclusive sneak peek at
LA **M**ADONNA **N**EGRA | **V**OLUME **IV**

The Don leaned in and gave his wife a kiss, patting her on the rump as she sauntered down the walkway. He was about to turn back when Johhny stepped outside and waved.

"Have fun," Johhny said to Gloria in passing. "She's still upstairs looking for an outfit."

Waiting for Johhny at edge of the main sidewalk, he greeted him with a grunt.

"You hungry?"

Johhny shrugged. "I could eat."

"Yeah, well, Gloria hasn't cooked all week," he grumbled. "She's on some cleanse."

"Gina's been doing it with her."

The Don made a face. "Really?"

"Nah," Johhny chuckled. "She hates cayenne pepper. But she didn't want Glo to feel alone. You know how they are."

Shaking his head, he gave his cousin a half smile. Gloria's cousin Gina was Glo's number one fan. The four of them had a nice thing going, living together all these years. It helped that the wives kept each other entertained, always finding something to do when he and Johhny were occupied with Family business.

"You gotta taste for something?"

The Don smacked his lips together. "Meatballs."

"You read my mind," Johhny said, rubbing his belly.

Snorting, the Don slapped his cousin's stomach. "You look like a meatball."

"Ah, go fuck yourself, Sammy."

He chuckled. "Why don't we go over to Angelo's spot?"

Johhny scratched the scruff on his neck. "Sound good."

A bird flew straight up into the air over Johhny's house at the corner of the property. The Don tilted his head when he saw it falling to the roof.

Only, it wasn't a bird at all.

Johhny's house exploded, the sound shaking the ground beneath their feet.

"Gloria?"

Johhny panicked. "Gina!"

The Don grabbed him quickly, holding him back by the arm as he fought and shouted his wife's name. Billy ran from the security hut, extinguisher in hand. Another small explosion came from within the house.

"That's the gas line, Johhny!" he shouted into his cousin's ear. "You hear me? They're gone!"

Johhny fell to his knees, rent his shirt and wept.

Made in United States
Orlando, FL
07 May 2022